USA TODAY BESTSELLING AUTHOR
DALE MAYER

Murder in the Marigolds

Lovely Lethal Gardens 13

MURDER IN THE MARIGOLDS: LOVELY LETHAL GARDENS, BOOK 13
Dale Mayer
Valley Publishing

ISBN-13: 978-1-773363-65-3
Print Edition

Books in This Series:

About This Book

A new cozy mystery series from *USA Today* best-selling author Dale Mayer. Follow gardener and amateur sleuth Doreen Montgomery—and her amusing and mostly lovable cat, dog, and parrot—as they catch murderers and solve crimes in lovely Kelowna, British Columbia.

Riches to rags … Chaos has never been so supreme … Now a suspect herself … No calm in sight …

Being a suspect in the murder of her ex-lawyer is not the fun Doreen thought it would be. And, of course, she's been ordered to stay away from the case, … but she can't help being interested. So she enlists Mack's brother, Nick—her *new* lawyer—to help.

Mack's first priority is to clear Doreen as a suspect. No one in their right mind would seriously believe she'd done the deed, of course. … But, the fact is, she had both motive and opportunity, so clearing her of suspicion isn't the walk in the park that Mack would like it to be. Especially not when she insists on sticking her nose into his case, where it doesn't belong.

And just when Doreen is certain things can't get any worse, answering her doorbell shows her that this nightmare has just started. Who just walked into her life? None other than her soon-to-be-ex-husband, … Mathew …

Prologue

Saturday Morning …

THREE DAYS LATER Izzy and Isaac, after promises were made to stay in touch, had been dispatched to Vancouver and a family who awaited their joyous reunion. Martin would be in jail for a very long time. He had finally confessed that he couldn't take his eyes off Izzy, when he was down on the coast for a trip stocking up, and had managed to snatch the girl from her parents and had kept her with him ever since. Nobody had been any the wiser, and, when Isaac had been born, Martin just made up lies about how he'd arrived, and everybody had basically accepted it.

If Izzy hadn't caught Thaddeus and hadn't put that message on his leg, she might still have been a captive there. It just didn't bear thinking about.

As soon as she got dressed and made her way downstairs, Doreen made coffee. Three days had passed since all that. Three days and her shoulder was finally nowhere near as sore. It still hurt to lift her arm above her head, but at least the oozing of blood had stopped, and it wasn't the gut-wrenching agony that she'd been dealing with. The pain was much lighter now, much softer, more distant. As she sat outside on the deck, she heard a vehicle drive up. Mugs immediately woofed a welcome. She looked down at him and laughed. "It's Mack, isn't it?"

Mack, instead of coming through the house, walked around the back, then smiled at seeing her. He had something large in his hand. She looked at it and asked, "What the devil is that?"

He lifted it up, and she saw that it was a table—he'd been carrying it sideways. He plunked it down on the deck beside her, and she cried out, "Where did you get that from?"

"One of the guys at work was getting rid of it," he said. "I said that you needed it, and he immediately offered it up. I've got the chairs in the back of the truck too." He disappeared and made two trips, carrying two chairs at a time. She just froze. Finally she had a table with four chairs sitting on her deck. She stared in amazed delight.

"It's just beautiful," she said. It was glass and acrylic, and it looked lovely. It was also the nicest outdoor set she'd ever had since living here. She immediately moved to sit down at the table with her coffee and grinned up at him. "Now, if only there was something to eat. And more coffee. I'm almost out."

He sagged into the chair beside her and stared at her. "I doubt it's that bad but if it is, I can stop and pick up a pack," he said. But something was strange about his voice.

"I'm really happy you came," she said, "and thank you so much for the table and chairs."

He nodded, but he was slightly distracted. He motioned at her shoulder that had been nicked by a bullet. "How are you doing with that shoulder now?"

"I'm better," she said, cheerfully lifting her cup and taking a big drink. Mack just glared at her. "Okay. It still bothers me. But not like it did." When he remained silent, she worried. "What's the matter?" she asked, her gaze sharpening. He shrugged and wouldn't meet her eyes. "More coffee's in the kitchen, if you want a cup."

"I'm fine," he said.

"Uh-oh." *Something was really wrong.* "And that means something pretty ugly is going on."

He nodded. "There is, and you'll hear about it soon enough," he said, his fingers tapping the table.

"What's the matter?" she asked.

"Have you—" And then he stopped.

"Have I what?"

He sighed. "You know the marigolds in the flower garden down at the big Welcome to Kelowna sign? The old one? There's talk of a new one north of the airport."

"Yeah, the one that I spent a lot of time on, trying to design a layout for the city? It was a pretty bunch of flowers, as I remember. I can't remember all of them, but some lovely marigolds were there, I think. They are tearing that one down? So that's why the contract didn't go through. Or maybe I misunderstood, and they were designing the new one." She frowned at that thought. It did explain why that scenario never moved ahead.

He nodded. "Yeah, that one. We found a body there this morning." He shrugged. "It's the first I've been there and was quite surprised the sign was gone."

Her eyebrows shot up, and she had to admit—even though it was ghoulish and wrong of her—that she was definitely curious as to what was going on. "I am too. I'll have to follow up on that garden design bid. And of course, I'm sorry for whoever it is," she said, "but don't keep me in suspense. Who was it, and what's going on?"

"Well, that's what I came to ask you about."

She stared at him in surprise. "Okay, now I'm confused."

"It might be somebody you know."

"Someone I know?" she asked incredulously. "Oh, dear, I hope not."

He pulled out his phone and slowly flicked through the photos there.

"So this is a delay tactic," she said, "and I admit you're scaring me."

"No, it's not that," he said, "but circumstances require that I ask you a couple questions." He proceeded to ask where she'd been an hour ago, where she'd been four hours ago, and if she had an alibi.

She sat back and stared at him in shock. "Seriously, Mack?" she said. "I woke up about an hour ago. I was home alone all night. Why? Who is dead?" Suddenly she leaned forward. "Is it one of the bad guys?"

"Well, maybe," he said. "I'm sure a lot of people would say it definitely was a bad guy, but a lot of people wouldn't."

"Stop now," she said, raising both hands in frustration. "Just tell me who it is."

Then he held out his phone.

She looked at it and stared in shock.

"That's the thing," he said. "This is our dead body. So where were you last night? And where were you early this morning?"

She stared at the picture of Robin, her former divorce lawyer. Her very dead former lawyer. "What on earth?" Doreen raised her gaze slowly to stare at him.

"And I'm sorry, but I have to ask," he said. "Did you murder her in the marigolds?"

Chapter 1

Saturday Morning …

DOREEN'S MOUTH WAS wide open, as she caught sight of Arnold and Chester, fidgeting where they stood behind Mack. "Are you arresting me?" she asked in a hushed whisper, her gaze zipping to Mack.

Immediately Mack shook his head. "Of course not," he said, yet he pulled out an official-looking document from the inside pocket of his jacket.

She looked over at Chester and Arnold to see them still standing there, afraid. They obviously couldn't hear what she had said, but they knew something was up with her. She shook her head. "That's just unbelievable."

"I know," he said, "but you also must understand that we have to check it out."

Her gaze slowly slid back to Mack. Inside, what she felt was almost anger, yet, at the same time, betrayal. "You know I wouldn't do such a thing."

"Of course I do," he said instantly.

Her shoulders slowly sagged, out of relief or despair she wasn't sure which. "I never thought I'd be in this situation," she muttered.

"Well, it's to be expected, if you keep interfering in these kinds of cases."

At that, her eyes opened wide, and she stared at him. "But I didn't do anything, and nothing in my cases was involved." Then her eyes opened wider yet again. "But your brother was."

He nodded.

"And you're right. The lawsuit obviously involved me." She frowned, her hand automatically stroking Mugs, who had come over for comfort. "What is it you need to know?" she asked quietly.

He rattled off a series of questions, but she couldn't give him any help with any of them.

"I went to bed around nine-thirty p.m.," she said. "Yes, I went to bed alone. Except for the animals, of course. Yes, I armed the security, but, no, I have no recording to say it was set and to confirm that I didn't leave. Nothing like that is available—as you well know, since you put in the system."

"We need to upgrade that apparently."

"Well, considering I was attacked inside the house several times, maybe that wouldn't be a bad idea," she muttered.

He nodded and made a note. That made her smile and regain a little bit of faith in her world. He wrote it on a small notepad off to the side, not on his official documents, as if it were a note for himself personally.

She sighed. "You know what the town will do when they hear."

"Some will laugh. Some will cry. Some won't believe it, and a whole lot won't care."

She studied the other two cops, who had seemed to relax now that she was easily talking to Mack, and she said, "As long as you know I had nothing to do with it." She slid a sideways glance at him, checking his reaction. Seeing the truth in his gaze, she relaxed further.

"I know that," he said. "We just have to make sure."

She nodded. "She really is dead?" she asked. How impossible that seemed.

"She really is," he said quietly.

She looked at him. "What about my ex? Did you check on his whereabouts?"

"Well, we're looking for him too," he muttered.

"Because he'd make a much better suspect, you know?" she said.

"The thought has crossed my mind," he replied. "Don't you worry."

"Well, of course I will worry," she said. "My ex's girlfriend, who also happened to be my unscrupulous divorce lawyer, has been murdered. We always know that the scorned partner is the suspect."

"Well, that's certainly true," he said. "We are looking at everyone with close ties to the victim. Especially if hard feelings or financial motives exist."

"Well, that's a pretty harsh thing to say," she said quietly. He just looked at her, and she shrugged. "Whatever."

"Do you think any of your neighbors saw you last night?"

"I don't know," she said. "I didn't even talk to Nan last night. I still haven't been feeling all that well, so I just went to bed."

He leaned forward. "You're still not feeling well?"

Her hand instinctively went up to her shoulder. "No," she said, "I'm not. I was doing well for several days, then suddenly I was worn out. Maybe I just need a few more days to rest."

"Have you had that shoulder looked at recently?"

She shook her head. "No, I should probably go to the doctor, but I haven't bothered." She looked at him. "So how was she killed?"

"She was stabbed."

At that, she stared at Mack, the color draining from her face. "Well, that's up-front and personal."

"Which is also why your name has to be considered."

"Can they tell if it was a right-handed or a left-handed person?"

His gaze sharpened. "We haven't gotten those results yet."

"Well, let's hope it's a right-handed person as my injury would have prevented me from doing this deed."

He looked at her injured shoulder and said, "That would be very helpful."

"And, of course, you won't let me work on the case at all."

"Nope," he said decisively. "Absolutely not."

She glared.

He shrugged. "Come on. You know how this works."

"Right, new cases are yours. Old cases are mine."

"And this is not an old case," he said. "And you remain on the suspect list until we have a better suspect. So don't add further suspicions." His glare added emphasis to his terse wording.

She shook her head, disagreeing with him. "But she's a visitor here right now. It's not like she even came from this area."

"That doesn't mean that we pay her death any less attention."

"Of course not," she said, with a wave of her hand.

"Don't mind me. You just shook me a bit. And here I've been sad and depressed about Isaac and his mom leaving and returning to the coast."

"And yet," he said, studying her carefully, "that's a good thing. She and her son can have a beautiful life. And she has her biological family to help her raise Isaac."

"It is a good thing," she said, "but, I guess, I was hoping to see more of Isaac."

"You really like the little guy, huh?"

She beamed. "He's a character, and he's very sweet."

"Well, he will have a much better life now," Mack said. "And just because he's gone to Vancouver doesn't mean he's out of your life forever."

"And that's a good thing too," she muttered. "At the same time, it's odd, you know? I find these people or make friends—or it seems like maybe I'll make friends—but then something goes completely wrong, and I end up destroying their lives."

"Well, you didn't destroy anybody's life this time," he said. "It's very important to remember that you did a very good thing here."

"True, they were in a terrible situation," she said, "but I don't know. I have just felt a little bit down."

At that, Thaddeus, who'd been on her lap, walked up closer and curled up on her belly. She stretched out a hand and gently stroked his beautiful feathers. "He's been better though."

"Good," Mack said. "Thaddeus, you doing okay now?"

Thaddeus immediately stretched up his wings and called out, "Thaddeus is here. Thaddeus is here."

She chuckled. "I don't know how people can live alone," she said. "These animals provide so many hours of joy and comfort."

"And it sounds like you need that right now," he said, his gaze low and worried.

She caught the odd note in his tone, and she smiled. "I'm okay. Really, I am. I just, you know," and she gave a wave of her hand at the policemen standing behind her. "This is a very odd day."

"We'll be gone soon," he promised.

"Well, good," she said. "I don't really have anything else to offer. I need to contact some people and see about getting some money from somewhere," she muttered distractedly, as she stared down at the creek. "At least the water is going down, so that's good."

"Yeah, you don't want to take any more crazy unexpected swims."

"I'd be okay not doing that again," she said emphatically.

He smiled, stood, and said, "I'll talk to you later."

"Good," she said. "You might bring some coffee, when you come." He snorted and she smiled. "Hey, at least I didn't tell you to bring groceries, although it seems like it is about time for another cooking lesson."

He stopped and looked at her with interest. "What do you want to make?"

"Well, I'm still eating tons of pasta, which is good, since it's keeping some weight on my frame," she muttered. "But there must be other things to eat too."

"Name them."

"Granola would be nice."

"You know you can buy that, right?"

She looked up at him in surprise. "Really?"

He nodded slowly. "Yes, really. It's just as simple as

picking it up at the grocery store."

She frowned. "Maybe it was the price then," she said. "I thought it was expensive."

"I guess it depends on what you call expensive, but, if you don't buy tons and if just you eat it, it won't be very much at all."

She nodded. "That might make me happy," she said, with a smile. "Maybe I'll walk down to the store and buy some then." She stopped with a quizzical look. "Just like any store or a specialty store?"

"Any grocery store, like, seriously any store," he replied.

She smiled. "Good to know."

At that, he headed back toward the guys.

She knew he turned to look at her again, but she didn't bother glancing back at him. Inside, she was still in this weird fog. The thought of her ex-lawyer being murdered just blew Doreen away. As far as she was concerned, her ex was probably involved, and that just made it something she thought of as an open-and-shut case; yet Mack and the others had come here.

They'd actually come here, asking about her whereabouts, and she didn't know what to do with that. It just hurt on so many levels. Yet it was something he had to check out, something he had to determine was nothing. And it was nothing, but she was an emotional wreck because of it. She didn't even watch as they left. They just disappeared, as she sat here, now with Goliath in her lap, trying to push Thaddeus aside. Instead the savvy bird had crawled up on top of Goliath, and Mugs was stretched out beside her on the deck.

"Well, now what do we do?" she muttered.

But then her phone rang. She stared down at it to see it

was Mack's brother, Nick. She groaned. "Ugh. I don't want to talk to him. Unless … does he defend the innocent? I might need a lawyer." She picked up the phone, answered it, and said, "Hey, so are you a criminal lawyer?"

"No," he answered. "Why?"

"Does that mean you can't do criminal law?"

He was confused, as he said, "No, of course it doesn't. I can do it. You're just better off having somebody else who's better trained and experienced in it. Why?"

"I think I may need a lawyer," she said abruptly.

There was sudden silence on the other end of the phone. "Maybe that ties into what I was calling about," he said, speaking carefully. "Is there something you need to tell me?"

She stared down at the phone. "Well, I didn't kill her," she said, enunciating clearly. "And Mack just left, after asking me a ton of questions, as if I were a suspect," she said. "I didn't appreciate that, and I don't appreciate your doubt either. I do understand it from you, at least a little, because we've only just met," she said, "but from Mack? No."

"Well, I'm sure he was just doing his job and trying to make sure he did it thoroughly because otherwise it would be assigned to somebody else, who would have had to do the same thing," he said, "and that may not have been anywhere near as pleasant."

"Oh," she said in a small voice. "I hadn't considered that."

"Well, maybe you should have," he said, "because Mack obviously believes in you and knows that you wouldn't do anything to hurt anyone. But, given the fact that it's your ex-husband's girlfriend, who was also your unscrupulous attorney who left you nearly penniless, it's a whole different story."

"Maybe," she said. "I mean, I certainly wanted to kill her at times. Both of them actually. In theory of course. Just venting."

"We always have people we want to theoretically kill," he said, with a note of humor. "It then becomes a matter of if you did it or not."

"Well, I didn't," she said almost absentmindedly. "And, of course, my vote for a likely suspect is my ex-husband. I'll bet he's the one who killed her."

"And that's almost too easy," he said. "You would think he would know a little more about trying to make it less obvious."

"Good point, which brings to mind the thought that it could be somebody wanting to set him up and to get him in trouble," she muttered.

"Which comes right back around to you again."

She winced at that. "Great, so even when I come up with theories on my own, they turn around and bite me in the butt."

He chuckled. "You need to trust Mack that he'll do what he can to make sure the suspicion on you is resolved and thrown elsewhere and that you're free and clear."

"I suppose," she said. "Did you have a specific reason for calling?"

"Well, I had heard about the body," he said. "The fact that I'm involved in all this in a peripheral way just means that it came up on my radar."

"You didn't kill her, did you?" she asked suddenly.

His startled gasp was heard clearly on the other end of the phone, and then he chuckled. "No, I didn't kill her either."

"Okay, just checking," she said cheerfully, "because, if

you think about it, she is somebody you really didn't like either." Suddenly frowning, she continued. "And, by that same token and following that logic," she said, "Mack is in that same boat."

"Well, I don't suggest you start slinging around the theory that Mack is a suspect either," he said, choking back a chuckle.

"No, Mack wouldn't like that, would he?" she said and started to snicker. "But then he would get the chance to know how I feel right now."

"But he was just doing his job, and that would be you just needlessly causing him trouble," he said, still sounding cheerful.

"Right, and I can't do that to Mack." She sighed. "Okay, fine. So how will we find this guy?"

Again came a moment of silence. Finally he said, "What do you mean? Hang on a minute. What are you talking about?"

"Well, we can't just have my neck hanging in the noose here," she said. "That's a very uncomfortable place to be, you know?"

"I'm sure it is," he said, "but you need to leave the police alone, so they can solve it."

At that, she laughed. "You're kidding me, right? This is what I do," she said, "or, at least, it's what I was doing."

"How much of that was cold cases?"

"Mack told you that, didn't he?" she accused.

"Okay, hang on a minute," he said. "Somehow I'm missing the train of thought in this conversation."

"Yeah, I've heard that a time or two," she muttered.

"What are you talking about?"

She shook her head. "Don't worry about it," she said. "I

MURDER IN THE MARIGOLDS

just need to make some inquiries."

"Whoa, whoa, whoa. What inquiries? Don't you go off doing anything rash now. You have no idea what Mack is doing, and what we don't want to do is cause him any trouble that messes with his ability to find out what actually happened here."

"Nope," she said, shaking her head. "I certainly don't want to do that."

"Oh, good, because I—"

"But I also don't plan on sitting back and doing nothing."

"That is precisely what you should be doing. Anything else will look like you're trying to muddy the waters and to make it look like you're not guilty."

"But I'm not guilty," she said reasonably, "so why wouldn't I?"

His voice took on a tone of alarm. "No, no, no, no. Don't do anything," he said. "You've got to let Mack handle this."

"Well, Mack was already here, and he hasn't a clue who did this," she said.

"And neither do you," Nick said firmly. "Please stay out of my brother's way."

She frowned into the phone. "Right," she said, "you don't know him like I do."

He gasped in frustration. "No?" he said. "Maybe not, but I know him pretty well, and he is very dedicated to doing what he needs to do."

"Sure, but that doesn't mean he can't have a little bit of help here and there." She looked down at her pets and smiled. "And we have a special brand of help."

"Oh, I don't like the sound of that," Nick warned.

15

"It'll be fine," she said. "He'll understand completely." And, with that, she hung up. She sat here on her new hand-me-down chair at her new hand-me-down table for a few minutes, just enjoying the view, as she thought about how her world could have completely flipped around so quickly.

"I don't know what's going on," she said to her animals, "but we didn't kill her, and so we'll find out who did."

With that, she got up, and, just as she did, her phone rang again. She groaned, as she stared down at it. "Goodness, it's turning into one of those days." She answered it, when she saw Nan was calling. "Hey, Nan."

"Did you hear?" Nan's voice screamed through the phone.

"Yeah. So I heard. She's dead. The B is dead."

"Oh, I don't think you should say it that way," Nan said.

"I know. I'm not allowed to say anything now because everybody will judge me for it. Now either I'm guilty or I'm gloating or something else," she said.

"Oh, dear. You're having a bad morning, aren't you?" she asked gently.

"Well, Mack was here, asking me questions about where I was during the whole time period that they suspect she was murdered," she said. "So how do you think that made me feel?"

"Well, you should be excited, since now you actually understand what it's like to be interviewed," Nan said. "And you absolutely know Mack doesn't believe you did it, so it should make you feel really good that he is at least covering all the angles to make sure he finds out who did."

She stared down at the phone in surprise. Then sagged back in her chair. "Oh," she said, "I guess I hadn't gotten as far as all that yet."

"Oh, dear, you were upset with him, I suppose."

"Well, it wasn't very nice," she muttered.

"Of course not, but he didn't do it on purpose."

"Not unless he killed her himself."

"Well, Mack has no reason for doing that," Nan said in a firm voice.

"No, I suppose not," she said, "but it did make me wonder."

"Well, how could you possibly think he would do a thing like that?" Nan asked.

"I don't know. He's definitely angry at what my soon-to-be ex-husband and my ex-attorney conspired to do, ensuring I wouldn't get a thing out of the divorce."

"So what?" Nan said. "You've also left that unhappy marriage and have been free and clear here ever since. So Mack has no reason to hold a grudge against them, and you've known him long enough to know that Mack doesn't hold grudges anyway."

"I know," she said. "I'm just feeling a little off this morning."

"Well, you know what the answer to that is, dear. You need to stand up and to figure out what you'll do."

"Well, I'm still trying to get details on it. Mack did tell me that she was stabbed."

"Ooh," Nan said, as if she'd just heard a secret. "That's interesting."

"It's also very telling," she said calmly, as she thought about it. "It does mean it's up close and personal, often somebody who is holding a grudge."

"Which could also go along with that ex-husband of yours? We don't know what all happened between them, but something certainly did, or Robin wouldn't have been here, attacking you."

"Yeah, well, it also lines up perfectly for anybody interested in putting me in jail," she muttered.

"But we know you didn't do it," she said. "Besides, what was Robin even doing here in town, besides bothering you?"

"I'm sure that's another part of this whole mystery we must solve."

"Did she contact you again?"

"Nope, I don't think so," she said. "I wasn't feeling good yesterday, and my shoulder was pretty sore, so I wasn't on my laptop or my phone."

"I'm not even sure you could have stabbed her."

"I probably could have," she muttered. "But not without some serious pain." She frowned at that. "Mack should know that I'm still not in very good shape," she said.

"Stop blaming Mack," Nan said firmly. "He is doing exactly what he needs to do."

Doreen groaned. "I can't help that it still feels so wrong, like a betrayal."

"No, honey. The betrayal is the fact that somebody killed her here in our town, making it look like it could have been you. How many people even knew your ex-lawyer was here?"

"I don't know," she said. "How many people even knew she existed? I certainly didn't want her here," she cried out. "I came here to get away from them."

"Well, in that case," she said, "maybe we can track down what else Robin was doing here." After a few moments of silence, Nan went on. "Any contact from him?" she asked.

"Who?"

"Your former husband."

"Ugh, no! Why would he contact me?"

"I don't know. It was just a question, dear," Nan said. "It wouldn't hurt to make sure you haven't gotten a clue somehow from someone."

"Yeah, will do," she said. "I should check my email at least. I haven't checked it at all today or yesterday."

"Well, you do that," she said, "and then come down here and have some tea with me."

"I'm drinking coffee right now," she said perversely. And then she looked down at Thaddeus and Mugs. "But the animals would really love a visit."

"We all would," Nan said. "So finish your coffee, check your emails, check to make sure your ex or someone else didn't contact you. Then come on down here and have some tea with me. It will do you some good."

"And, in the meantime, you'll check around and see if anybody at the home has any information?"

"I'd be delighted to," she said, with sheer joy in her voice.

Doreen was thankful for her grandmother, who could nearly always lift her spirits. Laughing, Doreen hung up the phone. She got up, refilled her coffee cup with the last of the pot, and went upstairs to change into company-ready clothing, since she had just thrown on a pair of shorts and a T-shirt earlier. She put on capris and a little dressier T-shirt, then slipped on her sandals. Sipping her coffee as she wandered up and down the garden, she was really just avoiding her emails.

With a sigh, walking straight to her laptop, she sat down and checked. And then groaned. Because, sure enough, her ex-husband had contacted her late last night. First, she took a picture of the screen, showing that the message was unread, and then she clicked on the email.

Coming to town and I need to talk to you. I'll make it worth your while.

She winced at that, took a photo of it, and forwarded both images to Mack. When her phone rang a moment later, she picked it up and said, "I didn't know. I just found it. Nan suggested I should check my emails."

"Is that all he said?" His tone was briskly efficient.

"Yes."

"And did he give a location?"

"Um …" She went through the email again and said, "No, nothing here. Just that he wants to meet."

"Check your phone," he said.

"Okay, hang on." She went through her phone messages and said, "No, nothing's here either."

"Does he even have your phone number?"

"I don't think so. But he'd remember Nan, of course, so would likely know to look for me here at her place, even if he didn't know that she'd moved."

"Right. I wonder if he's contacted her?"

"It's possible," she said, "but I don't know why she would give him the time of day."

"Of course not, but that doesn't stop somebody who's on a mission from doing it."

"I wonder what he wanted to talk to me about," she said out loud.

"Well, my brother filed some things on your behalf, as well as the complaints against your divorce attorney," Mack said, "so we should expect some pushback there."

"Maybe," she muttered, "but, at the same time, I would have thought it would have just been the lawyers haggling. It confuses me that he tried to contact me directly."

"Maybe he was trying to find something to make you feel guilty about or to appeal to your emotions."

"Maybe," she muttered. "It's hard to know what's on his mind."

"Did you often give in to him?"

"Oh, yeah, all the time," she said. "It was just so much easier. Besides, that's the way he groomed me."

"So, when he wanted something out of you, he would have gone to you directly. And that's what he's likely done in this case."

"Right, trying to get me to drop the whole thing, I presume, or whatever it is that Nick has instigated, and have it all go away possibly?"

"Exactly," he said. "The fact that his girlfriend, and your ex-lawyer, has been killed in the process is a whole different matter."

"And it doesn't make me feel any better at all."

"Of course not," he said, his voice gentle. "How are you doing?"

"Still bewildered. Still feeling upset and shocked."

"Sure you are," he said, his tone a little bit more distant. "She was with your husband."

"I'm not—" And then she stopped. "Look. I'm not upset about the fact that it's my husband's girlfriend or my ex-lawyer for that matter, although maybe I should be, and I guess I will be when I have a chance to really process what went on," she said, "but that's not why I'm upset. I'm upset that you came and had to ask me all those questions. Like I was actually a suspect or something."

"I get that," he said. "But remember, if I don't investigate and document the case properly, it will get thrown out, or I will get reassigned, and you'll be dealing with somebody else. So I had to ask those questions, with legitimate witness-es, in order to let everybody know that it was all aboveboard."

"Right," she said, taking a deep breath, "and I get that on one level. But, on another level, it feels like a terrible betrayal."

He sighed. "Well, I was hoping you wouldn't take it that way," he said, "because I certainly didn't intend it that way. Just the opposite, in fact."

"And I'll deal with it," she said. "I'm heading down to Nan's for some tea in a minute."

"You do that," he said. "Nan will rally the troops around you to make you feel better."

"I hope so," she said. "Anyway I've got to go." And she hung up on him.

Chapter 2

Saturday Midmorning ...

WITH THAT, DOREEN grabbed up leashes, deciding that Goliath on a leash was a bit of a distant memory, and maybe she should try it again. Goliath had other ideas, however, and Doreen finally gave up and tossed it to the side and said, "What a waste of money that was."

It had worked for a while, but then she'd gotten out of the habit of using it, and that just meant that putting it on the stubborn cat didn't go so well now, since consistency was the key in these things, but that was hardly Goliath's fault. With the animals in tow, and, as unsteady as Doreen felt, she better avoid the river, so she and her animals headed down the other side instead. When she got to Nan's, her grandmother sat outside, waiting for her.

The spritely old woman bounced to her feet and came running across the grass on the little stepping stones and gave Doreen a big hug, careful of her injured shoulder. "You don't look so well," Nan said instantly.

At that, Doreen grimaced. "Thanks."

Immediately Nan shook her head. "I don't mean it like that. I just mean that you look very disheartened."

DALE MAYER

"I don't know. I just feel now like I woke up on the wrong side of the bed this morning," she said. "And it's been going downhill ever since."

"And that was probably a premonition," Nan said, nodding wisely.

She looked at her grandmother and asked, "In what way?"

"Maybe somehow you knew that woman would die. She wasn't just your ex-lawyer, she posed as your representative in the divorce, then moved herself in with him the minute you were out. Not to mention the crimes she committed, bilking you out of your financial settlement."

"If I had known someone was out to murder her, I would have tried to stop it," she said.

Nan looked at her in surprise.

She shrugged. "She was a terrible person, sure, but I'm just trying to move on," she said.

Nan nodded. "That's because you're nicer than I am," she said. "Come on, dear." She walked Doreen back to the patio and said, "Sit down. Sit down. I've got a lovely surprise for you."

When Nan dashed back into her little kitchen, Doreen smiled, as she sat down at the patio table, and put Thaddeus on top. Mugs walked over to the side by Nan's chair and plunked down on the patio. "Right. We need something a little less depressing and a little less sad right now," she muttered. At that, Nan came back out, carrying a plate of little pastries. Doreen brightened. "Those look marvelous," she said in delight. "Where did you get them?"

"I went down to that little bakery, Sandra's, Sandrine's, whatever it is," she said. "It's downtown off Dilworth. Some lovely little baking is offered there."

"Nan, these must have been superexpensive."

"And I really don't care," she said firmly. "Honestly I didn't look at the price. I figured that, if I wanted to have a little pastry, these were about the right size, and this way I could have just one—or I could have two, if I wanted."

Doreen laughed. "Well, you could definitely have one or two, when they're not terribly big, like this," she said.

"Exactly, so just enjoy them," Nan said, with a smile. She pushed the plate a little farther toward Doreen. "And I bought two of everything. Now please take one, take one of each of them."

And, with that, Doreen complied, wearing a big smile on her face. "I haven't eaten breakfast," she confessed. At that, the plate was immediately rescinded.

Nan looked at her in astonishment and then scolded her. "Well, you can't have sugar if you haven't eaten." She stood, then disappeared into the kitchen with the plate.

Doreen stared sadly at the single piece she'd managed to pick off the plate. It was orange and round, and she had no idea what was in it, but it was brightly colored and made her smile. She sat here, with the tea getting cold, waiting for Nan to do whatever she thought she needed to do, worried that Doreen herself was woolgathering over the whole mess. Doreen hadn't eaten well for the last few days, and maybe that was part of her problem. Still, she really did want to enjoy the pastries, but Nan was right. Doreen probably shouldn't eat something like this on an empty stomach, already rolling with two cups of coffee.

Just then Nan returned, preceded by the smell of hot buttered toast. Doreen laughed when she saw it. "I haven't had that in quite a while."

"Well, you can have it now," she said, "and I even

brought out the cheese for good measure."

With slices of cheese now atop the toast, Doreen quickly ate breakfast, happy to calm down the caffeine bubbling away inside her stomach. "I just didn't feel like it this morning," she said. "And then, after Mack's visit, it was difficult."

"Of course it was," she said sympathetically, "but don't you worry about that now."

"Maybe."

Nan poured the tea and said, "I sure hope this tea is still okay."

"It should be," Doreen said. "So did you have a chance to talk to anybody?"

"Absolutely. I talked to several of them. Nobody knew who she was, where she was, or that she was even in town," Nan said, "but they're all congratulating you on the result."

At that, Doreen stared at her in shock. "Congratulating me? What result?"

"Oh, honey, it's simple," she said. "We know you didn't kill her, and that's great, but at least she's gone now. Did you think of that?"

Doreen stopped, looked at her, and shook her head. "No," she said, "I haven't gotten around to thinking that way just yet."

"Well, you would have gotten there eventually," Nan said encouragingly.

"I wonder," she muttered. "It seems like I'm not quite there."

"Well, it's been a rough morning. And honestly you've had a rough couple days. I gather that Isaac leaving was difficult for you."

"It was. Thaddeus was pretty upset."

"Of course he was. On the other hand, we do know that the boy and his mother will be in a much better situation."

"I know," she said. "It's another one of those cases where it all turns out for the best, but, at the same time, there is some upset and loss to adjust to afterwards."

"Of course," Nan said, with a smile. "But it's still good."

"I think it's just all coming down on top of me at once."

"Yes, and that makes sense."

"Not exactly something I want to deal with right now."

"No, and we have much more important things to think of, and that's your ex," she said, "because this completely changes everything."

"It changes nothing," Doreen said, staring at her. "What are you talking about?"

"Well, with her out of the way," Nan said, leaning forward, "you can get things straightened out with the settlement."

"I don't know how," she said. "I signed everything away. Remember?"

"Oh, but then the lawyer, Mack's brother, would get everything fixed, right?"

"Well, the courts will deal with that, and I don't know that her demise will make that more or less likely," she muttered. "Especially since I am apparently a suspect."

At that, Nan sat back, disappointed. "I hadn't considered that."

"Well, I hadn't really either," she said. "I haven't put any time or effort into this at all because, believe it or not, I'm still dealing with the news."

"And that worries me too," Nan said, studying her granddaughter carefully.

"Despite his obviously negative traits, I spent a lot of

years with Mathew," she said quietly. "So the idea that his legal lackey paramour has been murdered, and here in our town, is a bit disconcerting."

"That's understandable," Nan said instantly. "It's grief."

"Oh, Nan, I don't think I'm a good enough person to grieve my ex-husband's conniving little mistress."

"But you do need to separate the emotions a bit. Grieve the loss of your marriage, the betrayal you suffered from the both of them. Only then can you move on."

"Do you think?" Doreen asked. "I just don't even know why I'd be grieving that marriage now." She turned her hands, palms up. "Suffice it to say, I'm a bit confused right now."

"Good. As long as you're confused, and you're honest about it, then it's all good," Nan replied.

Chapter 3

Saturday Midafternoon …

DOREEN HOPED IT would work out that way, but she wasn't so sure. It seemed like everything was topsy-turvy and upside down right now. Still, she had thoroughly enjoyed the cheese toast and then the desserts with Nan. As they walked around Rosemoor a bit, Nan filled her in on the news here. The manager had a new girlfriend, and they were all trying to figure out if it was a good thing or a bad thing, but lots of joviality filled the place. The mood was high, and it seemed like the only one upset and depressed was Doreen herself.

Shrugging it off, she visited with several of the other residents, before heading back home again. This time she decided to take the river route, hating that the fear of her last swim had affected her more than she thought. Maybe this was something she could beat. She'd loved this creek—now a swollen river—before the last attack. She wanted to love it again.

She was pleasantly surprised when she went around the corner of the block to find that the river had gone down even farther. The pathway was there, a bit soggy if she stepped too close to the river, but near the fence line it was dry enough that she could walk easily. That's how Nan had been so comfortable going back and forth; there really had been a change in the weather, and that was lovely.

It was hard to believe it had been a crazy raging water funnel just a few days earlier, when she got dumped into it. But it was all for the good. Who knows what would have happened if the water level had been as low as it was right now? Doreen wouldn't have floated away, and she might have been shot, like a sitting duck—and probably not just once but many times.

Dismissing that morbid thought, she did feel happier, with the animals bouncing around behind her, so delighted to be back at a favorite haunt. She accompanied them all the way back home again, then came upon her backyard, where she walked to the deck and smiled. She had her lovely rocking chair now, with a footstool, plus the table and four chairs she got from Mack. Now all she needed was another chair or two that she could utilize for the little concrete patio area. Or a small couch. Then Mack could join her outside for a longer visit.

Still, she was delighted with the things she did have, and they were continuously coming to her free, or mostly free. Trying to throw off this residual case of the blues, she made a cup of tea, taking it outside with her. As she looked around at her garden, she realized she had missed working at Millicent's place as scheduled. And that was an income she couldn't afford to miss. Wincing, she quickly picked up her phone and called her. When Millicent answered, Doreen immediately apologized. "Millicent, I'm so sorry," she said, "but I missed doing your garden last week."

It took Millicent a moment, and then she said, "Oh my,

Doreen. You certainly don't need to be worrying about my garden. That's just foolish. You got shot, for heaven's sake. You need to look after yourself."

"No, no, no," she said. "It was only a burn. I'm fine. I'm just so sorry."

"You've been a little busy besides, my dear."

"Yes, and still busy," she muttered. "Do you want me to come today and catch up, or would you rather I just come on Friday as usual?"

"Well," she said, "if you want to come today, it wouldn't be a bad idea. No hard digging, maybe just catch up on those pesky weeds."

"Perfect," she said. "I'm in an odd mood anyway, so I'm hoping this will help get me out of it."

"Awesome. Come on over now, if you like," she said, then hesitated, "or do you want to come after lunch?"

"Now would be good," she said, hopping to her feet. "I just had some treats down at Nan's, so I'm full of energy and ready to go."

"Oh, lovely," she said. "I'll put on the teakettle, just in case." And, with that, Millicent hung up.

With an eye to her half-empty teacup, Doreen shrugged and tossed back the tea. Then she called the gang to her, grabbed her gardening gloves, and set off to Millicent's place. Mack surely couldn't get upset with Doreen for doing this much. It was his own mother's garden, after all. When Doreen arrived, Millicent was already sitting outside.

She smiled and said, "I do appreciate you coming, my dear. I know you're really busy these days. I just don't want you to overdo it."

"No, I'm not too busy to work," she said. "I don't have any income coming in, so I really can't afford not to work."

"Oh, dear, I sure hope those antiques come in for you soon."

"Me too," she muttered. "It's just that some things had to be repaired, and Scott wanted to wait and sell it all as a full unit." She shrugged, as if to acknowledge she couldn't do anything about it. And she didn't really want to push him.

"And what about your husband?"

"Oh, him," she said, rolling her eyes. "Nothing much to be said about him."

"But I do understand that there was a murder, and it might involve you?"

"Don't they all," she said, with a laugh. Then she sighed. "So, my husband kicked me out and moved my attractive young divorce lawyer in instead. I didn't know about it," she said, "until after we'd signed all the papers. And now unfortunately that lawyer has turned up dead."

Millicent gasped. "Oh my," she said, stunned. "Really?"

Doreen nodded. "Even worse, the little traitor had the audacity to die here in town. She lived on the coast with him, of course, but, no, she came up here to rant and rave at me over something. And who only knows what that was about. All I could figure out is that she was upset that Nick"—she turned to look at Millicent—"is helping me."

"Oh, that's right," she said in surprise. "I'd completely forgotten Nick was doing that."

"He had apparently filed some paperwork recently, and I guess that gave her a heads-up, or somehow she got an inkling through his investigative work that we were pushing back. So she came up here to rip into me about it all, and now she turns up dead. So naturally everybody thinks I did it." Millicent stared at her. Doreen shrugged and gave her a tiny smile. "Just for the record, in case you're wondering, I didn't do it."

Millicent burst out laughing. "Oh my," she said. "It never occurred to me that you would have done it, dear. You've spent so much time helping everybody else solve their murders," she said, shaking her head. "I can't imagine you adding to the backlog of mysteries to solve."

"Well, I'm glad to hear that," she said, "though I'm not sure your son Mack agrees."

Millicent just stared at her again, blinking.

Embarrassed, Doreen shrugged. "But I don't really know that, of course. It's like I said earlier. I'm just out of sorts today." She looked at the garden, grabbed her tools, and said, "Where would you like me to start?"

"Oh dear, those marigolds are looking awfully sad. Could you trim back the old buds for me? And the tulips. They were supposed to be trimmed ages ago. But I would leave the stalks, in case I want to pull them up instead to move to a new bed. It's so much easier to pull tulips when you have a stalk to tell you where they are. Once you trim them, it's almost impossible to know where they are, until you start digging them up."

Understanding what she meant, Doreen nodded and said, "Well, let's deal with the marigolds first then. You can just sit there and tell me what it is you want me to do."

For the next hour, Doreen worked and talked, cheerfully changing the subject whenever the topic at hand got too difficult or too depressing, and, by the time she was done, the two women were laughing merrily.

"I still can't believe Penny hired him to take you down," Millicent said, chuckling.

"Right, and from jail of all things." Doreen shook her head. "I know I wasn't exactly the friend she thought I would be, but really, was I that bad? Besides she didn't turn out to be that great in that department either." Then they started to laugh again.

"Well, you do seem to have a penchant for sending these people to jail," Millicent said.

"And that's where they belong too," Doreen said, with a frown. "Imagine all these killings going on around here. That's terrible."

"It is, isn't it?" Millicent said, "and I'm sure you'll get to the bottom of this one too."

Doreen looked at her in surprise. "Mack has made it pretty clear I'm not welcome to get involved."

"Of course he has," Millicent said, a smile blooming. "But since when do you ever listen to him?"

At that, Doreen gave a burst of laughter. "Well, I guess that's true," she said. "I hadn't really considered it that way."

"Well, you should," Millicent said. "This involves you, after all. The victim was your lawyer and was involved with your ex-husband, so she was obviously without morals. You can't have this going down in the annals of local lore as a crime you committed. Even if you don't get charged, it's just way too possible that they'll look at you that way."

"Which is the last thing I want," she said.

"Of course not! That would be terrible," Millicent said.

"I came here to make a fresh start."

"In the meantime," Millicent said, "we'll put our heads together and see what we can do to clear your name."

"Thank you," Doreen said, with a brilliant smile. "That does make me feel much better."

And, when she got home, she found it strange that she had blanked out that conversation, but then it came rushing back. Just what could she do at home with all this mess? She could track the lawyer. And, of course, that is something she should have looked at right from the beginning. Absolutely no reason for Doreen not to have done it already. How irritating that she'd left that undone.

But now that she felt a little bit better, while sitting with a hot cup of tea out on the deck, she created a timeline of yesterday, when she had seen her lawyer here in Kelowna. It was a little hard to think back as to what time Robin appeared here, but Doreen did her best. She wrote down as much as she could about the conversation, including the day and the weather, and anything else she could think to jot down. The thought that this woman was gone and how soon this all went down was terrifying.

It seemed Doreen had had more experience with death since moving to Kelowna than she had with life. Which is why the case involving little Isaac had touched her soul. Because it wasn't history, it wasn't a past-tense type of a thing. It wasn't a cold case to bring to closure, and it wasn't a current murderer to put behind bars; solving that case was actually freeing in a sense.

It made life so much better for both Isaac and his mother, and, for that, Doreen was overwhelmed with joy. It didn't make it any easier in some ways though, as she missed Isaac. Shaking her head, Doreen still needed to find out what was going on that got her ex-lawyer killed. But Doreen didn't have even the most basic information.

She frowned and then picked up her phone and sent Mack a text. **Did you find the vehicle my lawyer was driving?**

When she got no answer, she sent another message. **The green Jaguar.**

He sent her a response, but it was a short and cryptic

question mark. **?**

She shrugged and sent a short missive of her own. **Well? Not for you to worry about.**

That was his poor excuse for a response. She snorted at that and sent him another message. **Maybe not, but I won't sit by and do nothing.**

Immediately her phone rang.

"Doing nothing related to this case is exactly what you should do," he warned. "Remember? You're already on the suspect list."

"I might be on a suspect list," she said, "but nobody in their right mind would think that I did it. I have no motive."

"Are you kidding? You are the scorned woman for one thing," he said, "and Robin also wronged you professionally and cost you a boatload of money in the divorce."

"Yes," she said, "but she'd already gotten a dose of her own medicine, since my ex had apparently kicked her out already. Besides, he's the one who should be on the hook for this. Not me."

"Is he the kind to kill?"

"We already decided that he was, just not with his own hands," she reminded him.

"But a woman?" he asked. "A lot of people will kill someone, but it won't be a female. Some guys draw a line there and won't cross it."

"I doubt he has drawn such a line, and, if he did, I suspect he's crossed it already," she said. "Remember? My ex has no morals, no healthy conscious to stop him."

"Got it," he muttered. "I'll check and see if we've spotted the Jag."

"Well, if she was found stabbed at the Welcome sign, and her car wasn't there, then surely she was moved. She was probably either in a hotel or someplace where the vehicle was close by." She heard papers shuffled on Mack's end.

"Well, her rented vehicle was found near a coffee shop not too far away," he said. "Just off the main highway."

She winced. "Well, that's not very good," she muttered. "That's not good at all."

"Nope, it isn't," he said, "but that's what we must deal with."

"I got it," she said. "So, will you check out the vehicle? For hers, for any rentals? If she rented the Jaguar, surely she rented it at the airport, so she must have flown in," she muttered, her mind now starting finally to think. "But I don't know what hotel she was staying at."

"*If* she was staying at a hotel. It's not that far of a drive from West Vancouver to Kelowna," he reminded her.

"But still, what? Four and a half or five hours to drive that distance? And just one way? Both ways on the same day would be a lot of stress."

"It might be a lot of stress," he said, "but people do it all the time."

"The flight is only an hour. She had money. She had absolutely no reason to make that road trip and to make it take so long. She could have flown here, rented the Jaguar, thrown her temper tantrum, then turned around and flown back out of here, without even thinking about it."

"Maybe that's exactly what she did," he said. "It's really not that easy to know for sure yet."

"Well, it should be," she said. "You just need to focus on it a little bit more," she muttered.

He broke into a laugh. "Well, thanks for that," he said. "We really do know how to carry out our jobs."

"So you say, and I get that, but now it's a different story.

It's my neck on the line, and I can't have this case unsolved, with me sitting around, doing nothing."

Once she hung up, it wasn't like she would let it go because she was finally getting somewhere. "Okay, now let's track her," she said, "starting with the times." She checked into the airlines and, with a quick phone call, managed to find out that their victim was set to fly home that evening. She quickly sent the information to Mack. **So, no hotel needed.**

He didn't respond, and she figured that was a good sign. Okay, so that woman loved Chinese food. And armed with a photo of Robin, Doreen hopped into her car, leaving all the animals behind, then headed to the four or five Chinese food places that she knew were close enough, based on Doreen's location and where Robin's car was found, that Robin could have walked to and from. But then, since Robin flew here, she could well have rented her vehicle at the airport. Making a quick decision, she turned around her vehicle and headed to the airport, where she went to the car rental desk. There she held up the woman's picture and asked if Robin had rented a vehicle.

"Oh my, yes," the young woman said. "The cops were here asking about her earlier. Because we didn't get the car back."

"Right," she said. "I understand that. Did she say anything? Did she say how long she needed it for?"

"Only for a day. She said she was flying out that night."

"Right, and she was booked on the nine p.m. flight."

"It's so terrible what happened to her," the woman said. "Are you a friend of hers?"

"I was, indeed," she said quite honestly.

"But time is amazing," the rental car clerk said. "And it

just goes by so fast, and we never know when we don't have any more time ourselves."

"Yeah, I'm trying to track my friend's whereabouts to see who could have been involved in all this."

"Oh," the clerk said, with a shiver. "That's so scary."

"It is, but the sooner I have a little bit of knowledge, the better."

"That's so very difficult to even think about," the young woman said.

"I know, but she was a friend. Do you happen to know if she had any bags or anything with her?"

"She had one of those leather businesslike portfolios," she said. "The kind that holds laptops and paperwork. It was a beautiful bright blue. That's the only reason I noticed it."

"Right," Doreen said, with a smile. "I remember seeing that before."

"It might still be in the rental, but we haven't been allowed to see the vehicle. I understand it's in police possession."

"Maybe," Doreen said, "I'll go talk to the police about it." And, with that, she turned, walked out, and sent Mack a message, saying that the lawyer had this blue briefcase with her.

Mack called her right away. "What are you doing?" he snapped.

"I'm at the rental vehicle place at the airport. Apparently the rental clerk saw her with this striking blue bag," she muttered, as she ignored his question and then promptly hung up.

She put the phone in the holder in her car, as she drove back into town. As she did, she saw a new Chinese food restaurant, or at least new to Doreen. She immediately shifted lanes and drove into the parking lot. Robin had been addicted to Chinese food. If she were hungry, she'd have pulled in here for sure.

Doreen walked in to see an almost empty restaurant. At the counter, a young woman smiled at her. "Are you looking for a table or to order takeout?"

"Neither," Doreen said, but her stomach growled. "I'm looking for information." The woman's face fell. Doreen felt terrible immediately. "But having said that …" Her stomach growled again. She gave the young lady a horrified look. "Sounds like I need to order something."

The waitress handed her a paper menu. "Eat in or take-out?"

"Takeout for me." She perused the menu, her mouth watering at some of her favorite dishes. As she reviewed her options, she said, "I'm looking to see if a friend of mine stopped in here the other day." She fished in her purse for her phone and brought up a picture of Robin.

"Sure. She came in and had lunch." The waitress smiled. "She left behind a blue briefcase laptop bag."

Doreen's heart froze. "Do you still have it?"

"Yes, I was hoping she'd come back for it."

"Not happening. Robin was murdered."

The young woman cried out in shock. Then disappeared into the back. Doreen grabbed a pen and circled her favorite combo. When the waitress reappeared with the bag, Doreen's face lit up. She took it from her and handed her the menu. "Can I get this to go, please?"

The waitress disappeared again. When she returned, she looked at the blue bag in Doreen's hands and frowned. "I don't know that I should let you have that."

"You should," Doreen murmured. "I'll see that it gets to

the authorities."

"Oh, good. I honestly hoped she'd come back." The waitress rang up the order, and Doreen paid. All the while she was itching to look into the bag but didn't want to do that here. Nor did she want to do anything to make the waitress regret handing it over to her.

When the bell rang, the waitress disappeared into the back again and returned with her bag of food.

Doreen smiled. "Thanks." And left quickly. After she got in her car and drove toward home—the heady smell of Chinese food filling the interior of her car, making her even hungrier—she called Mack. Only she got a busy signal. She left a message, as she was almost at home.

He called her back immediately, even as she parked at her house. And before he had a chance to say anything, she said, "Okay, okay," as they continued their conversation a bit later. "I just figured, if we could follow her tracks, we might have a better idea where she was that night. By the way, she absolutely adored Chinese food, and, everywhere she went, she would get some. I picked up a dish to try myself."

He stopped and said, "What are you doing? I specifically told you to stay out of this!"

"I know, but I can't," she commented quietly. "You don't understand. It's driving me nuts."

"I do understand," he said, "but you're making things worse."

"By trying to find who did this? No," she said, "I'm not making things worse at all. It's what I do, Mack. I have no choice."

"No choice, my foo—"

"And besides," she interrupted, "I've got the bag."

"Don't you move," he growled. "I'm already in the truck

on my way."

"Oh, good," she said. "Are you trying to get here before I have a chance to open it up?"

"Don't you dare," he said, his voice soft.

She winced, as she recognized how serious he was. "Fine," she said. "I won't look inside." She slammed her phone down, but then her gaze caught sight of the Chinese food in the take-out bag, and she grinned.

"Food," she crowed. She grabbed a plate and served herself half of it. She was just hungry enough to eat the whole thing but didn't want to scarf it all in one shot, only to feel bad afterward. But she was really hungry. Maybe that was a good sign because, as the day wore on, she was coming out of the dumps. As she sat outside with her food at the new table and chairs set, Mugs was parked right beside her, his gaze on every forkful, just in case. Goliath was on the footstool of the nearby rocker, not caring, and Thaddeus was intently studying a piece of celery on the side of her plate, as she heard Mack's truck drive up. She groaned and looked down at her plate.

"Why is it that I didn't connect the fact that he was coming now to the reality that I left him half of the food? He's just going to eat it, and I won't have leftovers."

He came through the kitchen superfast, took one look at her, and nodded in approval. "You actually bought yourself some food?"

"I felt bad," she said. "The woman gave me the blue bag and told me about the lawyer, so I felt like I should at least put in an order to give her something back for her trouble."

"Well, that's not a bad thing," he said. "Wouldn't it be nice if you'd give me that consideration, like maybe give me the information *before* you picked up the bag?"

"Well, I didn't know about the bag until I spoke with her. And I couldn't leave it with her," she said. "That would be foolish."

"That is true, but you could have pursued other avenues. However," he said, "at least you're here, and you have it now."

"Yeah," she said. "I do want to see what's in there, you know?"

He groaned, realizing why she'd left it for him to pick up directly from her. "You know that I can't do that. As evidence goes, it's already tainted enough, thank you."

"You can too," she said, ignoring the scolding. "Just open it and pull it out the contents, and let's take a look to see if anything of importance is in there."

"If it's of importance, it won't be for here. It will be for my office." But he was already back in the kitchen, rummaging through things.

She smiled, as she watched him. "See? It can't be that bad," she said.

"Sure, it is," he muttered. "Right here, in the appointment book, it says that she was meeting you."

"And she did. She came here, but then she was meeting somebody else at the Chinese restaurant, and I don't know who that was."

"Well, maybe it was you," he said.

"After she barged in and blasted me so rudely? No way. Besides, it's not like she invited me. So it was someone else."

"Maybe," he muttered. "Some initials are here."

"See? There's always something." She watched, standing up with her plate and coming around into the kitchen, so she could take a look at what he found: a stack of loose papers, a notepad, and a laptop. But he still studied her little diary. "It doesn't say anything else?"

He shook his head. "No. It doesn't. Just that she had a meeting for dinner."

"I wonder who?" She frowned at that. "I really wonder."

"Who do you think it would be?" he asked curiously.

She shook her head. "I have no idea. It obviously wasn't me. She never invited me, though I have no proof of that," she muttered. "What are the initials?"

"It's just an *S.*"

She threw up her hand. "That's not helpful," she said. "That could be anybody then."

He laughed. "Or it could denote the place like the Starbucks close to where her car was. However, when people are murdered, rarely do the victims have a chance to set up the evidence, linking their murderer ahead of time, so that it's obvious who did it."

"Yeah, we should all have a little bit of warning," she muttered. "But that stabbing …" She shook her head. "Was she killed in the vehicle?"

"We don't think so," he said. Then he stopped, glared at her, and said, "Stop asking me questions."

"Well, I can hardly stop asking questions when it relates to me."

"Well, it doesn't," he said. "Remember that."

"I hope it doesn't relate to me," she muttered. She kept trying to see what he was up to but could see nothing, as he flipped through the paperwork. She sighed. "I don't know," she said. "It doesn't look like anything interesting is there."

"No," he said. "I'm just not sure what's going on. Well, I'll take this in," he said. "Forensics wants the laptop, and we'll take a look at the rest of this." He glanced at her and asked, "And you didn't look at it, did you?"

"No, for Pete's sake!" And she meant that. "And, other than her barging in here, I didn't meet with her."

"I know," he said. "We'll check the security cameras at the restaurant."

"The waitress said nobody showed up."

"So Robin probably went to meet them somewhere else then," he said. "We'll check the cameras anyway."

"Good," she said. "It still wasn't me."

"Good," he said. "Make sure it isn't you." And, on that cryptic note, he turned and left.

She frowned. He obviously was in a mood because he hadn't even tried to take some of her food. She grabbed the rest of it and dumped it onto her plate. She might as well enjoy a solid meal. It would be the first one she'd had in several days. She dug in.

Chapter 4

Sunday Morning …

THE NEXT DAY, Doreen woke up early in the morning with a heavy heart. Something was so weird about being involved in a case like this, where she was a suspect. Mack was studiously keeping away from her. Mostly because she kept asking questions, and then he ended up giving away information he wasn't supposed to. But they always talked daily, and, although she'd seen him last night, it seemed like he did not want any contact. She knew he wouldn't have been here at all if it weren't for the fact that she had Robin's briefcase in her possession.

Doreen hadn't even called Nan when Doreen was lonely because she didn't know what to say. Everybody was looking at her sideways. Or at least Doreen felt that way. She hadn't even gone for walks with her animals to see if anybody around here had comments, insights, information. Chances were, most people didn't even know about Robin's death yet.

Doreen sat up in bed, rubbed her face, and then smiled when she saw all the animals sprawled out on her bed with her. "Good thing we have this big bed, guys," she muttered, reaching a hand down to scratch both furry bellies. Eight legs faced the ceiling, and Thaddeus sat on the roost at the end of the bed, one of his many perches throughout the house. Obviously all of them were sleeping, as if this were an unaccustomed lay-in, which, if she were honest, it was. It wasn't that often they had a chance to do this.

And even now it wasn't that she necessarily wanted to do it, but she was still in a bit of a funky mood. Feeling a little bit better after some sleep and a snuggle with the animals, she got up, wincing at the stiff soreness in her shoulder. She headed to the shower and loosened it up in the heat. Once dressed and downstairs, she opened up the back door to the bright sunshine of the day and propped it open, so the animals could come in and out. She put on coffee, noting she needed to buy some more soon, and walked down to the creek with a cup in her hand.

"Look at this," she said to Mugs. "It's way lower now."

It reminded her of the way it had been when she had first moved in. They could even walk and play along the riverbank. She shook her head. "It's absolutely amazing how fast that can change."

She had to admit it was a little bit scary too. As long as she had a warning that it would rise as it had, it wasn't too bad, but, when it happened so fast with no warning, it became a scary thing. Still, bigger problems were in her world than the river rising again, and that was all about Robin. And what would Doreen do about her former lawyer who'd somehow managed to complicate Doreen's life even more?

"Of course she did," Doreen muttered. She shook her head, wondering what she should do about it. Just then her phone rang. Expecting it to be Mack, she looked down and frowned at the Unknown Number noted on her screen. She decided to answer it anyway. "Hello?"

"Nice," said a man, whose voice she recognized from her past. "At least you answered."

Her ex. She sagged down on a big rock, suddenly feeling unsteady. "Mathew?"

"Well, at least you still recognize your husband's voice," he said in a sardonic tone.

"Ex," she said instinctively.

"Not yet. Besides, it doesn't have to be *ex*," he said.

She frowned into the phone. "What are you talking about?"

"I want to see you," he said.

"Well, I don't want to see you," she said. "Don't call me again." And, with that, she quickly hung up the phone and put it down.

She stared at it, as if it were a viper or something. She didn't know where he'd gotten her number from or why he was calling, but this was a turn of events she did not see coming. Even as she thought about it, she had to wonder why he would contact her. And what was that bizarre comment about him not having to be her ex? No way he actually wanted her; he'd made that abundantly clear when he had tossed her out.

Not that she'd ever go back anyway. Not in a million years. That would be like returning to a life sentence in purgatory. But why had he called now, and what significance did it have? Particularly considering Robin's death. Hating to do it, but knowing she needed to at least let him know, she sent Mack a quick text. **Mathew called.**

When she got just a question mark back again, she answered, with a simple **My ex** and left it at that. If he wanted more information, he'd call her. She didn't have long to wait, as the phone call was instant.

"I know it's your ex. Did you think I wouldn't have figured out his name by now? What did he want, Doreen?" Mack asked, with both curiosity and an edge of something else she didn't quite understand.

"I'm not sure what he wanted," she said. "I was so shocked that he called me, and I was a bit stunned. I don't even know how he got my number," she wailed. "I didn't even—" Then she stopped herself. "Why didn't I ask him more questions?" she cried out.

"Hang on," Mack said. "Just stay calm."

"Easy for you to say," she muttered.

"What did he say?"

"I'm not even sure," she said, her mind drawing a blank. "Something about not having to be my ex."

An odd silence came from the other end. "Did he ask you to go back to him?" he asked in surprise.

For some reason, the surprise in his voice rankled. "Well, it's not that I'm so ugly that somebody wouldn't want me," she said.

He groaned. "I didn't mean it that way, and you know it. Come on. It's just odd that, after all this time, all the hard feelings, today he calls you up to ask you to come back."

"No, you're right. I get it," she said, sighing heavily. "Honestly I don't know what he's up to." She got up and started walking around. "He just really surprised me, shocked me even, and then I hung up on him."

"Interesting," he said, with a note of humor. "Good to know you don't just do that to me."

"Nope, I don't do it just to you," she said, with a half smile. "But I have more fun doing it to you. In his case, I just wanted to get away."

"Also good to know," he said, his voice suddenly more cheerful. "Did he say where he was?"

"No, he didn't, but it would have been good to know, wouldn't it?" she said. "I'm so sorry. I really messed that up. See? If I would have played it right, we could have gotten all kinds of information from him."

"Maybe," he said, "but maybe you did play it right because that was certainly in true character, wasn't it?"

She nodded, but he couldn't see her head movement, and added, "Yes. Actually, well, it is in line with the me who I am now," she said, trying for clarity. "But he may not have seen that person before."

"Still, you've been through a lot, so he shouldn't expect you to come back with open arms."

"Well, I would hope not," she said in disgust. "But it is him, after all, and he does have a massive ego." Staring at the river, she blew out a long breath. "It's because of Robin, isn't it?"

"Well, that would be my instinctive answer, yes. But that doesn't mean it's right. We really can't make any assumptions here."

She felt better, as she recognized what he was saying. "Exactly," she replied.

"But, if he calls again, I want to know about it."

"I don't know why he called in the first place," she said, "so I really don't know why he'd call again."

"Well, if he called once, chances are he will call again because he didn't get whatever he was looking for."

She snorted. "Well, rest assured, I don't have anything that rat is looking for."

"But he called you, so something's going on there."

"Maybe," she said. "I don't know."

"Don't worry about it. Just go back to sleep."

"I'm actually down at the river," she said. "It's really, really low again."

"That's life on the river. When it storms up above, the water rises fast, and, in that case, that's what carried you down toward the lake. Once the weather calms down and all the snow in the mountains has melted, the fluctuation in volume will be minor."

"Sure," she said. "I was pretty upset about it at the time, but, now that I think about it, it was actually a saving grace, wasn't it?"

"Not sure how you arrived at that conclusion, but if you say so," he said cautiously.

"Well, if I hadn't been carried away by the river, he probably would have just shot me dead."

"Ouch," he muttered. "Not something I want to think about."

"No, yet, at the same time, it's hard for me not to."

His voice was suddenly gentle. "Do you need to talk to somebody?" he asked. "You've been through a harrowing experience."

"Lots of them," she said. "Maybe they're starting to stack up. I don't know." She threw her free arm out wide. "I'm just really confused, and I blame you."

"Me?" he said in surprise.

"Yes, because I think all of this is because Nick opened up that door."

"That's possible," Mack said slowly. "And it's certainly not what we would have wanted to happen, but, at the same time, you also couldn't just leave things as they were."

"Why not?" she asked in a reasonable tone of voice. "Think about it though. I mean, who else would get hurt if we left it alone? It was just me."

"Well, that lawyer of yours, Robin, she wasn't just talking about what Nick had stirred up, was she? Wasn't it for something else that happened first? Nick said, when he first met with you on this matter, that he'd found a complaint filed against Robin for another issue."

"Well, she was pretty angry, and I'm pretty sure that's what was behind it all," she said. "When you think about it, everything in her life got flipped around because of it."

"Maybe so," he said, "but this is the hand we have now."

"I know. I know," she said, with despair in her voice. "It doesn't make me feel any better though. Anyway, rather than hanging up on you too," she said, "I'm getting off now."

"Wait," he said, as she wanted to end the call. "What are you doing today?"

"I'm not sure," she said. "I'm in an odd mood."

"I know," he said. "I can hear it in your voice, and it worries me."

"Worries you?"

"Well, like I said, you've been through an awful lot. Maybe you need to talk to somebody."

"Well, that takes money," she said, "and I don't know that I would trust anybody out there enough to talk to."

"What about Nan?"

"No, I don't think so," she said, feeling the pain in her stomach spread. "I don't think she would be the right person."

"We do have some specialists who are consultants to the force here, and they deal with people who've had to deal with some really difficult things. Maybe you should talk to one of them."

"I'll think about it," she said, more to get him off the

subject than anything.

"What about dinner?" he asked suddenly.

"What about it?"

"You had takeout last night, but maybe you're ready for another home-cooked meal."

"I'd love a home-cooked meal," she said, with a bright smile. "That would cheer me up here good."

He said, "That's done then. What do you want for dinner?"

She sighed. "I have no idea."

"If you were at home with your ex, what would you have?"

"Oh, it could be anything from steak tartare to duckling and orange sauce," she said, with a shrug. "That's hardly my budget anymore, is it?"

"Not really in either of our budgets," he said, with a note of amusement. "But, for a special occasion, we could do it."

"I'm just not sure I'm up for something like that right now anyway."

"How about something much simpler?" he asked.

"Like what?"

"Is there any food you wouldn't be allowed, rather than those kinds of things?"

"Yes, actually. What were you thinking of?" she asked.

He laughed. "Well, I'm fancying a good old-fashioned burger," he said, "if that appeals to you."

"I'd love a burger," she said, her mind instantly conjuring up the flavor of tomatoes and pickles on a bun with a big thick medium-rare burger. "And you're right. That was something I couldn't get before."

"You couldn't even have burgers?"

"*Peasant food*," she muttered.

"We're peasants then," he said, with a laugh. "As long as you don't mind me cooking there, it will be absolutely fine."

"I don't mind," she said in delight. "And thank you for even offering."

"So, what time then tonight?" he asked.

"Well, you're really busy at work, aren't you?"

"Yep, I sure am," he said. "Somebody around here keeps me busy."

"Yeah, sorry about that."

"Well, I'd believe you a little more," he said, "if you didn't keep going out and finding new cases for me, but, in the meantime, I'll probably be here until five or six."

"Fine," she said. "Whenever you're done, just come on over. I might get into the garden here. I haven't been in my own garden for a while. I was at your mom's yesterday."

"She told me," he said. "I'll bring some money along for you when I come."

"That would be good."

"Are you starving yet?"

"Nope, not yet," she said, "but I think it's just around the corner."

"That's fear talking."

"Well, it's also the fact that I've sent out hundreds of résumés and haven't heard a response yet."

"I think that's part of the problem with this new wave of applying for work. You put them in through these online application forms, and you never know if a job has been filled or not, unless you actually get a phone call. So you can potentially put in hundreds and never hear back from anybody. It also depends on what jobs you're applying for."

"Well, I'm probably applying for things I shouldn't be. However, I apply, so I can at least feel like I did something.

Then later I realize there really wasn't any point, and nobody will ever get back to me."

"Now you sound depressed again," he said, that note of worry back in his voice.

She boosted up her smile. "I'm fine," she said, "and really looking forward to that burger."

"Good," he said, "I'll try to get there before five, if I can, but I can't promise."

"Sounds good."

After she hung up the call, she sat here, feeling immensely better. "Well, guys, great news. He isn't ignoring us. He isn't mad at us. And, just think, we'll have burgers for dinner." She laughed at that because she did love a good burger—at least the looks of them—although she didn't have a whole lot of experience with what a *good burger* meant. But everything Mack had made so far had been absolutely delicious, and she was overwhelmed and frankly jealous at his ability to just create something. She thought about it and then said, "You know something, guys? Maybe we should make a dessert."

Immediately Mugs barked in agreement. Goliath looked at her in horror, and Thaddeus started to cackle, with that lovely sense of humor of his. She glared at the three of them. "What does that mean? I can try something. The internet is full of recipes and videos on how to make something simple, after all."

Of course the question was, what was something simple? She thought about all the things she loved growing up and decided that Nan would be the best resource. Doreen picked up the phone and called Nan, and, when her grandmother answered, Doreen asked, "What would be a very simple cake recipe to start with?"

Nan crowed in delight. "Oh my," she said, "I love this idea. And my first choice would be a pound cake."

"Is that simple though? Just because you love it doesn't make it simple."

"No, but you really want to spend time making something that you love, as well," she said. "Otherwise you'll make something that is simple but not very good."

Just enough logic was there that Doreen relented. "Okay, a pound cake it is then. I think I like pound cake, don't I?"

"You scoff it up when you're here."

"Okay, good enough," she said. "But I don't know what I need. I'll go back to the laptop and see what the recipe says."

"Originally it was just one pound of butter, one pound of sugar, one pound of flour," Nan said. "I'm sure a lot of tweaks have been made along the way. It needs lemon juice and some spices too. I used to love a lemon poppy seed pound cake."

"Oh, now you're making my mouth water."

Nan hesitated and then said, "Any chance I could come up and help you?"

Sensing the same loneliness Doreen felt and now heard in her grandmother's voice, Doreen said gently, "I would love that."

"Perfect," Nan said, with joy. "I'll be up in a few minutes." And not giving Doreen a chance to argue or to set a different time, she hung up.

Chapter 5

Sunday Noonish ...

BACK IN THE kitchen, Doreen surveyed the countertops. First, she needed to clean up.

"Even though I don't eat much, and I certainly haven't prepped anything, we somehow always end up with a collection of dirty dishes." She filled the sink with hot water and added soap and quickly started washing the dishes. Since Nan might want something to drink, Doreen put on the teakettle too. With the back door open and whistling gently to herself, she finished cleaning up the kitchen and was just wiping down the table when she looked up to see Nan coming up her pathway. She stepped out onto the deck and waved. When Nan reached the deck, the two women exchanged hugs.

"How are you doing?" Nan asked, looking at her with that bright, chirpy look in her eyes. "Oh look at that table," she crowed in delight. "And chairs." She danced around the set admiring the pieces.

"Mack brought them for me."

"You know," Nan said with a twinkle in her eye, "If you don't want Mack, I wouldn't mind trying my hand. That man is a keeper."

Doreen snorted. "Come on in. I put on the teakettle."

"Oh, good, a cup would be lovely," Nan said, with a bright smile. She looked around. "I haven't baked in a long time. This will be fun."

"Well, I've never baked," Doreen said. "So I don't know about the fun part, but I'm up for it."

"Of course. It'll be fun. I promise," Nan said, as she rubbed her hands together. "The question is, what do you have for cake pans?"

Doreen looked at her grandmother in dismay. "I don't know," she said honestly. "I cleaned out a lot of stuff because otherwise there was no room in any of the cupboards."

"Of course you did," Nan said, with a wave of her hand. "But Mack helped you, didn't he?"

She nodded. "I put everything in the living room, and he sorted through it, so I kept a collection of everything he thought I would need." She turned around in the kitchen and pointed at two cupboards. "I think the baking dishes went in there." Walking over, she bent down, opened up the cupboards, and showed Nan.

"Perfect. Generally bread pans would be my choice for a pound cake," she said, "and two are right there. Grab those."

Following Nan's instructions, they got the bread pans ready and brought out the ingredients.

"This is the only pound of butter I have," Doreen said, looking at Nan.

"Well, it will be gone now then," Nan said, with a laugh.

Doreen winced. "It's expensive."

"All food is expensive," Nan reminded her. "You must spend money to live."

"Yeah, but I haven't got very much though," she said,

with a quirk of her lips.

"But you have enough," Nan said. "Or at least I hope you do." And she turned, and her gaze pierced Doreen's heart.

"I'm fine," she said immediately.

Nan obviously wasn't convinced, but she let the subject drop. And, with that, they returned to the idea of a pound cake. Nan said, "I've got the recipe in my head, if you like the lemon and poppy seed version."

"You know I do, but," Doreen said, "that means I must write it down. Otherwise, it'll get lost soon."

"The idea is, you're supposed to memorize it."

"Well, if we count on my memory," she said, "we'll never save that sucker." She ran, got her notepad, and said, "Okay, let's do this."

At that, Nan grinned and said, "You need a mixing bowl, a whisk, eggs, butter ..." and she kept going on and on, and pretty quickly Doreen was overwhelmed.

"Stop. Go back to the simple stage."

"Fine, get a measuring cup and put five eggs into it."

Doreen grabbed her large measuring cup, went to the fridge, and pulled out five eggs, put them in the measuring cup, then put the carton back in the fridge. She turned, set the cup on the counter, and looked at her grandmother expectantly and said, "Next?"

Nan looked at her, looked at the eggs in the measuring cup, then back at Doreen's face. "Okay, so we need to go back to the real basics."

Doreen's eyebrows shot up. "I said that, didn't I?"

"Yes, but it's not quite the same as a visual reminder," she said, pointing to the measuring cup.

Doreen looked at her and asked, "What did I do

wrong?"

"You must crack the eggs first, dear."

Doreen winced and said, "Ouch, okay, that was a real beginner mistake."

She reached for the measuring cup, pulled out the eggs, put them on a tea towel, and quickly cracked and dumped the contents into the measuring cup. After that, Nan led her step by step through the process. And the next half hour was sheer fun as they blended the ingredients, whipped up the butter and the sugar, added in the flour and the eggs, and then the lemon juice and poppy seeds.

When she filled the pans with the beautifully whipped fluffy cake batter, Doreen asked, "So, what's next?"

"It goes in the oven," Nan replied.

At that, Doreen stopped and looked at her.

Nan stared at her. "Did you put the oven on to pre-heat?"

She immediately shook her head.

"Oh, dear. We should have done that first," Nan said, walking to the oven. "Come over here, and turn it on. Oh, let's see. I would say, probably 375 for this."

Doreen bent down in front of the oven and stared at the dials.

"What's the matter?" Nan asked.

"Honestly?" she said. "I've never touched the oven. I don't even know how to turn it on. Any cooking I do is on the stovetop."

"Oh, that should be easy," she said. "They're all pretty much the same." And Nan turned the oven dial, and a red light immediately came on.

"But doesn't red mean stop?" Doreen asked.

"No, in the case of an oven, it usually means it's turned

on." She added, "Now this one is newer than the old one I had. It might even tell us when it's up to temperature. Or this other light might go off, when it's up to temperature. Let's set it for 375," she said, and she showed her. "Now this is the only dial you need to turn on. Once you do that, it's all set," she said, "but let's check where the racks are."

She pulled out the racks and rearranged them. "Ideally you want to bake in the middle of the oven," she said. "If you're broiling, you want to be close to the top, but, if you're baking something like a cake, the middle of the oven is best." And, with that, they made tea, as they waited for the oven to warm up.

"Are we hurting the batter by waiting?" Doreen asked, her gaze on both filled pans.

"Well, it would have been more ideal if it had gone in immediately," she said. "But it wasn't ready, so no sense worrying about it. Only so many things you can control. Don't bother worrying about something in the past. Learn the lesson and move on."

She smiled at Nan. "That's how you've survived all these years, isn't it? By prioritizing the things that you worry about."

"It's called, *don't sweat the small stuff*," Nan said. "I think somebody even wrote a book like that." She shrugged. "Why people would write a book about something so basic, I don't know. But I think it was a best seller."

Doreen laughed. "Because a lot of people, like me, need to be reminded that we only have access to a certain number of molecules or brain cells or energy in a day, and we need to prioritize what we'll do with them."

"Maybe," Nan said. "But I never did understand why folks worry about things they can't change."

"Meaning, now that we already missed that opportunity to preheat the oven earlier, why worry, just carry on?"

"Exactly," Nan said. "Because we can't go back and change it anyway, so forget about it, and work with what we've got." And then she said, "But you also promised me a cup of tea."

Doreen laughed. "I did, indeed. So let's get that water back on again."

"That reminds me. My grandmother said we should never reheat tea water."

Doreen stopped and looked at her. "Seriously?"

"Yeah, but I don't remember the logic behind it now. It's just something we've always done."

"I guess it doesn't really matter, does it?" she said. "We certainly have it in abundance here." She dumped out the previously boiled teakettle full of water, only to refill it from the sink and put it back on again. Before long the oven was preheated, so the cakes went in.

At that point in time, the two women took their freshly made pot of tea outside and sat down at her new patio table set. Doreen took a seat and explained how Mack worked with somebody getting rid of this, so he brought it to her. She smiled when she thought about her cake and looked over at her grandmother. "Mack will be really surprised."

"Yes, I can imagine," Nan said, with a big smile. "He sure will. When is he coming?"

"I think tonight," she said. "We were talking about dinner. He told me what he was thinking of cooking, but I honestly can't remember anymore." She groaned. "It seems like my short-term memory is gone."

"Stress," Nan said wisely. "It'll do it to you every time."

Doreen laughed. "In that case, I probably don't have any

brain cells left."

"Well, the hits to your head certainly don't help either. But, when you're young enough, the brain cells will still rejuvenate. When you get to my age," she said, with a frown, "they tend to stay gone."

At that, Doreen burst out laughing. "I see no evidence of that, Nan."

Thaddeus hopped onto Nan's lap and then onto the table that Mack had brought them.

"Thaddeus is here. Thaddeus is here." He looked over at Nan and said, "Thaddeus loves Nan."

Nan burst into a huge smile, then got up and cuddled the beautiful parrot, until he hopped up onto her arms and snuggled up against her neck.

Doreen's heart warmed at the sight of the two of them.

"He is such a beautiful pet, and so lovely to have. I miss him terribly," Nan admitted. "But it was time."

Doreen wanted to ask what made it time but didn't really know how, and, besides, it was hardly appropriate when she was the one who had benefited from it all. "I just don't want you to have second thoughts about it or to regret the move," she said quietly.

"Not at all," Nan said. "Not at all. It was the best thing I could have done. And look. It brought you back into my life."

At that, Doreen winced. "I hope you didn't do it just so it would bring me back," she said, "because I could have just moved in with you."

"You needed to experience independence for the first time in your life," Nan said quietly. "And this was the way for you to get it."

Doreen's heart was torn because that was probably why

Nan had moved to Rosemoor.

But then, with a bright, cheerful voice, Nan said. "And besides, if I'd stayed here, I wouldn't have all the lovely new friends I have now," she said. "I wouldn't have all the fun with the betting that I'm not supposed to do," she said, her eyes twinkling. "And look at all the treats I get."

"Not to mention the boyfriends," Doreen said, with a roll of her eyes.

"Yes, well," she said, in a complacent tone, "that wouldn't stop no matter where I lived."

Doreen burst out laughing. "You're such fun to have around."

"Yep," she said, "that's what they all say too." Then she waggled her eyebrows at her granddaughter, who was lost in a fit of laughter.

Still chuckling a few minutes later, Doreen sniffed the air and said, "Oh my, I smell cake. I'm sure of it."

"And it's starting to smell delicious. Let's go check," Nan said, hopping to her feet and racing into the kitchen. With Doreen behind her, and two animals excited and running at their feet, Nan opened the oven and clapped her hands. "See? Look at this."

Inside the oven were two beautiful loaf pans, in which the cake batter had risen. Not high above the edge of the pans but enough to form a beautiful gentle curve of a slightly golden color.

"Now they still need a little bit more time," Nan said. "I'm thinking another twenty minutes or so."

And, with that, they went back outside. Doreen looked at her and asked, "Are you hungry?"

"Oh no, dear," she said, "I ate before I came."

"Good," she said, "because I don't have any food." And

then she burst out laughing. "I was supposed to go shopping, but I didn't get there yet."

"Didn't get there or couldn't afford to get there?" Nan asked, with her usual directness.

Doreen winced. "Well, I am a little worried," she said. "There's been absolutely no movement on the antiques yet. I know it's coming, but it'll still be months, and I did splurge on this deck, even though it was incredibly cheap because everybody pitched in. But it still cost me a fair bit."

"You had that bowl of money. Do you still have that?"

"I do, but I've had to tap into it quite a bit," she whispered. "I did work at Millicent's yesterday, so Mack will bring that money for me today."

"And is that enough to buy you some groceries?" Nan asked doubtfully. "Because I don't think so."

"It'll get me the basics," she said, "like coffee and eggs, plus bread and peanut butter."

"Are you still living on toast and peanut butter?" she asked in horror.

"Nope, I'm not. I do make a lot of sandwiches still though, and I eat a ton of eggs," she admitted. "I didn't think omelets would wear on me, but Mack promised to teach me how to make more breakfast meals that I could fix by myself."

"Good, but how about dinners and other things for lunch? Besides a salad and a sandwich I mean?"

"Well, the salad is easy, and it's healthy," she said, "so I'm not too bothered with that. I can cook hard-boiled eggs now because Mack showed me how to do those. Plus I have cans of tuna. Other than that, I do cobb salads or chef salads."

"Good," Nan said, with a bright smile. "And now you'll

have cake, and that'll make your tummy that much happier."

"Yes, and I think happy tummies are really good for keeping emotions happy too," Doreen admitted.

"Absolutely they are, dear. That's part of the reason people end up as drunks. Because the taste of the alcohol makes them very happy." At that, Doreen howled with laughter. Then right out of the blue, Nan said, "Did you find out anything more about Robin?"

"No," she said, "outside of the fact that she was stabbed and that she had a rental car and was due to fly back out the same day. I went to the new Chinese food place—or the one that I didn't know about beforehand, the one on the way from the airport back to here—and they said that she was there, waiting for somebody who didn't show, so she left after eating."

"Interesting," Nan said, fascinated. "I wonder where she went."

"Well, Mack thinks she went to meet this same person but at another location."

"And where would you go after a meal?"

"Well, for me, it would be coffee," Doreen said instantly.

"But not everybody drinks coffee after their meal," Nan reminded her.

"Maybe not, but a lot of people do. And, if the person didn't eat, maybe coffee is what they wanted instead."

The two women mulled over that possibility, and then Nan said, "You know what? If I'm thinking of the same Chinese food place, then a Starbucks is not far from there."

Doreen thought about it and said, "I saw one. It's inside a grocery store though. I don't think it's a real Starbucks."

"Oh, it is so," Nan said in a dry tone.

Doreen waved off her comment. "You know what I mean. It's not a place where you could go in and sit down to meet with somebody."

"Well, that's true," Nan said, "but there are so many in town. There's probably one within walking distance from anywhere in Kelowna."

"But neither her body nor the rental vehicle were found in that same area as the Chinese food place," Doreen said, "so she must have gone somewhere else, and then she was found a few hours after that."

"Ah, so the killer had to be whoever she went to meet then."

"Maybe not *had* to be but it sure makes that person the prime suspect," Doreen said. Then she went on, "Guess who phoned me this morning?"

Nan looked at her, one eyebrow raised. "Who?"

"Mathew," she said.

Nan's jaw dropped. "What?"

"Yeah," and then she told her about the odd conversation.

Nan immediately started shaking her head. "Good Lord, please tell me that you're not considering it."

"Considering what?" she asked.

"Going back to him."

"Oh, of course not!" she exclaimed. "Jeez, Nan. Ugh. No. I had a terrible time when I was with him. Why would I ever go back to that? Look what I have here," she said, and she waved her arm around at the house and the garden. "And thanks to you, I actually have a good life and fun," she said, "and I get to do things on my own."

"Good," Nan said, "because that makes the move to Rosemoor all the more worthwhile."

"Ouch," Doreen said, "you're making me feel bad."

"Nonsense," she said firmly. "It had been on my mind for a long time, but I never thought I would get you to leave him."

"No," she said. "I probably wouldn't have. Not until he actually made the move to do it himself."

"That's only because he had replaced you."

Doreen shuddered at the word. "Can we call it something else?" she muttered. "That's a little harsh."

"It's not harsh at all," Nan said. "It's reality."

"Ouch again," she said, "but you're right. It's one of those realities that I don't really like to look at very much."

"That's too bad because this is one that you need to take a good hard look at, so you don't ever get into that same situation again."

"And, once again, that's a bit too much reality for me," Doreen said.

Nan hopped to her feet and said, "Let's go check the cake."

And again, the two women trooped into the house, opened the oven door, and this time Nan exclaimed, "Oh, that looks wonderful."

Using the oven mitts, Doreen very carefully pulled out the cakes, put them on top of the stove, and then looked expectantly at Nan, who said, "Now shut off the oven." She pointed out how the dial worked and how to turn it off. Doreen turned it off carefully and even stood there for a few minutes to make sure the light didn't come back on.

Then she looked at Nan, with a triumphant smile. "Now that," she said, "looks like a cake."

Chapter 6

Sunday Dinnertime ...

DOREEN DOZED OUTSIDE in the sun, replete after more tea and a piece of cake, when a warm voice woke her up.

"Did you make cake?" Mack asked, with an odd note in his voice.

She smiled up at him, patted her tummy, and said, "Nan came up and showed me how."

"Ah, so Nan made it."

Doreen shook her head. "No, I made it, thank you," she said, "but Nan showed me every step of the way." Remembering the eggs in the measuring cup, she said, "And I mean, *every* step." He looked at her quizzically, and she shook her head. "No way. Some things are just too embarrassing to tell."

His grin grew wider. "I promise I won't tell anybody, and I really could use a laugh today."

She immediately shook her head. "No, sir. I've had enough of being the butt of everybody's jokes," she said. "If this ever got around town, they'd never leave me alone."

"Ha," he said. "What'd you do? Put something in the

wrong place?"

She shook her head.

"Put in salt instead of sugar?" he asked. "Everybody has done that at least once."

She looked at him and went, "Ooh, that would be gross."

"It is," he said. "I did that one myself. What then? Dang. What else could it be? It's a pound cake," he said, "so there aren't too many ingredients. Did you try it with a pound of frozen butter?"

She shook her head.

He said, "I won't let up. I surely deserve something to smile about today."

"Only if you promise to not laugh at me," she said in a warning voice.

Immediately his face firmed up. "I would never laugh *at* you," he said.

She said, "Fine. So Nan told me to put the eggs in the measuring cup, so I did. She failed to mention the part about taking the eggs out of the shell."

He looked at her for a long moment. Then his shoulders started to shake, and his lips quivered even faster, as he tried to press them tightly together. Then his shoulders really started to shudder, until finally he couldn't contain his mirth and burst out laughing, tried to stop, and then gave up and eventually sat on the deck beside her, while she lounged in the rocker, howling with unchecked glee.

She glared at him. "You weren't supposed to laugh at me," she snapped.

"I'm not," he said, gasping for air. "I'm laughing … with you."

"Do I look like I'm laughing?" she asked.

"You should be," he said, sitting up, "because, ... oh my, that one is priceless."

She looked at him, and a smile twitched at the corner of her lips. "Nan handled it very well."

"I'm sure she did," Mack said, sitting up and looping his arms around his knees to stare up at her. "That would have been worth the price of a ticket."

"Well, it was priceless but also educational. I guess you make those mistakes every once in a while in order to realize that you really don't know what you don't know."

"Exactly," he said. "And you've already tried it out, from what I see."

"Well, we had to taste it," she said, opening her eyes wide in mock innocence. "How else would we know if it's any good?"

"Exactly," he said. "Do I get to try some?"

She immediately frowned at him. "Oh, it was supposed to be dessert."

"Well, in that case, have you got some food first?" he asked, with an eyebrow up.

"Sadly, no, I do not," she said. "Didn't you bring something?"

He burst out laughing. "Yes, I did," he said, "and it's not what I had planned to bring either."

"What did you bring?" she asked.

"Well, you might be sick of it because of all we had when the guys were here, working on the deck."

She looked at him and then groaned. "Are you talking about pizza?"

He laughed. "Yes, but this is a little different."

She hopped to her feet. "Well, let's not let it get cold," she said.

"No, no, no," he said, jumping lightly to his feet and stepping in front of her, leading the way. "This is pizza that we make."

She stopped at the doorway. "We make it?" she asked. "Is that possible?" He looked at her, lips twitching, but then she held up a hand. "Don't say it."

"I won't," he said, "but the answer is yes. It's possible. In this case, I bought the dough from the little Italian deli down off Birch. They have beautiful homemade crusts." He pointed out the one he had placed on the counter, as he continued to unpack the groceries.

"Wow," she said, looking at it with interest. "It's got all these little fingerprints inside it."

"Yeah, but they have a purpose."

"If you say so. Why do you want people to already have poked it full of holes though?"

"They just punched in finger holes," he said, "better to hold the oil and sauce." She watched as he carefully poured a little bit of olive oil on it and spread it all over the top. "I brought ham, some tomatoes, fresh basil, and mozzarella."

Immediately she lit up like a Christmas tree. "And that's all going on top?"

"Yes, if that's okay with you," he said, looking at her.

"Absolutely! I was afraid you would have deluxe or supreme or whatever those kinds were last time. There just wasn't anywhere near enough meat, way too much crust, and way too greasy. Plus, just something about fast food makes my stomach feel like I've swallowed a rock."

"Some people thrive on fast food."

"Not me," she said, "but this looks very different." She watched with interest as he laid all the ingredients carefully on the top. "You put a white sauce underneath all this?"

"Well, I figured you might prefer a ranch dressing sauce on it," he said. "Whenever I make that spaghetti sauce next, we can take out some of the sauce, before it's done, and spice it up with Italian seasoning and fresh basil and keep that for pizza sauce too."

"Oh, wow," she muttered. "It seems like, if you know what you're doing, you can make one batch of something and have it for several different things."

"That's at the heart of cooking," he said, nodding.

Before long the entire thing was fully dressed, and it was bright red with fresh tomato slices and lots of white pieces of fresh mozzarella and fresh green basil leaves.

"It looks lovely," she said.

He grabbed the salt and pepper, and then, for good measure, he tossed some parmesan all over the top. Afterward he said, "Now, this can rest like it is for a while, or we can put it into the oven right away, but, either way, we'll need to heat it up."

"The oven might still be a little warm from the cake," she said. He walked over and turned it up to the temperature he wanted.

"Generally pizzas need high heat," he said, "so we'll put it up over 400 degrees because I think this one of yours runs a bit hot. I also brought some beer, and, if you don't mind, I'll put a couple in the fridge to get cold."

She nodded. "It's not like any were left from when the deck work was done."

"Nope, and you can't really expect guys who are working hard to leave any beer behind."

"So does that mean you'll be working hard tonight?"

"Heck no," he muttered. "I need some time off. But beer and pizza are too good to pass up."

When he had the beer in the fridge, he looked at the cake and then at her expectantly.

She shrugged and said, "Well, you showed me how to make pizza, so sure."

He went and carefully cut himself a slice, poured a large glass of water, and together they went outside. They were only out there for a few minutes, when he heard the buzzer on the oven go off, saying it was up to temperature.

"Wow," he said, "that preheat was fast. Let's get that pizza in." He walked back into the kitchen.

She traipsed behind and watched as he put it into the oven on a big hot stone he'd been heating in the oven. "Where'd that stone thing come from?"

"It's one I saved for you out of Nan's stuff."

"Wow, I wouldn't have known it was there."

"Well, I remembered it," he said. He closed the oven door and said, "Now we can go relax for a bit."

"How long?"

"It's a fairly thin crust, and everything else is more or less cooked," he said, "so we'll give it twenty to thirty minutes."

She nodded and said, "Perfect. I believe I could be hungry by then."

"Well, if you're not," he said, with an evil grin, "I've probably got room for your share too."

She just snorted and said, "That's not happening."

"I was just pulling your chain anyway," he said, as he headed out to sit on the one rocker she had on deck. "I'll just close my eyes here for a bit. Oh, yeah," he said, "I almost forgot." Reaching into his pocket, he handed over a small roll of cash. "Here's the money from doing Mom's garden."

She smiled and said, "Thank you. I'll go put this in the bowl, if you don't mind." He nodded, and she walked back

76

in and headed upstairs to where she now kept the bowl. As she put the money in it, she noted another roll and frowned. "Where on earth did that come from?"

She picked it up and removed the little elastic band around it. She quickly unrolled it and counted to find exactly twelve $100 bills. She stared at it in shock for a moment, and then she knew.

"Oh, Nan," she said. Earlier today, when Nan had disappeared to go to the bathroom, it had taken a little longer than usual. Now Doreen knew why. She picked up her phone, called Nan, and, when she couldn't reach her grandmother, Doreen left a message. "Thank you for the gift, sweetie. It is very much appreciated."

She pocketed her phone and raced back to Mack. When she stepped outside again, he was sitting back with his eyes closed, gently snoring away. She stopped where she was, wondering if she should wake him, but then he'd probably had a pretty rough day, and maybe he needed the sleep. Deciding that she'd leave him for a little bit, she walked down to the garden and checked on her flowers. She hadn't spent any time in her own garden, and it was starting to show. She bent down to pull off dead flowers from the marigolds and the petunias.

She quickly walked back inside, grabbed her gloves and a bucket, and got to work. The movement hurt her shoulder for the first few minutes, then eased back. Smelling pizza, a good fifteen minutes later, she got up and went into the kitchen and opened the oven. Immediately steam poured out. But the pizza was golden and melty and looked delicious. She frowned, wondering if this was long enough. She went back out and gently touched him on the shoulder. "Hey, Mack?"

Immediately he opened his eyes and stared up at her in confusion, blinked several times, then hopped to his feet. "The pizza?"

She nodded. "It hasn't been as long as you said, but it looks pretty good, at least as far as I can see," she said, with a shrug.

He took note of the gardening gloves in the bucket on the lawn and asked, "Have you been working?"

"I wanted to let you sleep," she said, "and I haven't had any time to work on my own garden for a while."

He nodded and stepped into the kitchen. He took the pizza out, looked it over, checked the bottom of the crust, and said, "You're right. It is ready."

He quickly turned off the oven, and using a cutting board he got from the nearby cabinet, he brought out the pizza stone itself and transferred the pizza to the board, setting the stone back in the oven.

She smiled at the pizza and said, "That looks absolutely delicious."

"It will be too, but it's way too hot to eat yet. So, if you want to finish off whatever you were doing for a few minutes," he said, "feel free."

She nodded and skipped down the deck steps, her heart light, as she returned to pulling the dead blossoms off the flower bushes. At some point, he stood behind her, studying the garden. "Problems?" she asked, turning to look up at him from down on her knees.

"Did you do any of this thing when you were married?"

She shook her head. "Nope. I directed a bunch of gardeners to do it for me instead," she said. "Sometimes my knees wish I had that option back again."

He burst out laughing. "I imagine they do," he said.

"You can get knee pads, you know?"

She looked at him in surprise. "Knee pads?"

He nodded. "To protect your knees, when you're working in the garden."

"Well, I wish I'd known that," she said in exasperation. She slowly stood, wincing as she straightened out her legs. "I need to get in here and do a bunch of weeding. I never did get anything else done, outside of all those plants I was given. I never had a chance to put anything else in here."

"What about my mother's garden?"

"I got a bunch from her," she said, pointing out some of the plants along the garden. "And the grass needs to be mowed."

"I can do that after dinner," he said. She looked at him in surprise. He shrugged. "It's no big deal. I do Mom's anyway," he said. "I rarely have time to do my own though."

"Right, it seems like the more we have on our plate, the less we get to do certain things."

"Yardwork always suffers," he said. "That's just a fact of life."

"I didn't really want it to, though," she said. "Especially now, having the beautiful deck and the fancy patio." She stepped onto her new patio that had been poured and did a little jig. She laughed. "It's such a great addition to the place."

He nodded with a big grin on his face and asked, "So now would you like to come up and eat?"

"Sure," she said. Mack got the pizza and a couple plates and set them up on the table on her deck. As she walked back up the steps, she asked, "What's happening with the kid who left the threatening notes?"

"Abner?"

She nodded. "I have mixed feelings about him, since he is also the one who led us to Isaac. Did anything ever happen to him?"

"The chief has him doing a community service assignment in order to stay out of jail and to keep him on the straight and narrow."

"Good," she said. "I don't think he's a bad kid."

"Nope, and he was just following what a bad adult did."

"Yeah, that guy was a piece of work," she said. "I still don't understand why Snoz bothered putting the rocks there in the first place."

"We also don't know for sure it was him. And not likely to confirm it now that he's dead either."

"Well, Abner identified him," she said in surprise.

"I know, but, like you said, it doesn't make any sense."

"No, it doesn't."

He looked over at her and said, "Go ahead. You can choose the first piece."

She picked out a big slice of pizza, folded it slightly, and took a bite of the melting cheesy tip. "Oh, my gosh," she said, with her mouthful. "This is really good." And, in spite of eating cake not that long ago, she scarfed down the entire piece. She sat here, still moaning in delight, when he pushed the pizza toward her.

"Look. We have the whole thing for dinner."

She looked at him in wonder and immediately snatched up a second piece. With the two of them sitting at her new table on the deck, they managed to eat three-quarters of the pizza.

As he looked at the rest, Mack said, "I don't think I want any more of this tonight," he said. "I'm pretty full, and, if you are too, that leaves you a meal for tomorrow."

"Thank you. That's great," she said. "That was wonderful pizza too. I liked it a lot better than what we had last time."

"I did too," he said, with a grin. "But we won't tell the guys that. Just something about a beer-and-pizza night doing work for a friend that makes it all very special."

"Everyone did a ton of work too," she said. "I'm still trying to fix little bits and pieces, collecting things and moving gravel, but it's just so wonderful. Next year the garden will be even that much better. It's just"—she gave a happy sigh—"perfect."

Chapter 7

Sunday Evening into Monday Morning …

DOREEN AND MACK deliberately didn't talk shop throughout the evening, and she didn't even grill him before he left. She prided herself on the fact that she hadn't bugged him with any questions regarding Robin's murder, and Doreen figured it was in part because he hadn't bugged her with questions about her ex. As soon as Mack was gone though, she pulled out her phone and sent him a text. **I forgot to ask if you found out anything new.**

He answered. **You were very good tonight.**

She responded with a smiley face. **You were too. You didn't even ask about my ex.**

Let's hope there's nothing to say about your ex.

Does it matter?

There was a long moment of silence, and finally he responded. **Yes, it matters.**

She stared down at that confirmation with a happy smile on her face.

"Okay, Doreen," she said to herself. "Talk about taking it slow." Mack had been very slow about the whole thing, but then she had thrown off all kinds of negative vibes early on, telling him more or less to get lost, so she couldn't really blame him for taking his time. On the other hand, she wasn't against it. She hadn't had anything like a slow intentional courtship with her ex-husband. On the contrary.

She wasn't sure that this was actually a courtship with Mack either, but it was definitely something special. With that thought in her head, she went to bed with a smile.

When she woke up the next morning, she felt like her normal self for the first time in several days. As she stretched, her shoulder didn't make her bite back a scream. She got up and had a hot shower and didn't feel like she needed to stay there forever to move about pain-free. When she got dressed, she had both the interest and the energy to put on something pretty. She bounced down the stairs instead of slowly dragging her sorry butt one step after another. In the kitchen, she put on coffee and opened up the back door to the outside world. She stood on the deck, took a big stretch in the sunshine, and cried out, "Good morning, world!"

Her neighbor on her left asked, "What's good about it?"

She chuckled. "Hello, Richard. How are you today?"

"I'm fine," he said, "especially now that you're in trouble." Then he laughed and laughed.

"Oh, I'm not in trouble," she said. "I didn't kill her."

Immediately Richard climbed up on whatever chair or stool he kept on his side of the fence for these situations, popping his head over the fence, so she could see him. "Didn't you?"

"No, I most certainly did not," she said, with a beaming smile.

"Why didn't you?" he said. "She was miserable. A horrible person."

"Yes, but you know something could be said for enjoying that misery," she said, with a laugh.

Richard considered that, looked at her with approval, and said, "You know what? I like that thought."

"See?" she said. "I didn't kill her, but it's interesting that she died."

"Why is that?" he asked, frowning.

"Because it makes you wonder if somebody was intentionally pointing the finger at me."

His jaw dropped. "Well, you do make a good suspect."

"Apparently," she said in a dry tone. "But sorry to disappoint you. I didn't do it."

Then he said something that surprised her. "Well, if you didn't kill her, who did?"

She looked at him. "I have no idea," she said in a dry tone. "And I've been told in no uncertain terms to stay out of it, since everybody already wonders if it was me."

"Well then, you can't stay out if it," he said. "People will crucify you. People who don't know you, like I do," he said.

She stared at him, thinking back to his accusation only moments ago.

Under the scrutiny of her unwavering gaze, he at least had the good graces to flush a lovely shade of crimson. "Well, I mean, obviously I didn't believe it," he said.

"Obviously not," she said. "And you did hear her attack me when she was at my front door."

He nodded instantly. "Of course, and she was pretty riled. I did see her later that day though," he said, "but you can bet I stayed well away from her. Wow, she was a fuse ready to light, if I ever saw one."

"Where did you see her?" Doreen asked excitedly.

"Down at the Starbucks on 97, Hwy 97," he said.

"About what time was that?"

He frowned. "*Hmm.* I don't know, maybe four o'clock. The traffic was ugly. I thought about pulling in there, but instead I went to the drive-through and was glad I did, when I saw her sitting in her car, with the door open, as I drove past. That green Jaguar is unmistakable."

"It was a rental," she said.

He looked at her. "They rent luxury cars in town?"

She shrugged. "I had no idea either," she muttered, "but apparently so."

"Well, she won't be driving luxury models anymore, unless it's a coffin," he said.

"True enough."

She thought for a moment and then asked, "Have you ever seen a guy going bald, with a little bit of gray around the top of his head?" Pulling out her phone and flicking through the pictures, she continued, "He's a little older than me and is always wearing a charcoal pinstripe suit or a charcoal suit with a tiny yellow stripe or very tiny red stripe? A very dapper-looking man?" she asked, walking off the deck, getting closer, and holding up the picture of her ex on her phone. "Have you ever seen this guy around?"

He looked at it and shook his head and said, "No. Do you think he killed her?"

"Well, it's possible," she said, "but I don't even know if he is around. I know he has had some issues with her."

"Better tell the police. They need another suspect to look at besides you."

"I told Mack," she said, "but I don't think I gave him a picture." Frowning at that, she quickly sent him a text and added the picture. **This is my ex, in case he is in town. He'd make a great suspect besides me.** Then she hit Send. She smiled and said, "I just sent that to Mack too."

"Good," Richard said. "I really don't want to deal with new neighbors. You're bad enough." And, with that, he dropped down from his perch on the other side of the fence and disappeared.

She gasped in the morning light. "I'm hardly being bad or difficult to get along with," she threw out.

"*Impossible* is more like it," he said. "So much noise, so much notoriety."

She had to admit he did have a point. She knew he hadn't been very happy when the Japanese tour buses had come into her orbit either. Or maybe she'd come into theirs? She didn't know. But at least she hadn't seen any of those lately. She wandered back to the deck, then headed into the house and poured herself a cup of coffee. When she came back out, a message from Mack was on her phone.

You're not a suspect.

She grinned at that and sent back a reply. **Yay. You could've told me last night.**

Couldn't. Last night you were a suspect. This morning we know the assailant was right-handed.

She immediately hit Dial, and, when he answered, sounding a little sleepy, she said, "Seriously, am I off the hook?"

He snorted. "Maybe, but if thinking you are keeps you out of trouble …" And this time he hung up on her.

She wanted to laugh and to cry all at the same time. She hated getting hung up on but knew she deserved it, where Mack was concerned. And he hadn't done it nearly enough times to get back at all the times she'd done the same to him.

But she danced a little jig and said, "I'm no longer a suspect. I'm no longer suspect. Yay." Mugs started barking, and Goliath immediately dashed by, trying to get as far away as possible. Mugs threw himself into the grass, where he stayed, Goliath giving him a disdainful look.

Thaddeus, never one to miss a celebration, danced around on the table. "No longer a suspect. No longer a suspect."

She stopped and stared. "Wow," she said, "you pick up the darndest things."

He cocked his head to the side. "Darndest things, darndest things, darndest things."

"Okay, enough of that too," she muttered.

"Enough of that. Enough of that. Enough of that."

"Stop it," she said, "or you won't get any cake this morning!"

"Stop it, or you won't get any cake this morning!"

She just glared at the bird, and, from Richard's side of the fence, his laughter rose higher and higher, until she imagined him rolling around on the ground, laughing his fool head off.

"That's fine. Very funny. I'm glad you got your morning's entertainment," she called out.

He kicked the boards of the fence several times, as if he were truly rolling down there, uncontrollably laughing at her.

She groaned and said, "Okay, that's fine. I will go grab coffee and cake, and you're not getting any." She went inside and poured herself a second cup of coffee and grabbed a piece of cake. As soon as she walked back outside, Thaddeus sat on the table, then looked at her and flapped his wings.

"Thaddeus loves Doreen."

"Oh no, you don't," she said, holding the cake up above her head. "You're not getting a single crumb. Cake is bad for Thaddeus."

"Thaddeus loves Doreen."

"No," she said, "you won't get away with any of that." She glared at the bird, as she sat down and popped a bite of cake into her mouth.

He tried one more time, looking at her with those big eyes. "Thaddeus loves Doreen."

She shook her head, "Uh-uh, not having it, no way," she said. "You're not getting my cake." She dropped her hand just to keep it away from the bird, when Mugs jumped up and took it from her fingers. "Mugs, don't you do that," she cried out. But he was too busy scarfing down the piece of cake and wagging his tail. She glared at the animals. Thaddeus immediately hopped to the ground, trying to get some of the crumbs out of the dirt that Mugs left. "You two are terrible!"

She groaned, got up, and walked back inside to grab more cake. When she came back outside, she heard the side gate. Figuring it was probably Mack, she called out and said, "You're not getting any cake this morning either."

When she heard no answer, she shrugged, sat back down again, and watched as the two animals still fought over the last little bit of crumbs. Then Mugs paid attention to the side of the house. He woofed several times, and, with his tail wagging, he took off.

"Great. Mack, you might as well come around. It's not like Mugs greets anybody else like that," she muttered. When there was still no sign of him, she got up and went to the corner of the house. She stepped around to the side to see Mugs going crazy over a stranger bent down over him. She stared at him in surprise.

"Mugs, come here. Come on. Get over here." But Mugs ignored her completely. She studied the stranger, and then her heart stopped. Slowly the stranger straightened and looked over at her.

"Hello, Doreen."

And, sure enough, it was her ex-husband.

Chapter 8

Monday Morning ...

DOREEN STARED LONG and hard at her ex, her heart sinking. She barely even recognized him. He still wore the same high-end luxury suits he always wore. But he looked older, thinner on top, and maybe even a little thicker at the waistline. She frowned, as she studied the man she had spent so many years with. "Mathew?"

He gave her that lopsided grin that had endeared her to him in the first place, but she was long past immune to it now. "What are you doing here?" she asked quietly. She didn't ask him in, as she leaned against the side of the house, trying to ignore the fact that Mugs was almost hysterical with joy at seeing him. But then that was a dog for you. They were loyal to a fault. Mathew looked down at the dog, and she watched the corner of his lip curl up.

"He looks disgusting," Mathew stated. "When did you last have him in for a shampoo and a nail trim? He looks so disheveled."

"Well, he looks natural," she muttered. She didn't want to take offense, but those visits to the grooming parlor cost hundreds of dollars. And that was food for weeks right now.

He shook his head, looked around at the house from the side yard, and said, "So this is where you landed, huh?" He shook his head again. "Unbelievable."

"Well, when you don't get any settlement after fourteen years of marriage," she said, stiffening her back ever-so-slightly, "you learn to find a new perspective on your life."

He gave a laugh. "That was my business. I built it," he said. "Nothing for you there."

"Why are you here?" she reiterated. She knew that Nick wouldn't want her talking to him at all. He pushed his hands into his suit pockets. Another mannerism that he used to do all the time, and then—wait for it. And there it was—that little rock back on his heels, as if he were somebody important, waiting for the rest of the world to figure it out.

"Is it wrong that I wanted to stop in and see you?"

"Yes," she said bluntly. "We haven't had anything to do with each other since I left the house."

"Well, you didn't leave willingly," he reminded her.

"No, I was kicking and screaming, as I recall," she said, not liking the reminder. "It was my home."

"No, it *is* my house," he said, with that shark smile. And then he waved a hand. "But that's all water under the bridge."

"And why is that?" she asked, her fingers tapping her arms, wishing she had a way to get out of this; yet she was curious and wanted to know what he was doing here. Why here of all places, and what did it have to do with her? And did he have anything to do with Robin's death?

"I was in town," he said. "I just thought I'd stop and see how you were doing. Is Nan here?"

"No," she said. "She's at Rosemoor."

"Ah, so she's in the home," he nodded, with satisfaction.

"Finally. That's where she belongs."

Doreen gasped at that.

He shook his head. "You know she was getting loony."

"She is my grandmother," she said stiffly. "Nan is very well loved."

"That's got nothing to do with it," he said. "She was off her rocker and needed more care."

"Well, she's fine where she is right now."

He looked out toward Mugs, who had wandered away a bit and appeared to see Goliath for the first time. His eyes widened. "Is that a cat or a bobcat?"

"It's Goliath," she said. "He's a Maine coon."

"Another one of Nan's lost strays?"

She winced at that because, if one of Nan's lost strays were around, it was Doreen. "Definitely one of Nan's pets," she corrected. "You haven't told me why you're here."

She looked around at the neighborhood to see several people surreptitiously looking at them, while she talked to him. She peered around the side of her house to look at the rental car. "Green Jaguar, huh?"

"Not much for rental cars here," he said, with a sniff. "This one's a private car I had to rent."

"Oh, do people do that?" she asked in amazement. "It seems a little off."

"Well, when people need money," he said, with a negligent shrug of his shoulders, "they'll do almost anything. Including renting out their vehicle."

"Interesting," she said, not quite knowing what else to say to him because he had yet to clarify why he was here. So she just stood and waited, trying to use Mack's patience strategy to get Mathew to blurt out something first.

He studied her for a long time. "You look different

without all that makeup."

"Well, I look like me," she said, with a bright smile.

He nodded, and there was a seriousness to his tone, as he said, "I like it. It's very fresh looking."

Her eyebrows shot up. "You used to tell me how I looked tired and old without it."

"And you did," he said, with another sharp nod. "So, whatever you're doing here has changed you."

"At that, I can agree," she said, with a bright laugh. "My life is very different, and I'm quite happy with it."

He looked at Nan's house, looked at the neighborhood, and shuddered.

"Nope, it's definitely not for everyone," she said, with a nod, "but I've made a place for myself."

"But you could also unmake it," he said. "It's obviously not up to your standards."

"It takes money to live up to the standards I used to live within, when we shared our home," she said. "But you weren't into sharing anything."

"Of course not," he said. "I earned the money. It's mine."

"Well, you didn't earn it all on your own," she said, glaring at him. She remembered what Mack and Nick had said. They were right. She had spent a lot of time helping him build that business. "Particularly when we first got married," she said. "You didn't have any big fancy businesses then."

"Exactly, but I spent the marriage building them. You didn't."

"You mean, the marriage where I got to be this little arm candy and look pretty every day, all day, and talk to your business associates and dig out little bits of information from their wives?" she said, with a sniff. "It was all part of the business."

"But it's not like you were making any money. It's not like you were doing any of the business work," he pointed out. And then he held up a hand. "And I can see that you've probably had a tough time of it. I mean, look at where you're living," he said. "And I'd be more than happy to talk about a settlement."

At that, she could feel a bolt of awareness go up and down her spine. "What settlement?"

"Well, I can see that the last few months have been rough on you," he admitted. "And I should have had more compassion for where you'd have ended up."

"Well, I think you were too busy looking at Robin's booty," she said, with a little tartness to her tone. "You two didn't even wait till the ink was dry on the paperwork before she was in my bed."

"No, that's quite true. She worked her way in there very quickly," he muttered. "But it's over between us."

"Nice," she said, with a shrug, wondering at his wording. Did he not know she was dead? "And I care about that, why?"

"Because your bed is empty again," he said. He looked at her with a manufactured, boyishly appealing expression. "And I'd like you to come back and to give us another chance."

At that, she stared at him, truly shocked. "What?"

"You heard me," he said. "I'd like you to come back. I'd like us to try us again."

"Why would you want that?" she asked, stunned. Was he just throwing out ideas to confuse her? Why would he mention a settlement and her returning, unless the return idea was just to get out of paying her settlement money. She looked at him, and, although she could see that he'd gotten a little seedier, a little chunky, and a little older, she didn't see that he was any more truthful, any more open, or the slightest bit honest, which is what she would much prefer at this point in time. "I mean, let's face it. You dumped me for her, so you'll just do it again with some other broad."

"Of course not," he said. "What being around Robin showed me was that she wasn't you."

"Well, she would never be me," she muttered. "And you made it very clear that you were looking for a much younger bride."

He winced. "Well, let's just say, I had it, and it wasn't as good as the old comfortable one I owned."

At that, she glared at him. "*Owned?*"

"Okay, that's not the right way to put it," he backtracked, holding up his hand, "and I certainly don't want to upset you. Can we maybe go for a coffee somewhere?"

She hesitated because the last thing she wanted to do was spend any time with him. But what wasn't coming across with his coffee offer was anything fake or put on about him. So what was he up to? "And yet you just said you wanted me to come back. I'm still really confused. Not to mention your talk of a settlement."

"Well, I thought maybe, if we spent a little more time together, it would help both of us realize we want to get back together again."

She shook her head. "Like I said on the phone, why would I want to get back together again with you? As soon as I thought I was secure again, you would dump me." Then she stopped, looked at him, and said, "You do know that Robin is dead, right?"

His face turned somber. "I did hear that," he said softly.

"Such a great waste."

"In what way?"

He looked at her in surprise. "Well, she was awfully young, you know?"

"Right," she said, "she was all of what? Five years younger than me?"

"Less, I think," he said apologetically. "And you have held up for your age."

"Wow, this is getting better and better," she muttered to herself, knowing it was five years. "I don't understand what your comment means about her."

"Well, she was the kind to get into trouble. She liked to live dangerously."

"Yes, I know that. I mean, she cheated me out of my divorce settlement and my husband and apparently would be investigated by the bar."

He looked at her with surprise, but she couldn't tell if it was a true reaction or not. "What?"

"Oh, you didn't know that?" she asked. "My understanding is that her, uh, *lawyership* or whatever you want to call it had been called into question, due to her unscrupulous practices."

"Oh dear," he said, with a heavy sigh. "In that case, I wonder if it wasn't suicide."

"I believe she was stabbed," she said, looking at him closer. "Hard to do that to yourself."

"So," he said, "rumors have found their way to your doorstep."

"Yeah, that stuff generally does," she said cheerfully, and again she hesitated as she looked at the animals. "Well, Mugs is definitely happy to see you."

"And I'm sure you are too," he said. "It's just the shock.

And, of course, you've had several of them lately. With Robin's death and all."

"Not to mention the fact that she came here screaming at me, before she was killed."

"Oh, that's so Robin," he said, with a shudder. "The things that you don't know about a person, until you live with them. She was definitely into drama."

"Well, that she was," Doreen said, "but then you were tired of the old gray mare."

"Well, you have let yourself go a little bit," he said, "and gray hair is coming through."

"And here just a few minutes ago you said I was fresh and natural-looking," she said, with a roll of her eyes.

"Well, you are that too," he said, "but there's no doubt that you're getting a little older."

She chuckled. "Yep, and I'm coming by it honestly."

He reached up and tugged at her hand. "Still, let's go for coffee," he said. "Let's get away from this. Leave the animals behind, and let's go out for a bit, even if we just go to the park for a walk."

She hesitated, but curiosity drove her. Finally she nodded and said, "Well, a walk in the park would be nice, but I want to bring the animals." He glared, as she shrugged. "Me and the animals or not at all."

He raised his hands in surrender. "Fine," he said. "I can't imagine taking the cat for a walk though."

"You might be surprised," she said cheerfully. She went inside and grabbed a leash for Mugs and said, as she rejoined Mathew, "Why don't we walk from here?"

He looked at her in surprise and then shrugged.

She headed down the driveway with the animals, and he hadn't even seen that she'd picked up Mugs. She'd also picked up Thaddeus and waited for Mathew to notice, but he didn't seem to see the bird on her shoulder. That just blew her away, but it was obvious that he was seriously focused on something else. Finally, when they walked around the cul-de-sac, she automatically headed toward Nan and asked, "Did you want to see my grandmother?"

"Lord no," he said. "That old bat never did like me."

She winced at his wording but had to give him credit for his perspective in noting that Nan never *did* like him. "Well, maybe she has gotten softer with age."

"No," he said, shaking his head, "not at all. Chances are she wouldn't hold back now either."

"Well, you did leave me high and dry for a younger woman and without any means to support myself," she said.

"No, I know that," he said, and she wondered if that was meant to be some sort of an apology.

"You mean, you didn't do it on purpose?"

"Well, of course I did," he said, "but it probably wasn't fair."

She just wasn't sure why this turnabout was happening, and it made her very suspicious. "I'm surprised to hear that from you," she said. "It's not what I would have expected."

"Well, times change."

She didn't think about that, but something had definitely changed. As they walked, she passed Rosemoor and said, "Grandma is in here."

"Ah," he said, "well, I definitely don't want to stop and visit her there—or anywhere," he muttered, picking up the pace. "Come on. Let's hurry up."

She said, "I'm not rushing. I walk this way all the time."

"But not with me," he said. "I don't even know why we're really out here walking, not to a coffee shop, where we could be inside, where it's nice and comfortable with the coffee."

"It's a beautiful day," she said comfortably. "So no reason not to be out for a walk. I didn't want to leave the animals alone."

"Well, you have to leave them alone soon," he said, "because you certainly can't take them into the coffee shop."

"My animals go with me everywhere," she said. "The town is used to it by now."

"Lord," he said, looking at her in horror. "Tell me that you haven't become the town crazy lady?"

"Huh," she said, as she thought about it. "You may have something there. That may be exactly what I've done. Not everybody knows who I am or what I'm like, but probably just enough do."

"Oh, dear," he said. "You know that always upset me."

"What? Rumors and being talked about?"

"Of course," he said. "To think that other people are gossiping about you? That's just terrible. Privacy is everything."

"It is to you. I guess that's why I'm wondering why you're even here," she said.

"I told you. I want to reconsider our future."

"And yet there's no reason for that," she muttered. "You haven't had anything to do with me in months, so why now all of a sudden?"

"When did you get to be so suspicious?" he asked in surprise.

She laughed. "You have no idea." He stared at her, as if in question, but she just shrugged and moved on. "The bottom line is, I am suspicious."

"I guess it must have been really tough for you these last

few months," he said sympathetically. "I should have considered that."

"Considered what?" she asked. He just looked at her quietly. "So something is going on. I'm not sure what it is."

At that, his phone rang. Something else that she remembered about him was how he was always on that phone. Not that she blamed him because it was such a digital age, but it seemed like, when they were together, he was always on his phone. He answered it while they were walking, and his voice rose sharply. She tried to block it out, but he sounded more and more like the Mathew she used to know.

"Well, find out," he said. "It has to be somewhere."

At that, her ears perked up. "What's going on?" she asked curiously.

"Oh, just lawyers missing documents," he said in disgust. "You'd think it would be simple to find stuff. We have digital storage, and we have paper storage, but no, no, no. Things still go missing all the time." He got off his phone with a huff.

"I can imagine," she said. She glanced around town, as they headed down to the corner of Lower Mission. "A Starbucks is up ahead," she said. "We can always grab a coffee there."

He nodded, but he was more absentminded now. "Did you talk to Robin at all when she was here?"

"She railed and ranted at me, but it wasn't exactly a conversation."

"No, when she gets off on her little moods," he said, "it's amazingly difficult to communicate."

She wondered about the phone call. "I didn't have anything to do with her, outside of her ranting and raving."

"So you didn't meet her for coffee? You didn't have

lunch with her?"

"Why would I?" she asked in surprise, quite shocked that he would even suggest that. "She screwed me over pretty badly."

"Well, she was looking after my interests," he said. "In all honesty, you should have expected that."

"Why should I have expected it?" she said. "I hired her to represent me, not you."

"Well, because we were already together."

"But I didn't know that," she said in surprise.

He looked at her in shock, and then he started to laugh. "She had to disclose that."

"Well, she didn't," she said bitterly. "I guess that I'm naive. I wasn't expecting that."

"Well, that's why she's was so irate when she contacted me then," he said. "She said something about you making trouble for her."

"What trouble was I supposed to make?" she said, shaking her head. "She'd already taken everything I had to give."

"Interesting," he muttered. But his voice was distant, as if he were thinking of something completely different. He started to chuckle. "No wonder she was so adamant about getting everything locked, signed, and sealed early."

"But was it early?" Doreen asked.

"Well, it seemed rather fast to me."

"Meaning, you thought I would put up a bigger fight."

"Well, our agreement was pretty simple," he admitted. "And, at the time, I was congratulating myself on Robin's ability. But obviously she had another plan going."

"What are you even talking about?" Doreen asked him in surprise. "What other plan?"

He looked at her and said, "Didn't you know?"

"Know what?" she said. "I haven't understood anything since that woman arrived at my doorstep. I get that you think that I don't understand business and think I'm pretty stupid, but it's hard to understand something if you don't actually get any explanations. Or even enough information to make a proper decision about something."

"No, no, no, of course," he said, "that makes perfect sense." But he started to chuckle.

"Will you explain?"

"No," he said. "If you didn't talk to her much …" Then his phone rang again. He looked at it, groaned, and said, "Just a minute." He took a few moments to step farther aside. She eased her way toward him, as he walked away. She heard the urgency in this voice. "You've got to find it. … No, no, I'm busy. … Yeah, I know. … I'll catch the plane. Don't worry. Make sure you do too."

And, with that, it carried on, but she didn't catch most of the rest, and he finally pocketed the phone, stared up at the sky, and then turned to look at her. "Something has come up," he said. He pulled out his wallet, handed her his business card, and said, "That's my new cell phone. If you think of anything that she might have said or done that made you suspicious, let me know, will you?"

"I will," she said, staring at the card in surprise, but inside she was thinking, *The heck I will.*

He smirked and said, "It's been really good to see you."

She studied him, and, this time, she wasn't even sure what she heard in his tone of voice, but it sure wasn't sincerity. It was more like the joke was on her. But then, that was the way he always treated her.

"Why did you really come?" she asked, looking at him. "It has nothing to do with me. Or getting me back."

"You never know," he said. He reached up a hand, patted her cheek, and said, "Something's very endearing about all that freshness."

"No, you used to call it gauche and embarrassing, when speaking of other women," she said. "You really came about the lawyer. It was all about Robin, right?"

He looked at her in surprise. "Of course not."

"Well, if you're looking for her laptop, the police have it."

He froze suddenly, and out came the husband that she recognized.

He snarled. "What are you talking about?"

"She was murdered, and they took everything. And that included the blue bag she had with her, including her laptop."

He just stared at her, his eyes narrowing to angry pinpoints.

She shrugged. "You could have just asked me at the beginning. It's not like I would fall for your BS now anyway."

He chuckled and said, "I think I like this spirit. You didn't ever talk to me like that."

"I almost never even talked," she muttered.

"And that's the way I liked it," he said, "but Robin was very different, so that gave me a different experience. And this spirit, I like it." He smiled. "Keep it up. Keep it up. And I'll see you in a little bit," he said. "I've got to fly back home, but I'll stay in touch."

Bemused, she watched as he turned and headed out without her. "Well, you might as well walk back with me," she said. "Your car is there."

He stopped, looked at her, and shrugged, then said, "Actually I'm here with somebody else, and they've already picked up the car."

"Ah," she said, wondering about that too. "I guess that makes sense. You didn't use to drive yourself around."

"Still don't drive much," he said, "just when I want privacy."

And, at that, she heard the purr of a powerful engine and watched as the Jaguar pulled up beside him.

"Robin was driving a car like that." He looked at her in surprise. Doreen shrugged. "I guess, like you, she's used to that luxury and couldn't get away from it. But I figured you wouldn't fund any more of it."

"No, I certainly wasn't," he said in a decisive motion. As he went to get in, she stepped forward and asked, "What broke up you guys?"

He just looked at her, as if wondering what to say. Then smiled and said, "She wasn't you."

And, with that, he got into the vehicle and drove away, as she stared in stunned disbelief.

Chapter 9

Monday Midmorning ...

AS DOREEN SLOWLY turned and walked past Rosemoor, Nan stood outside, waiting for her.

"Was that Mathew?" Nan snapped.

Doreen looked at her grandmother and nodded slowly. "I don't know what's going on though, so don't even ask," she muttered.

"Well, it won't be anything good. He's up to something. You can count on that."

"He's always up to something, isn't he?" Doreen said absentmindedly, wondering just what that could be. Nothing made sense.

"Absolutely he is," Nan muttered. "That man is simply no good."

"I get it," she said. "I just still don't understand the turn of events today."

"Well, it's scary that he even showed up at all. Maybe he killed the lawyer."

"Maybe," she said. "I did think of that."

"Of course you did. You're not stupid," Nan said.

She smiled. "You know what? You're the only one who

ever believed that," she said, with a laugh.

"Well, you should have believed it yourself all these years. But that man? That man is poison."

"Maybe. We definitely have to figure something out."

"Figure something out? What do you mean?"

She shook her head. "Sorry, I'm just thinking about some of the things I heard him say."

"Tell me. Tell me," Nan said, as she pointed at the patio. "Come have tea, and talk to me."

She looked at her and grinned. "You're just curious."

"I'm dying of curiosity. Wherever that man goes," she said, "trouble is in his wake. The fact that he's here and talking to you just terrifies me. I already told Mack."

Doreen stopped in her tracks. "You told Mack what?"

"I told him that your ex was here in town."

"Why would you do that?"

"Maybe the better question is," Nan said, turning to look at her in all seriousness, "why you didn't."

"Because," and then she stopped. "It wasn't … any of his business?"

Nan snorted at that. "That's because you're thinking like a woman. You're not thinking like a detective," she said. "Where's your head at, dear? Your lawyer gets murdered, and then your ex shows up. Of course they're connected."

"Well, I did think of that," she said, "but I couldn't really figure out why or how. Besides, I would text Mack now anyway," she said. Then she shrugged, as she sat down on the patio chair. "Honestly I was just flabbergasted that he was even here. He wanted to go for coffee, and I suggested going for a walk and automatically came this direction," she said, looking around. At that, another vehicle pulled up, and she watched as Mack got out of his truck and strode toward them.

"Great," she said, "now I'm about to get the fifth degree."

"And you better have an excuse ready," Nan warned.

"Why?" she said, glaring at her grandmother.

"Because you hurt his feelings, and Mack is a good man. You don't want to chase him away, making him think you're still interested in your ex."

She leaned toward Nan and whispered, "Mathew said he wanted me back."

At that, Nan stared at her, her mouth open. "He said what?"

She nodded slowly, as she watched Mack coming toward them with big long strides.

"What did you say to him?"

"I didn't really say anything because I knew it wasn't real. No way that's what he wants."

"Then he's up to something."

"I know," she said. "I just couldn't figure out what."

At that, Mack arrived and, glaring at Doreen, asked, "Figure out what?"

Immediately she glared back and said, "Trying to figure out what my ex was up to."

"Why was he here?" he asked and settled in a little bit, as if afraid that she wouldn't say anything.

"He didn't make that clear, and he is supposed to be flying out this afternoon." She checked her watch and said, "I think in about two or three hours."

"Any reason I should detain him?"

"I'm not sure. He didn't seem normal," she said.

"Meaning?"

"I think he was pretending to be nice, but I don't know

what he wanted from me. He wasn't here alone either, but I don't know who else he had with him. He was also on the phone a lot."

"All of this sounds very intriguing," he said, "but does it pertain to the case?"

She didn't like that stiffness to his tone. "Hard to say," she said, "but I do think that he was looking for something of Robin's."

"Like what?"

"Well, he kept talking to somebody on the phone about looking for something." Then she stopped and stared back in the direction of her house. "Oh my," she said. "I was really flabbergasted that he just showed up like that." Then she hopped to her feet. "Uh-oh, uh-oh."

"What?" Nan and Mack both said in loud voices.

"The Jaguar was parked at my house, and we went for a walk. He said that somebody else had picked up the Jag, yet, all the while, when we were walking, he was talking to someone about looking for something. I didn't put two and two together," she cried out in horror.

"Two and two what together?"

"He was searching my house. That's where they were looking for something." She stared at Mack in shock. "I just don't know what was there for them to find."

"Well, it must have been important," he murmured, "because he managed to get you away long enough for somebody to go in and check it out."

Chapter 10

Monday Midmorning ...

DOREEN CALLED THE animals to her, as she swept Thaddeus off the table, and raced off the patio, across the lawn, and headed toward the river.

Mack called out, "Wait, damn it. Wait!"

She said, "I'm going home."

"I have my truck right here."

She shook her head, lifted a hand, and said, "I'll meet you there." And she ran down to the river pathway. Keeping a steady pace, she moved along, past the houses up toward her own backyard. There she increased her speed because the ground was a little softer, as she raced up the path toward her house. She hadn't even thought about putting on the security system.

Why would she? She was just going for a walk with her ex. And, of course, that's the tricky part with her ex. *Now* all his stupid comments that kept her off-balance made some sense. Of course he didn't want her back. He just wanted her out of the house. It's not like she'd given going back to him a moment's thought anyway—although a part of her admitted it would be nice to know that she had no bills looming, that she had a secure roof over her head and a steady supply of food on the table. But that had been nothing more than a fleeting thought that was immediately gone. The life she had now was independent and free, and she marveled at the taste of freedom. It was incredible and was something she wasn't prepared to give up. At the same time, it was obvious that Mathew had been up to something, and she'd fallen for his ruse. Talk about stupid.

As she bolted through the kitchen door, she saw Mack coming through the front door. They both stopped and stared.

"Now stay where you are," he said, "and think. Has anything shifted? Has anything moved?"

She froze, even as Mugs and Goliath raced inside to greet Mack, as if they hadn't seen him in a year instead of two minutes ago. She shook her head at the animals. "I think they prefer you to me."

He bent down and gently petted them both. "It's nice to be wanted," he said.

She wasn't sure if he meant something by that or not, but she noted that odd tone in his voice. Then she remembered Nan's words. "You know that Mathew didn't actually want anything to do with me, right? He just wanted to get me out of the house."

"Well, I know that now," he said. "I wasn't sure if you knew that."

"I do now," she said. "I might be slow, but I'm not that slow."

"You're not slow at all," he said. "But I'm not sure how much you might have been taken in by the thought of going back to your old life."

"I'd be lying if I didn't say that, for a tiny fraction of a

MURDER IN THE MARIGOLDS

second, there was the thought of having no bills to pay, food on the table all the time without having to worry, and going to sleep at night and then to wake up the next morning knowing that I was okay," she muttered. "But I can tell you that it went into my brain and right back out again. I could never give up what I currently have."

"What do you currently have?" he asked curiously.

Her gaze, as it had been circling through the kitchen and around to her tiny little office area, zoomed back toward him. "Freedom," she said succinctly. "For the first time in my life, I'm free."

His eyebrows shot up, as he considered her words. "I guess that's important, isn't it?"

"I'm free to make breakfast, if I want. I'm free to decide if I get to eat or not, even what I want to eat. I'm free as to what clothes I choose to wear or whether I put on makeup. I'm free to do what I want during the day," she said. "I'm free to get a job, if I want." Then she muttered, "If I can anyway." She shrugged. "As someone on display in a gilded cage, I didn't realize how much of a prisoner I was, until I got a taste of freedom. Only then did I understand the difference and discovered how very restrictive my lifestyle was before."

"And I'm sure it was," he said. "That can't have been easy."

"I didn't see it happening at first, and, by the time I really understood, it was way too late."

"Let's forget about all that right now," he said, "and focus on your house."

Her gaze returned immediately to the office area and the papers there. She stepped closer and took a careful look. "Well, it looks like everything has been riffled a bit," she said, "but it will be a little hard to tell if anything's missing."

"Do you have any idea what he could be looking for?"

She thought about it and said, "Honestly I'm thinking that he's probably looking for anything to do with Robin."

At that, Mack turned and looked at her in surprise.

"He seemed quite perturbed when I told him that her laptop was in police possession."

"Where else would it be?" Mack asked curiously.

"I don't know, but maybe that's what he was looking for and thought she had left it here."

"Well, that all tracks," he said, "except for the fact that it's a murder investigation. You did find it, and you moved it on to us," he said, "although maybe it required a little persuasion."

"But the bottom line is, you do have it," she said.

"What are the chances that somebody saw you with it?"

She looked at him. "Anything is possible. The restaurant may have even told Mathew that they gave it to me."

"Quite right," he said. "I think it's safe to say he came here looking for that and maybe anything else he could find. Let's go check upstairs."

With that, they did a full search of the house.

"They obviously went through everything," she said. "Closet doors are open that I wouldn't have left open. Drawers are ajar that I wouldn't have left that way, things like that," she said. "But I honestly can't tell if anything is missing."

"And you didn't have much in the way of valuables, right?"

She raced over to Nan's bowl that she kept in one of the drawers. She pulled it out, shook her head, and said, "You know what? Really this is chump change for him."

"Maybe, but it wasn't him who did the searching, and it might not have been chump change to whoever that was."

"True, but Mathew would not have been pleased if somebody accepted a little something for themselves."

"Right. A bit of a stickler on things like that, is he?"

"In a big way."

She stared down, her fingers automatically going through the bowl of coins and bills, including the new roll from Nan. "I don't know what I would have done if I'd lost this," she muttered.

"You would have been fine." He gently squeezed her good shoulder. "Now, let's stay focused. Anything else to check?"

She looked at him, turned around to survey her bedroom, and said, "Well, the antiques are already out of here, and that's what was really valuable. Even the rare books. But I guess to be thorough, we should check the basement."

He led the way downstairs to the basement, and she searched the area and said, "I mean, nothing's really down here anyway."

"No, we did a good job emptying it," he said, with a note of humor.

She smiled up at him. "We did, indeed."

"And what about the garage?" he asked. We should check that as well."

They went out through the double doors to the garage. As she turned in a slow circle in the middle of the garage and all the tools, she said, "I don't think anything is missing in here either."

"Well, that's the good thing about not having much," he said cheerfully. "Not much to steal."

She rolled her eyes at him. "There is some truth to that.

He has all kinds of security systems at his place."

"Like what?" he asked.

"Surveillance cameras all over the property, alarm systems, things like that," she said, with a shrug. "I'm not even sure about all that he has."

"You never had anything to do with it?"

"No, not at all," she said, "just a matter of the need to always have them turned on. He was a stickler for that too," she admitted. "But then we had people on the property all the time who were looking after it."

"So would you say he was paranoid?"

"Absolutely. Of course, at the time, it just seemed normal. But, looking back, yeah, he was definitely paranoid. I don't think he's very comfortable in the world he's created for himself," she said.

"That's an interesting way to put it."

"I don't know about that," she said, "but, as I look around, and as I realize just how much I was confined in a way, he was also confined."

At that, Mack stopped, stared at her, and said, "That's an interesting take."

She shrugged. "Well, how else would you describe it?"

"I'm not sure, but he did have access to the security system, so he could turn it on and off at will, right?"

"Yes, but he didn't. When we were in for the night, we stayed in for the night. I don't know if he ever went out again."

"And what about when he was meeting the lawyer?"

She winced at that. "I'm not even sure when and how all that happened," she said, with a wave of her hand. "And I really don't want to go in that direction."

"Good," he said cheerfully. "Glad to hear it." And, this

time, his voice was more relaxed.

"Now that we've checked," she said, "I can calm down."

"More or less, yes," he said. "I guess I wanted to know for sure that he was actually gone."

"And why didn't you detain him?"

"I had no reason to," he said. "But now? I want to speak to him. I didn't really have a reason to before."

"That's not true," she argued. "We definitely have a reason. When you think about it, he needed to be questioned in terms of the lawyer's death. It's way too much of a coincidence for both of them to be here in the same time frame."

He just glared at her, and then his phone rang. He answered it. "Oh, good," he said, grinning at the phone. "I'll come down and have a talk with him myself."

"I thought—" She stopped and froze. "You lied to me," she cried out, when he got off the phone.

He glared at her.

"You were trying to throw me off the scent. You did pick him up, didn't you?"

"For questioning, yes. And he came quite willingly, without any trouble."

"Yeah, he is good at that," she muttered.

"Good at what?"

"Throwing people off that way. He's really good at deception."

"I'll keep that in mind. He does have a flight to catch later this evening," he said. "And he has requested that he be released in time for that."

"Of course," she muttered.

"If we need to get him back, we can always get him back."

"Says you. It would be much easier to keep him here.

117

Then you can nail him to the wall."

"Funny, you're the one who was out walking with him today, without first telling me about his arrival," Mack said, as he walked to the front door.

"Not fair," she said. "I was still trying to figure out what he was up to. The only reason I went for a walk was so I could figure that out. I was curious."

"Ha," he said, "and maybe, just maybe, you were a little homesick and a little lost and a little lonely."

"And you think I went with him for that?"

"Sure, it makes sense to me," he said. "Maybe this is too much for you here."

"What is too much?" she cried out, looking at him in surprise.

"Figuring out how to live on your own."

"Didn't you just hear me? I said freedom is what I was enjoying."

"But maybe it's not what you really want."

She glared at him, her hands on her hips, and said, "It is."

"So then you're never getting married again, are you?"

"I don't know if I am," she said, raising both hands in frustration. "It's too early to tell. I'm still caught up in this mess. Besides, what is it to you?"

He stopped, looked at her, and said, "Really?"

Something was going on here, and it had do with the relationship between the two of them. She just didn't know how she would say anything to him. "I'm not ready," she blurted out.

"And I get that," he said, "and honestly I'm good with that."

"You are?" she asked cautiously.

"Absolutely."

He got to the front door, and she said, "I don't want you to be mad."

He looked at her, his expression gentle, as he shook his head. "I'm not mad," he said. "If anything, this is actually encouraging."

She tilted her head to the side. "In what way?"

"Well, maybe you were looking at going back with him," he said cheerfully.

"I wasn't," she said.

He nodded. "And I didn't believe you the first time," he said, with a grin, "but I do now." He lifted his hand and said, "We'll talk later."

"If you're sure?"

"I'm sure," he said. "No pressure."

She smiled. "Thank you. You're really a nice man."

His head popped back in the doorway, and he shook it at her. "Don't say that to a guy. It's really not a compliment." At that, he laughed.

She ran to the door to watch, her heart twisting a little as he pulled away, mesmerized by that grin on his face when he reached a hand out his truck window and said, "I'll be back."

Chapter 11

Monday, Nearly Noon ...

DOREEN NODDED, CROSSED her arms over her chest, and leaned against the doorjamb. Since he'd come into her life, he'd shown her something completely different in a man. Something completely different in a relationship. They were friends. Could friends become lovers? They certainly did the world over. Was it a good idea? She knew Nan would be dying for Doreen to jump into bed with Mack. But it wasn't the whole bed thing that bothered her; it was what had happened afterward in her marriage that was the problem. That was where she'd become less than a whole person.

And how did that even work? How was she supposed to have faith in herself when she was the one who had made all these decisions that resulted in her being the person kicked out after all those years, the one who didn't even fight for her own divorce settlement. As she saw her ex for the first time since she had left, she now realized just how much she had helped build up his business and how much she was a part of what he had created. And, for the first time, what Nick had said to her made sense.

She pulled out her phone and called him. "I don't know if you know this," she said, "but my ex was here today. Mack is on his way down to the station to talk to him."

"Interesting," Nick said in surprise. "What did he want to talk about?"

"Well, it was bizarre because he actually mentioned twice that he wanted me back."

There was silence on the other end. And then he finally said, "So, are you going back?"

"Oh no, no, not at all," she said, laughing. "I went for a walk with him because I was curious to see what he was up to. You know? To figure out just what shenanigans he was up to because he is *that guy.* But he did mention it several times and, only after I stopped to see Nan, and then Mack showed up, did I figure out the real reason Mathew wanted to go for a walk. He had somebody search my house while I was gone."

"What?" Nick asked in outrage.

"Yes, and, of course, you'll confirm with your brother, but I think Mathew was after Robin, the crooked lawyer's, laptop."

"And why would he want that?" he muttered.

"Well, I can think of all kinds of reasons," she said, "but none of them good."

"Of course not. Interesting that he actually flew down."

"He has apparently asked to be allowed to get on his scheduled flight tonight," she said. "I'm hoping Mack has a reason to keep him."

"Me too. I'd love a chance to talk with him."

"But you don't get to, do you?"

"Only if he is willing," he said. "But, otherwise, no, we'll go through his lawyer."

"We did talk about the fact that he doesn't think I'm owed anything. But, at the beginning, he mentioned a possible settlement, but I think he was just trying to keep me off-center."

"Oh, ouch."

"No, it was a good conversation," she said.

"And I suppose now you want me to drop everything," he said in a resigned tone.

"Actually, no, I don't," she said. "As Mathew and I talked, I came to realize how much I had contributed to his business all those years and how I was actually a partner in things and not just plastic arm candy. Arm candy was the job description, and I played it very well, but it was almost twenty-four hours a day," she said, as she stared out at the deck. "I'm not sure what kind of money we're talking about, but I really don't want him to get away with all of it."

"Good," he said. "In that case, I'm glad he stopped by to see you. Maybe it helped to put things in perspective."

"That's exactly what it did," she crowed. "I think it backfired on him because I don't think that's how he thought it would go at all. I'm sure he thinks that I'm now wondering when he will call me again and invite me back into my old house."

"Good, and I know Mack would agree."

"Well, I don't know where Mack and I are at exactly," she said, "but I do know that we're really good friends. I don't want to ruin that."

Nick's voice was gentle, as he replied, "Just because you are good friends doesn't mean you can't be more."

"I don't have any references to draw from on that," she muttered. "Nan is always bugging me to push the issue, but I wonder about the judgment of somebody, like me, who I thought was intelligent, yet I was capable of falling for Mathew's ploys and becoming the person I was at the end of the marriage," she said. "I don't want to go back to that. I feel like I'm not ready or strong enough or aware enough to not let something like that happen again."

"Well, it's interesting that you're talking like that," Nick said, "because it sounds like you want a different future for yourself and that you're trying to work on the things you need to do to get that. That's really good to hear."

"Is it?" she asked in a dry tone. "It just makes me very confused."

"And, for that reason alone, I would suggest you talk to somebody."

"You mean, like a shrink?" she said. "My husband would have a heyday."

"And you're right. He probably would, and it would be ammo that he would likely use, but it's also ammo I could use as well. That there was so much mental abuse and physical abuse in your marriage that you needed help."

She laughed at that. "Mental, yes. Physical, no. At least not much."

"You know something, Doreen? I'm not sure about that," he said quietly. "In this day and age, a lot of people would look at what happened to you in a very different light."

"I lived in a gilded cage. Nobody has sympathy for that," she said, "so that won't wash. And I'm not trying to take from him anything that I'm not allowed to have. But I do feel like he owes me something."

"He does, indeed, and now maybe the government is more interested in what he's doing and why he is here too. I confess that it did cross my mind to wonder if he had killed the lawyer."

"Me too, but I really don't think so now," she said.

"Why not?" he asked.

"I think she had something he wanted, and she was here, so he thinks I might have gotten it from her, since she hated him at that point. I think it was a toss-up as to which of us she hated the most, me or him. I don't know," she said, confusing herself.

"Are you certain she didn't leave anything at your house?"

"I'm not sure," she said, spinning around and looking. "I haven't found anything new, but so far I haven't found anything missing either, after Mathew had my house searched. I'm not sure Robin even came inside the front door, to be honest."

"Well, see what comes up, when you have time to really think about it," he said. "Because, in a way, it would make sense that he should come to you to get that. And he surprised all of us by showing up."

"Right," she muttered. "But, if he didn't kill her, who did?"

"Maybe he hired somebody to do it."

"Or maybe it has nothing to do with any of this," she muttered.

"Do you know if she has ever been through here before?"

"I have no idea," she said. "I don't even know where she is from."

"Well, I can tell you that she was married before."

"She was?" Doreen stopped and said, "She was quite young."

"She was twenty-nine, turning thirty this year. She was married at eighteen."

"Oh," she said, in surprise, "that's young too."

"Exactly. She was married for three years."

"I wonder what happened."

"Like most things in life, it broke up."

"She didn't kill him, did she?" she asked, wondering at the potential irony.

"I highly doubt it," he said, "but, in the world you walk in, who knows?" And then he laughed. "Maybe I'll just take a quick look and find out."

"Oh, please do, to get my mind off this mess here," she said, with sudden fascination. "What's his name?"

"I'll text it to you," he said. "And I'll do a bit of digging on my own."

When he hung up, she was a whole lot happier. As a matter of fact, Doreen actually felt like she had a whole new lease on life. How exciting.

Chapter 12

Monday Noon …

DOREEN PUT ON a pot of coffee, got out her laptop and a notepad, and jotted down notes. First, she put down everything she could remember of the conversation with the lawyer. Ex-lawyer. Doreen didn't even want to use her first name. She was just *the lawyer*. It allowed a little bit of distance in Doreen's mind from the hurt and the sense of betrayal. Not just professionally but also as a friend. At which point, Doreen realized there was no friendship. That's not what friends did to each other.

Then she wrote down everything she remembered of her husband's visit. *Ex-husband, maybe not in deed yet but mentally…* And the details of her suspicion that someone had gone through her place while they were out. That completed, she opened up the laptop and started researching the lawyer's past. Indeed, she had been married, and, as the text from Nick confirmed, it had lasted three years, and then her husband had gone back to school. So had Robin, and apparently that had been the end of it. She went through law school, followed by all kinds of suspicious rapid rising success in the law firm.

As Doreen read about it, she wondered because two divorces followed, involving other partners in the law firm. As she read some of the gossip columns, she found some reports of liaisons between Robin and the partners in the law firm where she worked. That would make sense, if she had slept her way to the top.

Apparently Robin had slept her way into other advantageous positions as well. Maybe that's the only way she knew how to be a success in life. Sad if that were the truth. But Doreen wouldn't get hung up on that right now. There was just so much else. She searched the first husband because that could make for another suspect. But, as she searched, she didn't find a whole lot. He was a lawyer in Vancouver, married, with two kids. She frowned as she searched for anything more, but she found nothing. She quickly sent Nick a message back. **The first husband seems clear.**

Agreed.

And she kept searching, looking for anything, but nothing was to be found. She groaned, as she sank back. "Come on," she said, to no one in particular, though Thaddeus looked interested. "If you got involved with any of the lawyers in your firm, then potentially one of the wives did something about it. That would be awfully hard to find out for sure." On impulse Doreen picked up her phone and made a long-distance call to the law firm where Robin worked, until her death. When one of the receptionists asked who was calling, Doreen said she had heard about Robin and that she was an old friend.

"I'm so sorry," the receptionist replied. "It's been a shock to all of us here."

"She said her boyfriend was one of the other lawyers there. Could I talk to him, please? I really want to know she was happy her last few months."

"I'm sorry." The receptionist's voice turned stiff. "To the best of my knowledge, she didn't have a boyfriend."

"Oh, yes, she most definitely did," Doreen said in a gushing voice. "I know she did. She told me how wonderful he was and that they worked together all the time."

"Sorry," the receptionist said stiffly, "I wouldn't know anything about that."

"I'm sorry," she said, with an innocence to her voice that she was really proud of. "I'm really not trying to step on toes, but she was a really good friend of mine."

"I'm so sorry for your loss," she said, "but I can't help you any further."

"Wait, could you at least put me through to him, so I can talk to him myself?"

The woman hesitated.

"Surely it won't hurt anyone," Doreen whispered. "My heart is breaking for my friend."

"I'll pass on the message," was all the receptionist said, and then she hung up.

"You'll *pass on the message*," Doreen said out loud. "Fascinating. So the receptionist knew that Robin had a relationship with somebody. Too bad I didn't get his name." She quickly texted the information to Nick. It wasn't helpful, yet it was affirming.

Nick called her and said, "You know that Mack won't be happy with us."

"Ah, but you can see just how addictive this sleuthing can be?"

"Very," he said, chuckling. "But all we know is that she had an affair with some lawyer in her office."

"Plus several others earlier, I believe, but then she also

had an affair with my ex," she said. "So, what if some disgruntlement is there?"

"Then we lay the names and places in Mack's lap, and he can find out."

"I suppose," she muttered, "but I'd really rather find out myself."

"It is a current case. Remember that," he said.

"Right, in which case Mack will be mad at me." She sighed. "Is there anything suspicious about her and her ex?"

"What do you mean?"

"Well, if there was a cold case involving her and her ex-husband, then I could look into it."

He started to laugh. "I have no idea," he said. "How would we possibly find out? We both did some initial looking without any luck. So what do you suggest?"

"If only their names came up in connection to something," she muttered.

"Well, his parents were murdered, but I don't know that it's a cold case."

Her ears perked up, and she sat up straight, a big grin on her face. "Seriously? We'll need to find out," she said urgently. "That would be huge."

"Whoa, whoa, whoa," he said. "You're not getting me hooked into this. I don't want to get on the wrong side of my brother."

She snorted. "Are you scared of him?"

"Absolutely, and you should be too," he warned. "We definitely do not want him upset at us."

"Nope," she said, "I don't. I've mostly avoided that, so far. But, if it's a cold case, then I would be fully justified in going down that pathway."

"I'm not sure how the justification works," he muttered,

"but I can give you the names of the parents."

"Perfect," she said. "That'll work."

"In what way?"

"I have my ways and means," she said. "What are their names?"

"Ralph and Jennifer Waldorf," he said. "And their deaths were over a decade ago."

"Oh boy," she muttered. *Hmm.*

"What does that mean?"

"As cold cases go, a decade isn't too bad, but it can be hard to get accurate information. Twenty years ago, we had that switch from paper to digital, and then after 2010 and beyond," she said, "we would have social media to mine."

"Oh, that's interesting," he said. "I hadn't thought of it that way."

After the call, it took quite a bit of digging, but finally she found what she was looking for. It was apparently a breaking-and-entering case gone wrong. The parents were supposed to be at the symphony for the evening, but Jennifer hadn't been feeling well, so she'd stayed home, and so did Ralph. The intruders snuck into the basement. The father went down to investigate; there was a tussle, and he fell down the basement stairs, broke his neck, and died almost instantly. The wife heard the fight and called the police but then panicked and raced down the stairs after her husband, where they knocked her out. But they broke her nose and ended up killing her instantly, as a bone pierced her brain. So the burglary ended up being two murders.

Doreen stared at the information on the page and shook her head. "What a waste," she said. As she continued, she realized it was, indeed, a cold case. The murderer had never been caught, and the local authorities had very few suspects.

Doreen knew that the son would be a suspect by default, since he was the one who inherited.

And he was married at the time, to her lovely ex-lawyer.

"Interesting," she muttered. "Law school is expensive. Is that how she funded it?" And that, of course, led to Doreen wondering if both Robin and her husband had funded college that way deliberately. Doreen hated to think that anybody would kill their parents in order to get the money to go to school, but she had seen murders for less. And she knew Mack had seen murder cases with much less motive. She frowned as she sat back.

What motive would there be, besides money? The burglars apparently got away with handfuls of jewelry and a painting, all of which had yet to show up later. And just like that, she was fascinated. She got up and paced her kitchen and then the living room. In a comedic array, Mugs matched her, step by step by step. Goliath, in true fashion, settled himself on the bottom step of the stairway, and she watched his tail twitching, as she went past him again and again and again. Thaddeus was on the kitchen table, doing a stiff-legged march along the tabletop, keeping time with her. She laughed. "I don't think any of this is helping us, guys."

"Helping Thaddeus. Helping Thaddeus."

"Are you helping, Thaddeus? Well, in that case, do you want to go find something shiny for us?" she asked. "I feel like we need a break in the case."

"Break in the case. Break in the case."

"Well, I said we needed a break, and, being a cold case, the details are quite sketchy."

She wondered if she dared ask Mack to take a look at the file. She did as much research as she could and found various snippets of information, including an obituary on the parents, but, as far as actual forensic information, it was pretty skimpy. Nick might help too. Delighted to have another resource, she quickly forwarded the information she had gathered on the case and sent it to him. **Is there any way to track what happened to the money they received?**

Nick called her right away and said, "Not really. That was a long time ago, and, once the inheritance is paid, and no further investigation involves them, nothing much anybody can do about it."

"And it wasn't insurance money, right? It was just that they got the house and personal belongings, correct?"

"Again, I haven't seen the will, and I don't know what the estate looked like, but, in a case like that, if they're not considered suspects, they have every right to inherit."

"What if they *are* considered suspects?"

"Which they aren't," he reiterated. "Nothing in any of the files indicates that. The authorities had no evidence to move in that direction."

"Well, what I find interesting," she said, "and maybe you can help with this, is that both of them went to law school."

"Well, that makes a lot of sense," he muttered. "Most people have a defining moment in their life that changes the course of what they were planning on doing, and, in this case, the murder of his parents probably sent them both looking for justice."

"Oh," she said, then sat back and thought about it.

"What were you thinking?" he asked curiously.

"I was thinking they were looking for money for school."

He gasped in shock.

"I know it sounds bad," she said, "but you know that

people have committed murder for a lot worse reasons. Surely we can find out if they had student loans, can't we?"

"And you're thinking, if they didn't have student loans, that would support the theory that they murdered her in-laws?"

"Well, I mean obviously, if they got the money free and clear on the inheritance, they would have used that for law school, depending on how much it actually was, and both of them got an education. Still paying cash seems suspicious."

"If they paid cash maybe, but maybe not. Maybe they worked several jobs," he said. "You can't assume anything." Hearing the same rebuke in his tone that Mack always used on her, she groaned. "I'm not trying to assume," she said. "I'm just trying to figure out how we can prove that."

"I don't know," he said. "So far, none of the jewelry or the painting was ever found again."

"That would be something too," she said. "I wonder how we could find out about that."

"Well, if they haven't shown up in ten years, you can bet it won't show up anytime soon."

"No, but there's got to be a reason. If it was theft, then maybe people are just sitting on it, until they can sell it."

"It's hot, meaning, that as soon as it's identified through a sale or something public, then people will know the seller had something to do with the murders."

"Right, so whoever it is maybe took it out of the country or something," Doreen said.

"You mean, like take it to another country and sell it?"

"Yes, depending on how much it is worth," she said. "I mean, it's pretty easy for a woman to wear jewelry onto a plane, and you'd never really know if it was stolen or not."

"I guess it depends on what jewelry it was."

"Right. Which is exactly why I need the cold case file," she said triumphantly.

"Well, you know exactly who to ask then, don't you?" he said. Then he hung up on her.

She stared at the phone. "Oh no, you don't," she said. "Not you too." She glared at her phone, but then it rang right in her hand. And, sure enough, it was Mack.

"What's up?" he asked suspiciously.

"You called me. What do you mean, what's up?"

"You sound odd."

"I was just talking to your brother," she said, with a groan. "He's a little bit too much like you for comfort."

"Meaning?"

"He hung up on me," she wailed.

After a moment of startled silence, Mack laughed. "You must have got to him, if he did that."

"Apparently I can get to anybody," she said, with a dark tone. "Can you pull a cold case file for me?"

"Nope," he said cheerfully.

"It's related," she said.

"I doubt it," he snapped. "You're just trying to get your nose in my business."

"Is it working?"

"Nope, not at all," he said once again in a cheerful voice.

Then she remembered what he had been doing. "Hey, what about my ex?"

"What about him? He decided to stay in town for a couple days."

"Ooh," she said, "that's fascinating."

"Well, I don't know about *fascinating* as much as potentially irritating, but, hey, we'll keep him close. He is coming back in to answer a few more questions tomorrow."

"Why did you let him go today?"

"Because we didn't have any real reason to hang on to him, and we don't want to tip him off and let him know we're suspicious."

"Right, you want his cooperation," she groaned. "But that means he's still in town, so I will have to deal with him."

"Why do you think that?" Mack asked curiously. "Do you think he will contact you again?"

"Yes. He already searched my house, but that doesn't mean he found what he was looking for or that he wants something else as well. Or is afraid I know something I'm not telling him." And she had to wonder if maybe she did. She looked around her home.

"Did you let Robin in the house?" Mack asked.

"No, not really," she said. "It was mostly a big confrontation on the front steps." At that, she walked to the front door, pushed open the screen door, stepped out, and looked around. "And you've got her laptop anyway. Can you not get into it?"

"Forensics has it," he said easily. "And remember. I'm not telling you anything."

"So, back to that cold case," she said. "Could you get me the file of the murders of Ralph and Jennifer Waldorf, on August 17, 2000?"

"What difference does it make?" he asked.

"I think it'll be interesting."

He said, "Is it related? You said it was related."

"And you said it wasn't."

"I'll take a look at it," he said, "but chances are it's a no." Then he hung up on her.

Doreen sighed and came back inside. As she slowly put her phone on the kitchen table, she looked around the kitchen, ran her fingers through her hair, and said, "I need coffee."

She walked over and put on the coffeepot, wondering what Mack would decide. She didn't have long to wait. No sooner had she hit the Start button on the coffeepot than her phone rang. She walked over, took a look, and started to laugh.

Chapter 13

"HEY, MACK," DOREEN said, feeling pleased with herself.

Where did you find this?" he snapped.

"Well, that's why I wanted more information because I hardly found a thing. I mean, until we actually get anything, we don't know squat, right? That's how you always look at everything, right?"

"Where did you get this information?"

"Well, you'll just get mad at him, and I don't want that."

"My brother?" he asked, incredulous.

"Well, not so much your brother as I did worm it out of him."

He groaned. "Nick doesn't know what you're like. He didn't stand a chance."

"Thank you very much for that," she said. "You make it sound like I'm some weasel."

"Not a weasel at all," he said, "but you weasel information out of people."

She huffed. "Isn't that the same thing?"

"No," he snapped. "A weasel is like a rat, somebody who

tells on another person."

"Oh, so like you."

Silence.

She snickered. "Never mind that. What's your answer?"

"The answer is no. You're not getting into this one. It's connected to my case, so the answer is no."

"But we don't know how much it's connected," she said.

"Well, if you're involved, chances are it's very connected," he said, speaking in a rapid voice. "I will take a look, but, if nothing's there, we'll drop it, okay?"

"Fine, but, while you're taking a look," she muttered, "you should check to see if the son and his wife, Robin, actually paid for law school themselves or if they managed to get through without having student loans to pay for it. Of course they'd use their inheritance to fund their futures."

"Well, if they inherited a lot of money, they wouldn't have had to pay for college."

"Obviously," she said, wondering where he was going with this.

"What are you talking about?" he snapped. "Don't start talking around in circles again."

"I'm not. You are."

"Stop it," he said.

"What if they wanted to go to law school and couldn't afford it, and maybe the parents wouldn't help them?"

"You think they murdered the parents so they could go to law school?"

"I don't know. We've certainly seen worse motives."

He stopped and thought about it. "Well, I'll give you that. I mean, people do the stupidest things for the darndest reasons sometimes."

"Exactly, and, of course, they can't turn each other in

because then they would incriminate themselves."

"I wouldn't have thought they would have gotten divorced at that point."

"No, I think they're both climbers. Who knows? They might even have still been involved with each other, but the bottom line is that they're climbers."

"Meaning?"

"I think any relationship they had would be to move themselves up the ladder."

"Like with your ex?"

"Exactly. Maybe she was getting information or wanted to be one of his many lawyers. Maybe she was after information, or perhaps she just wanted to feather her nest a little bit."

"Or all of the above? he asked.

"Precisely. But I don't know anything about her husband."

"And he hasn't been on the scene for a long time."

"Maybe," she said, "but, while I was going through online images, I did find her with quite a few different men," she said. "I saved what I found. I think I've got thirty-six various men here. If we had a picture of her ex, it would be interesting to see if they've spent time together in the last decade since they split up."

"Well, of course they have. They were married for three years."

"Sure, but what about in the last ten years, the last five years even?"

"Not all the divorces are nasty," he said. "Lots of people have relationships with their ex-spouses, you know."

"Uh-huh," she said, "still, it's a pathway to follow-up."

"Not necessarily."

"Do you have anything else?" she challenged.

"Well, I certainly don't have to go back ten years to a cold case to find any suspects."

"Right," she said in a dry tone. "The one you looked at first is likely the one you'll follow, right? I have better things to do than be your suspect, Mack."

"I told you before that you're not a suspect. I just had to make sure you were clear."

"Well, now make sure that these two are clear," she said.

"No. I don't have time to deal with this," he said.

"Which is why I asked for the cold files," she said. "Just let me take a look. I'll know pretty quick if anything is there or not."

He stopped at that.

"Mack, come on. You know I've got a talent for this," she wheedled.

"Well, you might have that," he said, "but that doesn't mean you have the jurisdiction."

"But you do," she said cheerfully. "So I'll just go through the file to see if anything's there, give you anything I find, and you can get the credit."

"I don't care about getting the credit," he snapped. "You know better than that."

"I know," she said. "I have just one more little notch on that motive line that I was hoping to twist to get you to do it. But you're right. You don't do things like this to make yourself look good. But it doesn't mean that these people didn't kill his parents so that they could have a better life." She paced around as she spoke, trying to reel Mack in and to get his interest in the case.

Getting no response from him, she continued, "And then it seems weird that they'd go to school. Because I don't think there was a ton of money in the entire inheritance. For all you know, when they actually robbed the place, maybe they got the jewels assessed, and maybe they found out they were fake. Maybe what they thought was a fortune waiting for them wasn't. Maybe it was just enough for them to do something serious to improve their lives, and so, becoming lawyers, they could keep themselves out of trouble."

"Well, that makes a twisted kind of sense," he said, "but who would kill their parents for just enough money to go to school?"

"We don't know if that was the first implication or reasoning behind it or if something else was involved," she muttered. "But I'm not terribly comfortable walking away from this thread until we know for sure."

"And how will you know that, when Robin is dead?"

"Which is why you need to get into that laptop, her bag, her pockets, and everything else and see if anything there matches any of this jewelry that was taken because she probably would have kept one piece, even if just for sentimental or some trophy value. And it'd be easy for her to toss it off and say that her mother-in-law had given it to her and that somehow it accidentally got onto the stolen property list."

"You know that is almost something doable," he said, muttering to himself.

"See? You know how bad paperwork is. How easy it is to lose a piece of jewelry, how easy it is for insurance to, oh, let me think, pay for it? But what if there wasn't a whole lot behind it? What if there was no insurance involved? Maybe Robin and her husband just thought there was, and, when they found out there wasn't, it just upset them even more?"

"Again, conjecture," he said automatically.

"Noted, Counselor," she said simply.

He started to laugh. "You're getting very good on those one-line comebacks," he said.

"Good," she said cheerfully. "I don't think your brother appreciates me though."

"No, but that's because he doesn't know you," he said affectionately. "What are you doing about dinner?"

"Is it dinnertime already?" she asked. At that, her stomach growled. "Oh, my God, food. Now that you brought it up …" She groaned. "I'm not even sure what time it is, but I did just put coffee on."

"Good on the coffee," he said. "Maybe I'll come over."

"Ha," she said, "unless it's dinnertime."

"It is dinnertime," he said. "We could do a quick pasta dish, maybe with pesto."

"Sure, I'm up for anything," she said. "Especially if you bring the cold case files."

And, with that, she hung up on him.

Chapter 14

Monday Dinnertime ...

ONCE DOREEN ENDED the call, she poured herself a coffee and walked out to the deck. She sat down, with her notes, and started working out any and all possible alibis and motives that she could come up with. Obviously there was the potential for insurance money; there was money from the house and goods; there was the ability to do something with their lives, the possibility to take on the world and to change it. It all started with money; the absence of which, people often found to be the biggest hindrance. She worked out what she could, and, when nothing else popped to mind, she got up, refilled her coffee. As she returned to the deck table, the doorbell rang.

Mugs immediately started barking and barking. She walked over to the front door because no way Mack would have rang the doorbell. As she walked through toward the door, Mugs immediately shifted from barking to whining, and she knew with a sinking heart who it was.

"Wow," she said, opening the front door. "I didn't expect to see you again."

"I told you that I'd be back," Mathew said, leaning comfortably against the railing, a broad smile on his face.

"I hear you were down at the police station."

"Yep," he said, "but you've got to expect that. I mean, Robin and I were an item."

"Well, and they do say that the most common murderer is the spouse."

"Well, in that case, that will be you and me," he said, with a smile. "I never married her."

"You didn't think about it?"

"God no, she was a lawyer. You've got to watch those people."

"And yet you were totally okay," she said in wonder, "having an affair with her."

He looked at her in surprise. "Of course," he said. "One is just sheer fun. The other one is a duty."

She winced at that. "Oh, so that's how you look at it. Interesting."

"Not a problem," he said. "Though we did have fun in our time."

"We did when we were young and stupid," she said, with a smile.

"Absolutely." And he smiled back at her. "I was going to invite you out for dinner."

She stopped, not sure what to say. "Oh," she said in wonder, offset by the invitation. What was he up to? "I just refilled my coffee."

"Forget your coffee. We'll go out for dinner."

"I'm a little busy at the moment," she said, wondering what to say because she knew Mack was on his way.

"That's okay," he said. "I can come back in a little bit."

She climbed onto that idea. "That might be better," she said. She looked at her watch, and it was already six. "How about in an hour?"

"Perfect," he said, as he nonchalantly turned, walked down her front steps to the Jaguar.

"Nice car," she said again. She remembered the days when she drove around in such class. There was just something so comfortable about having that level of a vehicle.

"You know I like to travel in style," he said, with a big grin. "I'll see you in an hour, maybe even an hour and a half. Which would be better?"

She considered it, shrugged, and said, "Maybe an hour and a half."

"Okay," he said. "In the meantime, I'll just see what this town has to offer for a restaurant. Not sure there's a whole lot."

"Not sure there is either," she muttered, as she watched him get in the vehicle and drive away. She should have told him to stay here with her. But then Mack would arrive, and who knew how that would turn out.

She'd barely reached the kitchen, when she heard Mack drive up. Sighing, and wondering what she was supposed to say to him, she walked back out the front door.

He stood there, staring down the driveway.

She winced. "You saw him, huh?"

He looked over at her, frowned, and said, "Yes. What did he want?"

"To take me out for dinner."

His eyebrows shut up. "And are you going?"

"Yeah," she said. "I wasn't sure what to do."

Mack just gave a nonchalant shrug. "Well, go, of course. I mean, after all, he is your husband."

She glared at him. "Ex-husband, if you don't mind."

"Well, you're separated, but you're technically not divorced yet."

"Why are you being difficult?" she asked. He glared at her. And then she got it. "You can't be jealous, are you?"

His glare deepened. "I never said I was jealous," he replied stiffly.

"Because I don't want anything to do with him. You know that."

"I don't know that," he said. "Having that lifestyle back again is pretty appealing."

"Remember the gilded cage part?"

He glared at her.

"Look," she said. "I just feel like he knows more and like he's after something."

At that, his anger turned to fury. "Are you serious?" he said. "Because that's the last thing we want. If he is the killer," he added, "that puts you in danger."

"He would have someone else do his dirty work. And, when he wants something, he won't be that obvious. I think he will just try to pump me for information."

"Why would he think you have any?"

"I think it stems back to the fact that I spoke with Robin. I think he is afraid that she said something. I just don't know what he's afraid of."

"Well, it's got to be something to do with her murder case most likely, which means you could be in danger."

"I'll tell you what restaurant I'm at," she said, with a smile, "and you could always sit there yourself."

He laughed. "I just might."

She grinned, happy that things were better between them. "I've got fresh coffee," she said. "Come have a cup."

"Well, I thought we were doing dinner," he said, holding up the grocery bags.

She gasped and winced. "And I forgot," she said. "I'm so sorry."

He looked down at the groceries, shrugged, and said, "Well, I guess we can do it another night. But it still leaves me not eating."

"I wasn't kidding," she said. "I can tell you what restaurant we're at. If you feel like I'm in any danger, you can always come keep an eye on me."

"No, then he'll know I'm stalking him."

"Does that matter?" she asked. "Maybe it would keep him on his best behavior, if he thought you were there."

"No," he said. "I don't know." He looked a little disgruntled, as he walked over to the kitchen and put down the grocery bags.

"We did talk about dinner, and it completely slipped my mind when he just showed up like that."

He just nodded.

"Not because I wanted to be with him," she said in exasperation, hating that it looked like she chose Mathew over Mack. "But because it completely flummoxed me that he was back and so soon. And then all I could think about was that he wanted something, and I needed to know what that was."

At that, he spun on her and said, "You get so involved in these cases, you never give a thought to your own safety."

"No, I guess I don't. You're right," she admitted; really that fear for her safety was his overarching emotion. "I generally don't, which is why I end up getting hurt. I know. And, so far, you've been the one who's come along and saved me every time. You have no idea how grateful I am."

At that, he snorted.

She poured two cups of coffee and handed him one. "And you're right. I should have thought about that this time. But it was a dinner invitation."

"And dinner at a level that you haven't had before, or at least not in a long time."

"We used to go out for dinner all the time," she said.

"But Vancouver is a very different place for restaurant selection than here."

"That doesn't mean it's bad though," she said. And then she added, "I like it when you're jealous."

He stopped and stared, his eyebrows lifting.

She shrugged. "At least I know you care."

At that, his gaze softened, and he shrugged. "Of course I care. You know that. We're friends."

"I know we're friends," she muttered, as she headed for the deck outside. "But are we more than that?"

"Wow," he said, "I'd say no because you have to ask."

She flushed because she'd spoken loud enough for him to hear. "We are friends, the dearest of friends," she said. "I just, I'm not so sure that I'm ready for anything more."

"No, you're obviously not because you're questioning it," he said. And he shrugged. "Just my luck."

"What?"

"I find a fascinating, irritating, very unique woman, and she's not ready for a relationship."

"I am ready for a friendship though," she said quietly. "I've never had one before."

He looked at her in surprise, then reached across. She smiled when she saw he held out his open palm, with fingers toward her. She immediately put her hand in his.

"Seriously?" he asked.

She nodded. "Seriously. You have to remember the life I led. I wasn't allowed friends, outside of him."

"Madness," he muttered, as he squeezed her fingers gently. "I still don't like you going out to dinner with him."

"No, but understand why I'm doing it, and maybe that'll make it easier."

"No," he said, with a derisive laugh. "Hell no. Just think about it. It'll just put you in his target zone."

"Yeah, well, I already am," she said. A moment later, Doreen looked at him and asked, "What about the cold case file?"

He glared at her.

She beamed. "It might be connected, huh?"

"No, I can't guarantee that."

"So tell me. Do they have student loans?"

He shook his head.

"Aha," she crowed.

"That proves nothing. They inherited a lot of money. So they put it to good use. You can hardly call that criminal action."

"Do I get a list of the jewelry that was stolen or the other items?"

"There was one attached," he said thoughtfully. "That's public knowledge. I can get that for you."

"That would be good. Also, what about alibis?"

"They didn't live in the same house as the parents. James and Robin were at their home, together, having a nice quiet evening as a married couple. In other words, they alibied themselves." She nodded. "But remember. That doesn't make them guilty."

"Nope, but it doesn't mean they're innocent either," she said. "I really like this idea."

"That's because you're just guessing. You want it to fit because you want to have some reason to go in after them."

"Of course. I know, and I get that," she said, "but maybe

you should ask the husband about it."

"Ask what?" he said. "What we need is a way into the victim's life."

"But that's your job," she said, with a bright smile. "You can look at her bank accounts, her assets, debts, … safety deposit boxes. You can look at all of it. Including whether she has any little hidden secret folders on her laptop."

"Maybe," he said. "I'm waiting on forensics for that."

"They haven't got back to you yet?"

"They are busy, just like I'm busy," he said, pulling out his buzzing phone, but then he winced. "But I've got a message from my guy."

"Call him," she urged. "The sooner we find out, the better."

He rolled his eyes, picked up his coffee, had a sip, and then called the number that sent the message to his phone. She waited, but he looked at her, and she shrugged, then appeared to pull out her phone to look uninterested in what was happening. The fact that Robin was murdered, and now to find out her in-laws were murdered too, meant that was two cases too many. Most families went through an entire lifetime without being touched by murder.

"Got it," he said in a low tone. "Yeah, send the report, please."

She looked at him in surprise when he hung up. "That was fast."

"Only in the sense that I have a lot to pore over," he said. "Looks like I'm heading back to the office. I'd have to cancel on dinner anyway."

"Something on the laptop?"

His face turned grim. "A lot is there," he said. "I'm even more worried about you going out with your ex tonight."

She hesitated, then shrugged. "He's had lots of opportunities to kill me," she said quietly. "I think he is looking for something, and he is really hoping I have it."

"What happens when he finds out you don't?" he asked. "What happens when he finds out that you have absolutely nothing on any of this?"

"Then what? I guess I'll face that when I get there," she said, "but I can't imagine that anything is different about tonight."

"He hasn't had anything to do with you in eight months. His mistress, who replaced you, comes here and is murdered, and now he shows up out of the blue, and you think it's got nothing to do with this?"

"I just don't see that, after all those years of marriage, when he could have done something easily to me, why would he wait until now? I've been privy to all kinds of information," she said. "I probably still have some of that." At that, Mack stopped and stared, until she shrugged. "I had some USBs full of information. They came with me, but I hadn't actually found them until recently, when I discovered them in one of my old purses."

"What information?"

"I'm not exactly sure," she said. "I haven't taken a close look."

He stared at her. "You know you just dropped a bombshell, right?"

She shrugged. "For all I know, it's just his accounts. You know? The water bill," she said, with a laugh. "I really don't know what it is."

"Why do you have them?"

"He gave me a bunch to use at one point in time, and I know a couple of his got mixed in because I put one into a laptop to transfer some information that I wanted, and it was already full. At the time I just shrugged and tossed it in with the rest of my stuff."

"Where are these USBs now?" he asked, the intensity in his gaze growing stronger.

She looked at him in surprise. "Upstairs."

He nodded and said, "Go get them, please."

She hopped up and said, "I still don't think anything interesting is on them though."

"But you never know until you try," he said, giving her a wolfish look. "Wouldn't it be nice if you actually found some dirt on your ex?"

"Maybe, maybe not," she said. "You might want to consider it could make him more dangerous."

"You might want to consider that yourself," he said, fixing his glare on her. "Those may be what he's looking for."

She stared at him. "You mean, when he searched my house?"

He nodded slowly.

"Oh no," she said, "it just might be."

"Does he know you have them?"

"No, but if he went looking for them, at any point in time since I left, he might assume I've got them."

"Exactly," he said. "Now I really don't want you to go out to dinner with him."

Chapter 15

DOREEN WENT UP to her bedroom, taking the stairs two at a time, as Mugs raced ahead of her; so did Goliath, but then he stopped and lay full-length across the top stair, almost tripping her up. "Goliath, why must you do that?"

Of course he didn't answer. He just looked at her; she moved quickly through to the master bedroom. There she stopped and wondered because things had definitely been disturbed in her closet. She dug for her old suitcase, pulled it out, and, in the side pocket, pulled out the small purse that she'd kept as a spare when she had moved. It had a firm triangular bottom instead of one that collapsed. She pulled it out, popped open the metal clasp, and dumped out the contents on her bed. Out came four USB keys. She shrugged, picked them up, put them back in the purse, and walked down to Mack. She showed him the purse. "This was inside my suitcase," she said. "I was wondering if it was something I could sell."

He looked at it doubtfully.

She said, with a smile, "It's a Prada, worth about seven grand." He just stared at her in shock. She shrugged. "It's my old life. What I wouldn't do to have that seven-thousand dollars now," she muttered. "If I could sell it," she said, "I might get a couple hundred for it."

Mack looked at her again and said, "You know that a couple high-end consignment stores are downtown. Some people here are megarich, so they do take quite a few things there that you might not expect."

She looked at him in surprise. "You mean, not just Wendy?"

He shook his head. "I don't know why I didn't think of it before, but there are several similar stores."

"Well, Wendy was quite happy to get a lot of the stuff I had."

"And she might sell that for you too," he said, nodding at her Prada purse. "The stuff that she doesn't sell, what happens to it?"

Doreen looked at him in surprise. "You know what? I never even thought of that."

"Well, maybe contact her, and, if she hasn't sold certain things, you could always try these other places."

"I never thought of that," she muttered.

"May I?" he asked. As she nodded, he opened the purse, and he whistled. "Three of them."

"Should be four."

Peering through the purse, he dumped them on the table and said, "Yes, four." He looked at her laptop and asked again, "May I?"

She shrugged, pushed the laptop toward him. "Sure. Why not? I don't know what, if anything, is on them."

"Well, let's take a look." He opened up the first one. "Look at this," he said. "All kinds of information on living alone and surviving a divorce."

She flushed. "Like I said, I was saving information for myself."

He nodded, and his gaze warmed. "Nobody would blame you," he said. "It's not like you had very many tools to survive this, and yet you've done better than most. Plus, many people would have had a support system behind them. While you've had Nan, otherwise you've been on your own, and you've done really well for yourself. Don't knock it."

Feeling a little glow around her heart, she settled in, as he searched through that USB key and then pulled it out and handed it to her. She put that one in her office alcove by the printer. And she left it conspicuous, in case somebody came back looking for a USB, so that particular one would be the one that they found.

Mack inserted the second one and whistled. "I don't think you realize what you have here."

"Well, even looking at it, I don't realize what I have," she muttered, peering over his shoulder.

"They are all accounts," he said, opening up folder after folder. "The trouble is, I don't have enough time or knowledge to figure it out right now."

"Even if it is accounts, so what?" she muttered. "It doesn't mean anything illegal is there."

"And you're right," he said, "but, if something is illegal, I can see that he would really want it back. Maybe even if that isn't what he's seeking."

"Well, he didn't ask for it."

"That's because he didn't know you had it." Mack gave her a curious look.

"And honestly neither did I," she said. "It's not like I had much chance to pack up and purposely steal something."

"Nobody is accusing you of having taken anything."

"Good thing." She had a terrible feeling, like she'd done something wrong.

"I need to take these to the office and have a good look. We have specialists there."

"Some of it should be fairly explanatory," she said, as she leaned forward to study the screen. "I mean, look at that landscaping billing." She shrugged. "How complicated could that be?"

"Yeah," he said, "and that's four years ago. Did you have anything major done on the house?"

She shook her head. "No, we haven't done anything major to the house in a long time."

"Well, here it says that he spent $175,000 in landscaping."

She looked at him in shock. "That much?"

He nodded. "For just one year. If nothing else, this looks like tax stuff."

"I don't know how many properties he has, so, if it is the combined total of his landscaping bills, that might make more sense."

"Right, another good point," he said. "I think I need to get somebody who knows what they're talking about to look at these."

"Okay, well, let's take a look at the other thumb drives." The next one had similar accounts, although an awful lot more of them was here. And it went back for a few years. One of the files he opened up because it was labeled BM.

"Why would you open anything that says BM," she said, shaking her head at him. "To me, that would be like the last thing I'd want to open up."

"Because, instead of what you were thinking," he said,

"my mind immediately went to *blackmail*."

She gasped. "You don't think he was blackmailing people, do you?"

"Blackmailing or being blackmailed. People in power are often involved."

"That's just wrong," she said in shock. "If they got the money honestly, they should be allowed to keep it."

He burst out laughing. "Oh, I agree with you," he said, still chuckling, as he leaned forward to look at the listings. "It doesn't mean that is the way of it." And then he stopped and frowned. "What was the name of your lawyer's ex-husband?"

"James, I think. Why?"

"Because he is listed here."

"Oh, interesting. Why would that be?" She studied the screen again. "It doesn't really say anything, does it?"

"No, it sure doesn't. But we have regular payments here of five thousand a month."

"But five thousand to my ex is nothing," she cried out. "To me, it's the world, but, to him, it's not."

"But five thousand a month for every month for"—and he scrolled back—"a lot of years adds up."

"I can't see him getting involved with her, if he knew that she was involved with somebody that he was blackmailing," Doreen said.

"Or being blackmailed by," Mack said. "I can't tell from this if it's money in or money out."

"Some code is being used," Doreen noted. "I wonder if that's why they had the falling out. Maybe the lawyer found out about it."

"Or maybe James found out about Robin's part in something else," Mack suggested, "because why would Mathew be paying James? For that matter, why would James be paying Mathew?"

"Well, the reason that comes to my mind, off the top of my head," she said, "would be the murder of his parents."

Mack groaned, sat back, and looked at her. "You're a pain sometimes. You know that?"

She beamed. "Thank you." She hopped up and poured herself another cup of coffee; as she walked back, he held out his cup.

She moaned. "You do know that I'd have coffee to drink every day, if you didn't keep stealing it all."

"Are you that short?" he asked, looking at her under furrowed brows.

She shrugged. "No, not really. It's just something to bug you about."

He chuckled. "Well, you better find another topic then," he said, "because I won't give up on my coffee any more than you are."

"Right," she muttered. "I'm definitely not giving up on my coffee."

"Exactly." He flicked through more and more accounts. "I am not sure what's going on here," he said, "but this is fairly in-depth." He went back to the BM file, taking pictures of her screen.

She waited until he was done and then asked, "What about the other two?"

"I'm getting there." And he opened up the next one, which was full of accounts too, and then the last one was photos. He whistled at that. "Well, this explains a lot."

"What does it explain?"

"*He* was blackmailing others." She looked at Mack in surprise; he pointed out various people in the photos. "All of them were engaged in something that looked very shady."

"Interesting," she muttered. "Well, that would be why he was always hiring the private investigators. I never could understand what his involvement was."

"What investigators?"

"He told me that he kept a team of them on staff, just in case."

"Nobody keeps a team of investigators on staff, unless you're actively investigating," he said, staring at her.

"Remember that part about I didn't have anything to do with his business?"

"Of course," he said, "unless you knew that you couldn't be arrested to testify against him."

"I've got nothing to say," she said, throwing up her hands. "I really don't know anything."

"And that was a safe way to keep it," he said, with the nod. "The less you knew, the less you could talk."

"And now he's what? Decided that I'm disposable?"

"I think you were always disposable, my dear," he said. "The issue has only come up now that the lawyer was murdered. And that brings us back to whether Mathew did it or not."

"So, in that case, I really need to go out for dinner with him."

"You really don't," he muttered, staring at her. "It's even more important now that you have nothing to do with him."

"Yet that's not possible," she said quietly. "And it also isn't very smart to not utilize something there to be utilized."

He stared at her, not comprehending. He shook his head. "And that's where you're wrong," he said. "I want to keep you safe, not have you attacked by this guy. He is still looking for something."

"Why don't we set a trap?"

"What kind of a trap?"

"I'll mention that there's still a bunch of stuff I haven't even gone through and how I found some USB keys that might be his. I mean, in the spirit of being a nice wife and maybe getting back together again, of course."

"And what? Leave yourself wide open for him to come back here and attack you?"

"Or he will get his little henchman to come down and search while I'm away."

He studied her for a moment. "And all we would get though is somebody who is potentially breaking and entering."

"Maybe but that would lead you back to Mathew, wouldn't it?"

"It's hard to say, depends if the guy doing the B&E talks or not. He might easily go down for such a minor charge."

She frowned at that. "You know what? It really shouldn't be a minor charge, when somebody goes into my house without my permission while I'm away."

"In the grand scale of things," he said, "it's a minor charge, particularly if it's a first offense."

"What if he was hired to do it?"

"You'd have to prove that, so we must find a payment transaction or get a confession from him."

She nodded. "Can you give me a wire?"

He looked at her. "What are you talking about?"

"Like in the TV shows, have me wear a wire, while we're there at dinner, and maybe I can get him to talk."

Mack hid a grin. "Do you really think he will talk to you about all the things that he has done wrong at this point?"

"I don't know," she said crossly. "I'm looking for ideas.

You're not helping."

"That's because I don't want you going down that pathway," he said, shaking his head.

"Well, I don't have much time to make a decision," she said, looking at the time on her cell phone. "I want to go because I need to know what he is up to. So the next best thing is for you to come to the same restaurant.'

"And that won't be easy either," he said, "because I won't know where you're going."

"No," she said, "and I need to find that out too, don't I?"

"You sure do," he said, "and fast."

She frowned, looked down at her phone, and said, "I could call him. He left his new number."

"I don't really want his number on your phone. The last thing we need is for you to have been the last one to have called him, if he does get caught in some sting."

"I don't think like a criminal," she cried out.

"No." Then he sighed. "I really hate to see you go."

"Follow us," she said. "I'll tell him that you're jealous." He just glared at her. She shrugged. "What do you want me to say?"

"I don't want a confrontation that puts you in the middle."

"Well, you don't have much time," she said, "because I have to go get changed real fast. So what'll it be? Although you also have to go to the office." She hopped up and said, "I will go get changed right now."

His eyebrows shot up. "What's wrong with what you are wearing?"

"This is my ex-husband. Remember?" she said, with a dry look. "I don't want to appear too far off from what he used to know me as."

"I'd go as yourself," he said. "It's never a bad time to start being you."

She stopped, stared, and sat down hard. "You know what? You've got a point."

"I do," he said, "and a good one. He needs to know who you are now, not who you were."

"But shouldn't I still appear submissive?"

"Why?" he said. "That's not who you are anymore. I think it'd be much better if you went as you."

She smiled and said, "You know what? That might not be a bad idea." She looked down at her jeans and shirt. "He would be quite offended."

"Good. Maybe he'll cancel dinner then."

She laughed. "I wonder. A good test to see just how sincere he is."

"No," he said gently. "It'd be a test as to how desperate he is."

"Ooh," she muttered, "I like that."

Just then the doorbell rang. Mugs took off toward the door, barking like a crazy man. She looked at Mack, stood, and said, "Here goes nothing." He frowned; she shook her head. "It will be fine."

"Famous last words," he muttered.

She walked to the front door, opened it up, and said, "Hey, good timing. I just finished."

He nodded in a bright cheerful way and said, "I'll wait, while you get changed."

So typical of him to see her as not acceptable as she was. "Where are we going? I wasn't sure if it would be a fish-and-chip shop or if we would go to a high-class restaurant."

"Well, the Capri is supposed to have a nice restaurant.

Also The Yellow House Restaurant's downtown too," he said. "I wasn't sure about that one."

She nodded. "Either of those would be lovely," she said. "I'll go change." Because, in fact, she would go change for a dinner at either of those places, and it would still be a nice evening out. Just with the wrong escort. She quickly went upstairs, put on a simple dress, brushed her hair back, and put on lipstick. She was downstairs in a few minutes. After that, she grabbed the little purse that she had given Mack, sans the USB keys, dropped in her keys and her phone, and noted the two men stood like pit bulls, staring at each other.

"Oh, have you guys met?" she asked.

Mathew looked at her and snapped, "What's he doing here?"

"He stopped by, and I asked him if he would feed the animals and look after them, while I was gone," she said. "He'll be leaving in a few minutes." She smiled at Mack, gave him a three-finger wave, and said, "Thanks so much." With that, she turned, and she walked toward the front door. She could almost hear him gnashing his teeth behind her. But her ex quickly caught up with her, as they stepped out the front door and down the porch steps to the Jaguar. As she approached, she murmured, "I forgot how much I love these cars."

"That's the life with me. Remember?"

She kept her response to herself, but she absolutely didn't want to remember so many other things about life with him. She got into the front seat and allowed herself a moment to just sit here and wiggle in joy at the luxurious leather interiors. "So what did you do all day?"

"I told you," he bit off, "I was down at the station."

"Well, that's one thing about Mack," she said. "He never

discusses cases. He is not allowed."

Mathew looked at her searchingly and then relaxed slightly.

"I don't know anything about the case. But you're in town when somebody was murdered. You were the last person in her personal relationships," she said, "so I guess a little questioning is normal."

"Maybe," he said, settling in a little bit more into his seat. "Just something about seeing cops like that makes my back go up."

"Well, I just haven't had any reason to be sideways of the cops," she said, "and he's always very nice to me."

"That's because he wants you," he snapped.

She looked at him in surprise. "I don't think so." Well, she hoped so, but she still wasn't quite ready, and that just took her down that pathway of how she was a confused mess.

"Any guy can see it. That's the only reason he is hanging around."

"Well, it's nice of him still," she said. "Being here on my own has been a challenge."

"It has, but, like I said, it's not something that you have to do anymore."

"Well, that's romantic," she said in a dry tone.

He chuckled. "I think we're well past that."

"I don't know," she muttered. "It does feel a little wrong, when you've been out of my life for so long and after your ex has just been murdered."

"Well, I didn't do it," he growled.

She sighed, shrank back slightly into the seat, and said, "I never said you did."

He pulled up in front of the Capri. "Will this work?"

"Of course," she said. In fact it was better, as she didn't

think they could get into The Yellow House without a reservation. It was a small catered scenario over there, where they only did so many dinners for so many people in the evening. She'd walked past their building once and had stopped to study the menu and had wondered what it would be like.

But the Capri would work just fine. As she walked toward the front door, he rushed forward and held the door open for her. She smiled her thanks, wondering at his actions. He'd done things like that early on in their courtship but had very quickly stopped. As if he already had her, so why bother with niceties. She'd always found that difficult. Now it was almost more difficult to let him do it. He was after something. … He was also perturbed at Mack's presence at her house. She had to admit to feeling a certain joy over that too.

They were given a table with a view. Mathew smiled. "This is nice. I mean, it's a small hick town, so you can't expect much."

"Nope, you sure can't," she said, agreeing with him.

"I don't know why you couldn't have stayed on the coast."

"I didn't want to," she said simply. "It wasn't the life I wanted to lead anymore."

"So you wanted to come to this little hick town and be a country girl?"

"Well, it's hardly a country-girl life I live. I'm here in a town, not raising chickens on a farm."

"Well, that'll probably be next," he said, with a wave of his hand. "I think I even passed cows on one of the roads. Like somewhere off Benvoulin or some such thing. *Cows*," he said, pointedly looking at her. "Did you hear me? Like they actually have cows here."

She burst out laughing. "Well, you'll probably order a steak for dinner," she said, "so it does make sense that they have cows here."

"That's just wrong though," he said. "Steak belongs on your table, but cows do not belong in a field beside me."

"Everybody wants the food lot to be in somebody else's backyard," she said simply.

"Of course and thankfully it's here because then it's not my backyard," he muttered.

She chuckled. "I don't mind seeing the cows, and the horses are a joy, as is all the other wildlife. I've seen quite a few things since I've been here." That was to put it mildly.

"I'm sure you have," he said, with the shake of his head. "I mean, it's not as if you stayed in the same social circles, the same level of lifestyle."

"Yeah, how would I do that?" she said. "I didn't have any money. Remember? All our *friends* dropped me, when they heard that."

He smirked. "Well, you could have it again though."

She didn't answer him. Why would he even dangle something like that, when it's obvious he didn't care about her? What was this all about? The maître d' came around and brought a drink menu and a regular menu for them. Doreen looked quickly and decided that one of the things she hadn't had in a very long time was fresh tuna. So she ordered a glass of white wine, and, when the waitress came, Doreen placed her order, and her husband approved.

"That's always a good dish, isn't it?"

"Well, I haven't eaten things like that recently," she said, "so I will enjoy it."

"Good," he said. "Anything that reminds you of the lifestyle that we had together is helpful."

Again she said nothing. When everything was delivered, and the staff left them in relative peace, he said, "So what's going on between you and the detective?"

"Nothing," she said in surprise. "We're friends."

"Yeah, friends," he said sarcastically.

"It is possible to be friends."

"Not really," he said, "he wants something from you."

She stared at him. "Well, I'm sure he'd probably say that about you too."

At that, his eyebrows rose. "I told you that I wanted something," he said. "I want you back home, where you belong."

"Robin's hardly even dead," Doreen murmured. "Isn't that a little fast?"

"We'd already split up," he said. "Thankfully. Otherwise the cops would be looking at me a little more intently."

"Well, I don't think Mack wants anything from me," she said. "I'm more of a pain in the butt to him instead."

He laughed. "Well, that's the thing about relationships, you know? Either it goes the way you want or it's the opposite, so that you don't want anything to do with it."

She frowned. "That's a pretty rough assessment."

"I know people," he said, "and I definitely know men. And I know what he wants."

"I think you're wrong."

"That's because you always were naive. He obviously wants a relationship with you."

"Well, being friends is a relationship."

"And now that's being naive again," he said, "and foolish. You've never been foolish."

She narrowed her gaze.

"You used to do foolish things," he said, "but I could always trust your judgment of people."

"And that's why I'm telling you that Mack is a good guy."

"He might be a good guy, and that just probably makes him a good cop," he said, with a sneer. "People who deal with criminals are not the kind of people we associate with."

She winced at that. She'd been associated with them, with Mack and his team quite a bit. Not to mention Mathew was hardly an angel.

"That little old house of yours is quite the run-down shack too, isn't it?"

She bristled. "It's Nan's house," she said, "and I really love it."

"Well, I mean, if you dropped it and built something new maybe," he said, with a shudder. "But, other than that, it's just this hokey piece of crap that should have been demolished a long time ago."

"Well, thankfully it hasn't," she snapped, glaring at him.

He held up a hand. "I forgot how defensive you are about that old lady."

"She is my grandmother, and she's special to me," she said, as she sat here, feeling this growing wish to reach across the table and just smack him one. She'd probably be charged with assault. Or maybe the police would be too busy cheering on the sideline, when they heard what she'd done, to charge her. But, at the same time, she didn't dare do anything to cause a commotion.

He was here for one reason, and she was well past the point of believing that it was because he wanted her back. He wanted something from her, but he had yet to play his hand and to let her know exactly what it was.

Chapter 16

B Y THE TIME they finished eating dinner, Doreen was none the wiser of what Mathew was up to. Finally, when she ordered coffee and a piece of pie—something that she rarely afforded herself—she asked, "So why are you really here?"

He leaned forward and said, "You don't believe I'm here for you?"

"Remember that part of being a good judge of character and understanding people?" she said. "No, I don't believe anything yet."

He shrugged. "It was worth a try."

"Not really," she said. "So what's this about?"

"You have something of mine."

She stopped and stared at him in surprise. "Seriously what? And why didn't you just ask for it, instead of this elaborate ruse?"

"Because I figured that you wouldn't give it to me."

"Well, I don't even know what it is," she said, turning her hands, palms up.

"I'm missing a USB key."

"A USB key?" In her mind, she was like, *Just one?* But, if

it was just one, that was perfect. "I have only one key," she said. "When I realized you were divorcing me, I collected information and spiritual affirmations on how to survive it."

"Oh my, that must have been pretty rough," he said, giving her a small smile that almost looked like quashed delight to think of her suffering. The longer she stared at him, the more she could see the facade cracking. She didn't have a clue how she had even fallen for this guy in the first place or why she'd stayed. But that was one of those mysteries that would take a lifetime to sort out.

"That key you're definitely welcome to have," she said, "but I don't think anything of yours is on it."

"Well, I want to take a look."

"Sure. It's at home. I don't have a problem with that."

"Good," he said. "So we can leave."

She snorted. "You mean, now that you are telling the truth, you want to get out of here?"

"Of course," he said, yet he remained seated.

"You and Robin were more alike than I thought," she muttered, eating her apple pie. They'd always been in a rush. "It still makes me angry that I didn't see the two of you carrying on around my back."

"Ah, it was pretty easy to do. We used to meet at work most of the time."

"And, of course, I never knew anything about your work because you never talked about it."

"No, and she never came to the house, until you and I were more or less done."

"Right," she said, not wanting to hear any more details; it didn't matter that the woman was dead or that this was a long time ago. It was still her marriage, and she wanted to keep a few illusions that hopefully they weren't cavorting in her own bed. The fact that Doreen and her husband had shared separate beds had always confused her. But it's the way he'd wanted it, and, only over time, did she understand. "Well, as long as you guys were happy," she said.

"Not even for five minutes," he retorted. "The minute she moved into my place, she became this whiny, demanding witch."

She stared at him in surprise and started to giggle and then laughed out loud.

"Hush," he said, glaring at her. "It's not that funny."

"Well, it is," she said, chuckling. "I mean, really? After all you put me through, I'm allowed to have a little bit of satisfaction in knowing you weren't living happily ever after."

"Of course it wasn't happily ever after," he said quietly. "I didn't want her there at all, but I needed to keep her close."

She stopped and stared. "What? Why?"

"Because she was trying to blackmail me," he said in an angry hushed voice.

She stared at him. Now they were actually getting somewhere. "That's terrible," she said. "I can't imagine what that was all about. It's not like you've done anything criminal." And, wow, she deserved an award for that performance.

"Exactly," he said, "and, when I wouldn't play her game, she got really angry. But then I found something on her, and she found something on me, and it just got ugly."

"I'm sorry," she said, "because the two of you could have been quite happy together. If you'd worked at it."

"No, not likely," he said, shaking his head. "Not at all."

"You don't know that," she said. "You were both Type A

personality people, both driven to succeed, both the kind who like to manipulate people to have it all your own way."

"Exactly," he said, "so no way both of us could even be in the same room for long."

"But you managed for quite a few months."

"Sure," he said. "I took what was offered and thoroughly enjoyed it," he said, "but I wasn't a fool to get sucked into it."

She nodded slowly. "And, if she was trying to blackmail you, did you get her to stop?"

"Of course," he said, "Fair play meant I found out something on her." At that, he chuckled. "That was a great conversation. But not quite as much as the sex afterward. Makeup sex is wonderful."

She shook her head. "I don't think I ever lived in your world."

"You never did," he said, with a wave of his hand. "Come on. Eat up," he said. "I need that key."

"Fine," she said. And she brought the last bite of apple pie into her mouth.

He stood up immediately, tossed money on the table, and said, "Let's go."

Chapter 17

MATHEW USHERED DOREEN out of the restaurant into the car a little too quickly for her comfort. She protested when he slammed the car door with more force than necessary. He got into the vehicle beside her, and she said, "What's the rush?"

"I want that USB," he said, with a snarl.

She nodded. "And you can have it, as soon as I get home, but I don't think anything on it is yours."

"We'll see," he said. "That witch took it."

She stopped and stared. "Took what?"

"Several USBs from my office."

Her stomach sank, and she stared at him. "Oh, my God, do you think she did it on purpose?"

He looked at her and gave a bitter laugh. "Absolutely, she did. That's the problem with taking something and enjoying it. In a moment of weakness, a shark, like her, took advantage. I presume one night, when I was sleeping, she snuck down into my office and took stuff."

"That's terrible," Doreen gasped. And, in truth, a lot of honesty was in her horror. Because that wasn't what one did to another person, particularly if you cared about them. But it sounded like her husband and her lawyer had more of a shark-eat-shark relationship. "I'm sorry," she said sincerely. "Sounds like she was even more unpleasant than I thought."

"You have no idea," he said, "and I admit that, for a little while, it kind of appealed."

She stared at him, eyebrows raised and her eyes wide.

He nodded. "You're just so much honey and sweetness. After a while you kind of want a bitter taste of lemon to cut through it."

She sank back in the seat and turned to stare forward. "Well, I hadn't considered it that way." Besides, she felt like she'd found a little bit of lemonade in her spirit too.

"No," he said, "and I was surprised how quickly I would tire of it."

She shrugged.

Very soon they drove up to her place. When they got there, he said, "The lights are on."

"Mack probably left them on," she said absentmindedly.

"Do you have any security on up there?"

"Yep," she said. "Not sure he turned it on though."

"What kind of hick town is this where you don't even worry about security?" he asked, with disgust.

"One where not a whole lot of crime happens."

Then she winced because she'd proven that was absolutely not true. She stepped out of the vehicle and walked quickly up the front steps, pretending to take care of the security system on her phone. Then, when she stepped inside, Mack *had* set the security system, so she quickly shut it off. She didn't know if that was the smart thing to do or not, with Mathew following close behind. She headed toward the kitchen, hoping that Mack had taken the other USBs. Then she set down her purse and said, "I'll go to my room and grab it. Oh, wait—" And then she stopped and said, "I think I put it in the office."

She spun, then headed toward her little nook that served as an office, as he stopped and stared. "Good God," he said, "you don't even have a chair in here."

"That's why it's an office," she said. "It's not like I need one anyway."

She reached out, picked up the USB that she found, and handed it to him. He snatched it from her hand and stared at it greedily. She shrugged. "Like I said, I don't know that it has anything on it."

"That's fine," he said. "I will head back to the hotel."

"Hotel?"

"Yeah, remember? I decided to stay overnight."

"Okay," she said. "Have a good night."

As he stepped out the front door, he didn't even answer her. She watched, as he raced down the steps, got in the Jaguar, and headed down her driveway and up the cul-de-sac. She immediately closed and locked the door and reset the security alarm. She didn't know what he would do when the truth came out. Interesting that he'd finally realized all the USB keys were missing, but chances were he was missing what Doreen had, not what the lawyer Robin had.

She quickly texted Mack. **Call me.**

When her phone rang, he asked curiously, "Why call you?"

"Because I have a bunch to tell you," she said, then quickly relayed everything that happened at the restaurant.

"Wow," he said. "What kind of a relationship is that?"

"One where they use each other," she said smoothly. "Not my kind at all. But the fact of the matter is that I gave him the USB key that I had on my divorce search findings, and he is busy looking for the ones that the lawyer had. Or that he thinks the lawyer had."

"And you think it's the ones that you had all along?"

"It's possible there's more, so maybe the lawyer did have some of them," she said. "I mean, he does a lot of business, so he could have any number of USB keys."

"True. I don't think there was anything like that on her person, but I'll check in the morning."

"And did she go anywhere else, meet anybody else, where she could have put it somewhere?"

"Was she alone at your house? Did she ever leave your sight?"

"I don't think so. She was busy throwing a temper tantrum on the front steps, and she was a little bit wild and gesturing about, but I don't think she had anything with her." She stopped and frowned and said, "But maybe."

"What does that mean?"

"Well, I don't know," she said. "I mean, I haven't looked in the front garden at all."

"You think she buried something in the garden?" he asked incredulously.

"No, but, if she had it in her purse, it's quite possible that she flung it or dropped it or something, as she was quite riled. I'm sure she was hitting the door with her purse. Who knows what might have popped out?"

"Did she take off her coat? Did she drop her bag or anything?"

"Both of those things," she said. "But I didn't notice anything fall out."

"That doesn't matter," he said. "It could be anywhere."

"Well, I won't see anything tonight," she muttered. "It's dark."

"I'll be there first thing in the morning," he said. "Now make sure you lock up and stay inside, and, if you get any unwanted visitors, call the police."

"Sure will," she said. "You'll be the first one to call."

"I'll probably be the first one to get there anyway," he said in a resigned voice. But then his voice thickened considerably, as he said, "Have a good night." And he hung up.

She smiled, staring down at the phone. "Good night, Mack." And then she wondered if she should have asked if he liked lemonade or just honey. And thinking it was such a stupid question, she deliberately tossed it from her mind and headed to bed.

Chapter 18

Tuesday Morning …

SHE WOKE UP the next morning to pounding on her front door. She hurriedly dressed and raced down the stairs to see her ex standing there. She rubbed the sleep out of her eyes. "Hey," she said in confusion. "What's going on? Why all the panic?"

"Are you sure you don't have any other USBs?" he said, almost desperately. She looked at the one that she'd given him and shook her head. "No," she said, "that's the only one. Why?"

"Because there's nothing on it," he said in disgust. He handed it back to her and said, "You really need help if you think that garbage on there will benefit you at all."

"Well, I thought so at the time," she said. "Unlike you, I was not quite ready for a divorce."

"No," he said, his voice softening. "I guess it was a shock, wasn't it?"

"Not that you cared," she said primly. "Now if you don't mind, I need to go put on some coffee."

"Good, I'll have a cup," he said, stepping inside.

She automatically stepped back, as he crowded her.

"Why?" she said. "I don't have anything else for you."

"Well, I don't know about that," he said, turning his gaze on her. "You look mighty fetching, still half asleep."

She immediately flushed. "Don't even go there," she snapped. "You can stay for a cup of coffee, and then you'll be on your way," she said. "I've got to go out today."

"Really? What are you doing?" he asked, with a sneer.

"Applying for jobs," she said primly. "It's not easy to get work, when you don't have any job skills."

"Well, you had the perfect skills for my job," he said. "You were great at making people comfortable."

"Maybe."

"You also opened them up, getting information at an amazing rate," he said. "People just love talking to you. It's a skill I really miss." He looked at her suddenly. "I could hire you to do more of that."

She shook her head. "No. The only reason it worked," she said, "was because I was your wife, and I believed in the business and what we were doing. I just didn't realize that it was your business and that there was nothing in it for me, even after you threw me out."

"Well, we could change that," he said, smiling at her. "Remember?"

"Nah," she said, "you didn't mean any of that. You're just trying to find whatever it is your mistress took from you."

He shook his head.

"Did she make friends with any of the staff? Would she have hidden it somewhere in the house? Could she have paid the staff to move it?"

"She wouldn't have dared," he said, and then his tone darkened. "They wouldn't have dared."

She nodded, again clearly seeing the man she used to know. "In other words, you pay them for their secrecy."

"And loyalty," he said. "Remember that. It's everything to me."

"I get it," she said. "What about a safe deposit box?"

He looked at her and said, "We checked. She doesn't have one."

"Well, maybe she doesn't have one under her name, but what about another name?"

"What other name would that be?" he asked.

She shrugged. "I know that she was still friendly with her ex-husband."

He stopped and stared at her for a moment. "I wonder."

She shrugged. "Just an idea."

"And a good one," he said, tapping the table, as he sat down heavily on a chair. He propped his chin up on his other hand, as he kept thrumming the table with his other.

Thaddeus immediately popped up onto the table, pacing back and forth, bobbing his head. "Thaddeus is here. Thaddeus is here."

Mathew looked at him in disgust. "Seriously, you have a bird? And you let it on the table?"

"That's Thaddeus," she said, "and be nice to him. Otherwise you'll hurt his feelings."

He turned to look at her with an incredulous expression. "Seriously?"

"Yes, seriously," she said. He snorted at that. "Hey," she said, "it's very important. My friends I keep close, even if they're feathered."

"Wow," he said, "I didn't realize it was that bad."

"And be nice to the dog and cat too, while you're at it."

"Well, Mugs of course," he said, bending down to

scratch the basset hound behind the ear. "Although he definitely needs a bath." He looked at his fingers and made a grimace. "I mean, he is deadly dirty." He got up, came over to the kitchen sink, and scrubbed his fingers.

"Time to take him to the river then," she said cheerfully. Mathew stared down at Mugs and looked at her again. She shrugged. "He loves to go in there."

"The water is dirty," he said, as if explaining something simple to a child. "You can't just take a dirty dog and put him in a dirty river and expect him to come out clean."

"Well, I do actually," she said. "Quite a decent amount of fresh water flows in there. And, if I can keep him out of the mud afterward, he is amazingly fresh-smelling."

"Oh, my God," he said. He looked at the coffee she was making. "I'm surprised you even know how to make a pot of coffee."

"I've learned a lot of things in the last few months," she said, steadily refusing to get riled by him. He'd been very good at making her feel like she had absolutely no value and had completely demeaned her in public. It had been her ability to smile and to carry on that had won her the most respect, but, behind her back, everybody had laughed at her. It was only later when she found out that his behavior was not all that unusual among the rich and wealthy set.

She reached into the cupboard, pulled out a cup, poured him some coffee, and handed it to him. "There you go," she said. "Fresh coffee."

He took it gingerly, as if not sure that it was drinkable. "Do you have any milk or sugar?"

"I have a little bit of milk and sugar," she said, bringing out the bag of sugar and the milk jug. He looked at it, then at her. She said, "Sorry, no fancy coffee service set here."

"Wow," he muttered under his breath, as he liberally added two heaped spoons of sugar to his coffee.

"Wow," she said, "I don't remember you taking it that sweet before."

"Yes, but, at home, it's always served to me, as I like it."

She nodded without saying anything, then pushed open the back door and stepped out. "You want to sit out here?"

He stepped out with her.

She immediately took up her favorite spot on the steps, leaning back against the railing. "I know it's not much yet," she said, "but I've done a ton of work back here."

"It doesn't look it," he said. "Weeds are everywhere."

She remembered how utterly offended he was by weeds. The gardeners had to go over the pathways and sidewalks all the time to make sure it was 100 percent clean. "You know what? I'm happy to get along with nature instead of go against her," she said, with a smile. "I need to get back out here and take care of a bunch more, but you can see how far down I got."

"Yeah, that's obvious," he said, pointing to the distinctive line where different levels of weeding had clearly occurred. "Also, it looks like you haven't worked on it for weeks."

"Probably not," she said. She reached out and rubbed her shoulder, wincing at how it twinged every once in a while, almost like a warning. "But I'll get there eventually."

He nodded, took a sip of coffee, and winced. He took another sip, shuddered, and put it down on the deck.

"It's good, isn't it?" she said cheerfully, taking a hefty swig of her own. She smiled as the extra caffeine hit her nerves and upped the wattage of her view of the world. "Hard to get started in the morning without it."

"That's like thick sludge for fuel," he said. "Remember? I drive a luxury car and only get premium."

"No premium around here," she said, hating the smugness in his voice.

He stood and said, "Well, I gave you back the USB key. If you can think of nothing else?"

She immediately shook her head. "Outside of her having talked with somebody on the property, like one of your security guys or something," she said, with a shrug, "I have no idea what she might have done with it."

"Well, I'll check my staff, but I pay them very well to be loyal."

"Yeah," she said, "but don't forget she had *special equipment*, and, while you were taking advantage and enjoying yourself, it doesn't mean somebody else wasn't too."

He stared at her, a shadow darkening his features, as he turned his gaze toward the river. "She sure as hell better not have."

"The only way to find out would be to check with your staff," she said.

He nodded. "Well, I will hit the police station this morning to ensure they need nothing more," he muttered, "and then I'm heading out."

"Good," she said, "it was nice to see you."

He looked at her, startled momentarily, and then smiled. "You're the only woman I know who doesn't bear a grudge. Always smiling, always happy," he said. "For the longest time, I hated it. Now I realize how soothing it is to my nerves."

"Well, too bad," she replied. "Like you said, you wanted that hint of lemon, and you got it."

"Yeah, and now she is dead, and that was before I got a

hold of her." He shook his head. "I'd like to find the guy who offed her."

"I'm sure the cops would too," she said, "so if you have any idea …"

He shook his head. "Nope, I have no idea. But I wish I did." With that, he smiled at her and said, "Until we meet again." Then he strode out to the side yard and around the house.

"Well, you could always leave me some money," she said. "I'm sure you don't want to see your wife suffer."

He laughed. "You seem to be doing just fine on your own."

And, with that, he strode down the sidewalk and headed to the car. She cut through the house from the deck, stood on the front porch, and watched, deliberately waiting until he left, before she investigated something twinkling in the bright sky. The early morning light had hit something down there in her garden bed, but she didn't want to give Mathew any inclination that she might be looking for something. He drove down and around the cul-de-sac and took off. Seconds later she heard Mack's truck rattling upward. She stayed on the front steps, with the animals around her. Thaddeus was walking up and down on the railing, calling out, "Thaddeus loves Doreen. Thaddeus loves Doreen."

Richard opened his door and called out, "Why are you making so much racket this early in the morning?"

"Well, we weren't making any racket," she said, "until you started yelling." She motioned at Mack. "Of course, the cops are here, so you can always complain, if you want."

Mack hopped out, looked at her quizzically, then looked at Richard and asked, "Is there a problem?"

Richard harrumphed, then walked back inside and

slammed the door.

"He was just about to make a noise complaint," she said helpfully.

He rolled his eyes at her. "So, you're in trouble again?"

"Not deliberately," she said honestly.

He laughed at that. "Says you."

"My ex just left."

He froze on the spot and then slowly fixed his gaze on her face. "Why was he here?" And then he swallowed hard. "Or did he stay overnight?"

Her eyebrows shot upward. "That'll never happen," she said and then shook her head. "He woke me up, pounding on the front door, just about twenty-five minutes ago."

"Why'd he come?"

"He wanted to return the USB key." She held it up in her hand. "When I started making coffee, he invited himself to stay for a cup, but he didn't like it much."

"Why is that?"

"Because I made it as black as sin," she said, with an evil grin, "and even his two overly heaping spoons of sugar didn't help him get it down."

Mack started to chuckle. "Ah, so you like dark coffee now, huh?"

"Always have," she said, "and it is a bit strong, but I would never let him know that I didn't like it."

He reached out, took the cup, from her hands, and took a sip. "Wow, that's good," he muttered, staring at it, and then looked at her. "You just get better and better at this stuff."

"Well, he didn't finish his, and there's still some in the pot."

Mack nodded. "I'll go grab a cup."

She smiled. "You do that, and here, in the meantime, I will pick up that thing that I can see over there in the grass."

He froze immediately, came back, and said, "What are you talking about?"

She pointed at whatever was shining down in the garden, caught between the marigold blooms and the bark mulch behind it. He immediately retraced his steps to the bottom riser and over to the marigolds. Digging into the back, he pulled it up. "Aha!"

"Well, look at that, another USB stick. Or is it? It's odd-looking, isn't it?" she said, frowning, because it was mostly just a smooth slim piece of metal.

"It's more expensive," he said, "but these things hold a lot."

"Well, I don't know where it came from but—"

"But," he said, with a big smile, "let's hope it's all about the right person."

"I hope so. I was waiting for Mathew to leave, before I investigated it. Then I heard your truck coming, so I thought, if I waited for you, then it wouldn't look like I planted evidence."

"Well, it could be that you planted it and then asked me to go pick it up." She glared at him, and he just laughed.

"Come on. Let's go grab some coffee and see what's on this. Besides, you already have the other USB keys," she said.

He nodded. "Absolutely. But they've been turned over to forensics. And now we'll see what's on this." He pushed her gently through the door, with all the animals crowding in as well. "Let's take this to the kitchen."

Sitting down on the table, he pulled her laptop to him, looked at her, and she smiled and nodded. That was the thing about Mack; he was always respectful. Well, he was always respectful, except for when he wasn't, like when he was hanging up on her. But then she probably deserved as much of that as he did. He popped in the USB and quickly opened it up and found a single file. That was it. He popped it open and immediately it came up. It was a one-page letter, yet Doreen could see that the document was several pages long.

"What's behind the letter?" she asked, because the letter was just one page.

He flicked through it. "Wow, look at this," he said. "It's her Last Will and Testament."

"Aah," she said, staring at it. "Why is it on that key?"

"Well, she is a lawyer, so maybe she felt she needed it. If anything happened to her, it would be on her person."

"Which means," she said, staring at him, "that she thought her life was in danger?"

He nodded slowly. "I'm afraid so. And, if you read the letter, you'll see who she thinks it is."

Chapter 19

Tuesday Midmorning ...

DOREEN READ OUT loud from the beginning.

"*To whom this may concern. If I am dead, you need to look at Mathew. He was my latest relationship and a meganarcissist, the craziest I've ever met. He is dangerous. He is dark, and he is involved in many criminal activities of which blackmail is only a part. I thought I was treading into the shadows, before I met him. But something dark and ugly attracted the two of us together. And, like anything, it was combustible to the point that we couldn't put it out. Now I'm running for my life, and I'm sure he is hunting for me—and maybe for good reason.*

Part of being in the dark criminal shadows is that I can look for information I can sell. Then I sell it to somebody else, who takes care of it, and they pay me a cut. I'm not telling you who that is. It doesn't matter because obviously I won't be giving them any more information if I'm dead.

But you need to look at Mathew. He will be the one who kills me, and his ex-wife is likely to be his next target. And that's possibly my fault too. If I am heading to God to be accountable for my sins, then I need to be honest. It will be because of me that Mathew goes after Doreen. When he accused me several times of looking for information and stealing from him, I said that probably Doreen had taken the information.

I was also instrumental in their divorce and in Doreen getting nothing for a settlement. And I do feel bad about that. The trouble is, she is one of those sweet-as-sunshine bright songbirds of the world, and I am one of the ravens in the dark. I could have eaten her for breakfast, and honestly I more or less did. I didn't have any remorse, until I realized what it was like to be hunted myself. And now I know just how wrong what I did to her was. If I manage to survive, and nobody reads this, then I'll try to turn a page and to become a better person. But, if you are reading this, it's already too late. Remember. Go after Mathew.

Doreen slowly sat down and stared at Mack. "Oh, my God," she whispered.

He nodded. "That's quite a confession letter. She doesn't really state what she did to you, except that she cheated you out of your proper settlement and marital rights in the divorce."

"Right," she said, staring at the letter. "No wonder he wanted that. It directly points to Mathew as being her killer." And she stopped, shook her head, and said, "But that's not right. It wasn't him."

"You really don't think so?"

She shook her head. "No, I really don't think so. I mean, he is flummoxed and angry, and he wants to know who killed her, so he can get a hold of the guy himself. More or less to find out if he got any information from her and then to kill him."

"Interesting. So somebody got to her first."

"And I wonder if it wasn't the one she was feeding the blackmail information to."

He looked at her in surprise. "Why would he do that? That would be like killing the golden goose."

She leaned forward and tapped the bottom lines of the letter. "But here she says she will try to turn over a new leaf. What if she would refuse to get more information? What if she had suddenly grown a conscience?"

"Did she sound like she'd grown a conscience, when she was throwing her fit on your porch?"

"She sounded terrified," Doreen replied. "She was angry, frustrated, and really scared."

"Well, she had reason to be. Because eight hours after seeing you, she turned up dead."

"And we still don't know who killed her."

"No," he said.

"Hey, what's in the will?"

He quickly scrolled through it, without giving her a chance to read anything. When he got to the last couple pages, he said, "It's actually very simple."

But an odd tone was in his voice. "So, what does it say? Come on. Here's a different theory for you. Whoever stands to inherit is probably the one who killed her."

Mack looked at her, and his lips twitched. "You might want to watch what you say."

"Why is that?"

"Because she left everything to you," he said quietly.

Doreen burst out laughing at the joke, but the expression on his face didn't change. She stared and then pulled the laptop toward her, so she could flick through the pages herself, and there it was. *"I leave everything in my bank accounts, all my property, and my complete estate to the woman who was my friend and who I screwed over at the very end. I am fully responsible for her not receiving any marital assets. No alimony or anything else from the more than 100 million dollars her husband raised throughout their marriage. It felt good at the time to trick her into signing away her rightful settlement, but then I realized what a madman Mathew was and what I'd done, and, for that, I am very sorry. The only thing I can do is make restitution in this way."*

Doreen stopped and stared at him. "You know the courts will think I did it," she said helplessly.

He nodded. "But I did find the key. It's not like you put it there," he said, as he looked at her, one eyebrow raised.

She immediately shook her head. "No, I didn't. What if my ex had found that? That doesn't bear thinking about."

Mack nodded. "What I don't know is whether that version of her will has actually been filed."

"Meaning, it's not legal?" she asked.

"That's what we have to figure out. But it is witnessed, although I don't know who the witnesses are." Then he laughed and said, "It's actually digitally signed online here in Kelowna. This is a copy of the original, so we'll find out who the witnesses were."

"And in Kelowna?"

"What do you want to bet that's who she was meeting?"

She shook her head. "But this is just too unbelievable."

"Well, as I'm searching her holdings online," he said, "what you won't believe is the amount of money that she left you."

"Meaning?" she said. When he didn't say anything, she added, "Does that mean I need to hand out the thousand résumés I printed off yesterday?"

He looked at her, then at the stack of papers she pointed to on her desk, and started to laugh.

"What does that mean? Why are you laughing?"

"Well, let's just say, I don't think you'll have to worry about money anymore."

"Was she rich?"

"Not in the same league as your husband by any means, but she definitely had money in her bank account, plus stocks, bonds, and an apartment in Vancouver. That will net you quite a bit."

She continued to stare. "Seriously?"

He nodded solemnly. "So I'm not sure how this works," he said, "but it looks like maybe you have landed in the roses."

"No," she said. "Marigolds."

"Marigolds?"

She looked over at him and said, "Hang on a minute. Wasn't she found in a marigold bed too? That's why you dubbed it *Murder in the Marigolds*. Remember?"

He nodded slowly.

"But still, to find the key in the marigolds in my front yard," she shook her head. "What if this was planted?"

"But why would somebody do that?"

"What if Robin did it?" she asked. "What if she tossed it when she was having that little fit of hers? What if she did it on purpose?"

"If that's the case," he said, "she wanted to be found out, and she wanted to be forgiven. She just didn't know how to do it."

"Or she wanted to point her fingers at both Mathew and me, get us both charged with her murder."

Chapter 20

IN A SUDDEN movement, Mack stood, disengaged the USB key, and said, "I'm off," as he pocketed the key.

She looked at him in surprise. "Where are you going?"

"I'm taking this to the office," he said, "before anything happens to it. I will book it in as evidence. Remember? She's on a slab in the morgue."

Doreen winced. "Great way to remind me." She looked at the key. "Any chance I can get a copy of what's on that?"

"I'll see," he said.

"Hey," she protested, "if I found it first and hadn't shown you what was there, I would have just kept a copy."

"I know," he said, "and I did take a picture of it."

"Sure, but you didn't take a picture of everything on it, did you?" she said, "and that's important too."

He frowned, thought about it, and said, "Fine."

He sat back down and popped the key into her laptop and quickly copied it over for her. And then he said, "Now remember. This is forensic evidence. The only reason I'm doing this is because it's a will, and you're the inheritor. But we don't know for sure that it's her *last* will and testament and that it's perfectly legal."

"But, if it was her *last* will," she said, with a bright grin, "maybe she did turn over a new leaf. Although I don't know what would have caused that."

"Well, according to the letter, she had an awful lot in there that caused it. And you can read the letter again on your own," he said, "but I want to get this to the office."

He stood, hesitated, and she asked, "What's the matter?"

He shrugged. "I shouldn't have given you a copy of that."

"I promise," she said calmly. "I won't do anything with it, until you tell me to."

He looked at her directly. "It could cost me my job, you know?"

"I would never do that," she said gently. "I'm perfectly happy here at Nan's house. It's not like the potential money would change me."

His gaze searched hers, and then he nodded slowly. "It'll go to probate, and you wouldn't get it for a long time anyway."

"What's a long time?"

"Nine months for probate, once it actually gets started," he said, "and the executor of her estate would do that. So potentially you're looking at a year."

She sat back down on the kitchen chair, raised both hands, and said, "See? It's not like I could buy groceries with it this week anyway."

He burst out laughing. "Let's take it one step at a time." He walked rapidly to the front door, turned back to look at her, and said, "Remember now. Don't tell anyone about it either."

"I won't," she said.

"And make sure you don't pass it around."

She looked at him in surprise and shrugged. "There just doesn't seem to be enough there that would explain why Mathew would want it," she said. "Accusations but no facts. I just don't get the feeling that this is what he was after."

Mack looked at the key in his hand and nodded. "I guess a couple reasons come to mind," he said, "and none of them are good."

She looked at him in surprise. "Like what?"

"He might have known about the will. He might have known about her confession letter. He might think it holds other secrets that aren't there. It might not be what he is looking for, but it still could be something he would utilize."

"Maybe," she said doubtfully, following Mack to the front door, "but I don't know why he would care."

Mack, at that, stopped, looked at her, and said, "You're still so innocent."

She stiffened and glared at him.

He smiled. "It's very endearing."

"Oh, please," she said, rolling her eyes. "So why are you thinking I'm missing the point?"

"Because it's a really big one and something that I really don't want to contemplate."

"Now what?" she asked.

"What if you're not there," he said, "what if you aren't there to inherit?"

She shrugged. "Then I'm sure it'll go to somebody in her family."

He nodded. "Okay, I get that," he said, "and what if you are there. What if you inherit, and then you die?"

For a moment there was just silence, as she stared at him. "You're thinking Mathew might kill me in order to get his hands on … what though? This money is peanuts to him."

"I don't think it's so much the peanuts," he said slowly, "but maybe whatever else she has in her possession, like in her safe deposit box, hidden in her home, or wherever it is that she's got the stuff stashed that he is looking for. He's been pretty patient. Look at the game he is playing here already."

At that, she winced. "Okay, I can see that," she said. "Is there any way he can move the probate faster, so I would inherit earlier?"

"No, not necessarily," he said, "but I don't know estate law, and he certainly has a team of lawyers, so I'm guessing the answer to that question is maybe. But, what if he is friendly, gets back in your life to some degree, and wants to help you sort out this mess? And he finds out where her stash of goods is, then goes after it himself, because that's what he is really after."

"So we're back to thinking that he's here because of her, and he's only coming around me because he thinks that she gave me something."

He waggled the USB key. "She did."

She crossed her arms over her chest, as she contemplated it. "I guess," she said quietly. "There's another easier answer too. What if he can make another will, dated later than that one, with his name on it. Using the same document and just change out the details?"

He smiled gently. "And I can see that he might want to try to at least alter this document, so that your name isn't on there. That would certainly be easy enough to do. It depends on whether she had a chance to file it or not."

"And could he change that one?"

"He'd just file one between the time that she filed this

one and her death."

"As if she would have immediately changed her mind and filed another one?"

"It happens," he said, as he stood on the front step and looked out at all the neighbors. "Families are weird, and, when they find out they are or are not in a will, they can change. People have changed their wills in a heartbeat, just from finding out something about somebody or what somebody did to someone else," he said. "So I wouldn't put it past him."

"In other words, we still have a lot of digging to do," she said. "And now you're making me even more freaked out about my ex."

"You should be," he said seriously. "I didn't like you going out with him last night. I really didn't like to see that he came here this morning, and now? After seeing this? I think you're in even more danger."

"What about Robin's ex-husband?" Doreen asked.

"That's another reason I'm going to the office," he said, now pocketing this latest USB. "I will contact Vancouver and see if I can get that file and get some follow-up to look for any current history on him."

"Good idea," she muttered. She beamed and said, "And, of course, you'll tell me all about what you find out, won't you?"

"In your dreams," he said cheerfully, as he quickly jogged down the steps to his truck.

"I helped you," she called out.

"And I'm helping you too." He walked to the driver's side, hopped into the truck, then, leaning through the open window, said, "Remember to stay safe."

And he turned on the engine and backed out of the

driveway, as she watched him go. As soon as he was out of sight, she immediately went down the steps, and, with the animals at her side, snuffling through the tall grass, she searched among the plants.

Almost immediately Richard stepped out and asked, "What are you doing?"

She sat back on her heels, looked up at him, and said, "Checking out the marigolds. Why?"

He crossed his arms and frowned at her. "I heard him. He pretty well said, *Stay out of trouble.*"

"Weeding my marigolds is hardly trouble."

He looked at her suspiciously. "Anything that's a plant seems to cause you trouble."

She burst out laughing. "Hey," she said, "I've been doing a lot for plants around here."

"Yeah, sure," he said, with a grumble. "Remember. stay out of trouble." And he stepped back inside and slammed the door. As she sat here on her heels, wondering at the craziness of her neighborhood, she had to wonder if he was worried about her staying out of trouble for her sake or his own.

"I bet it's just because he doesn't want the Japanese tourists back again," she muttered to Mugs.

Mugs barked and then barked again, rolling around on the tall grass right beside her. She reached over, scratched his belly, and then, overcome with emotion and enjoying having him close, she gave him a great big hug. He whimpered and got riled, as he got free of her arms and started to do zoomies on the front yard. She sat here and laughed and laughed, until he finally collapsed beside her, panting. Goliath, far too superior for such displays, had just laid in the tall grass beside her the whole time. As soon as Mugs collapsed nearby, the big cat reached out with long claws and whacked Mugs across the forehead. Mugs yelped and immediately backed up out of reach. And Goliath stretched even farther out in the grass, as if claiming the space.

Doreen smiled, as she looked down at the two of them, but Thaddeus wasn't here. She hopped her feet and called out, "Thaddeus? Thaddeus!"

At the far end of the garden came his cry. "Thaddeus is here. Thaddeus is here."

She walked over to see what he was up to. "Are you getting into trouble?" she scolded.

"Are you getting into trouble?" he said back at her.

She groaned, dropped to her knees, and said, "No, I'm not in trouble. You're the one that's been getting into trouble lately."

"Are you into trouble? Are you into trouble? Are you into trouble?"

"No," she said. She reached down, and he immediately hopped onto the back of her hand and climbed up her arm. When he sat on her shoulder, he crooned up against her cheek and said, "Thaddeus loves Doreen."

She smiled and cuddled him closer. "Well, I'm really glad to hear that," she said. "Because Doreen really loves Thaddeus."

They sat here in the grass, as a family, and she thoroughly enjoyed the moment. Just then her phone rang. She pulled it from her pocket and smiled. "Good morning, Nan."

"Good morning, dear," she said. "I have fresh warm croissants and clotted cream."

"Oh," she said, "clotted cream. I haven't had that in," and then she stopped. "Well, let's just say, in ages."

"If you come down here with the animals, I'm sure we have a few for you."

"Any other reason for the visit?"

"Well, I've been asking around a bit," she said, "and there's definitely some interesting gossip."

"I'll be there in a minute," she said, laughing.

She got up, walked through the house, locked up, and this time chose to go out through the cul-de-sac. Maybe it was because of Mathew's visit, or maybe it was because of finding the USB key out in front of her house. She couldn't walk past the garden without checking to see if anything else was there. It blew her mind to think that maybe Robin had actually thrown it into the garden on her own.

Was Mack right? Had it been more of an apology from Robin because she didn't know how to fix things? It seemed strange, given the personality of the woman, at least the side Robin had shown to Doreen when Robin had shown up here. But prior to that, they'd been friends, and that was something else that blew Doreen away. The ranting visit wasn't the behavior of friends either. Still, Doreen could hardly blame a dead woman, and obviously Robin had had a change of heart somewhere along the line.

"Thank you, Robin," Doreen whispered aloud. "I'm not sure where this all ends up, but, if, indeed, that will is yours, and it is legal, thank you for thinking of me and trying to make amends."

A warm breeze drifted toward her just then, and she smiled, as strands of her hair lifted across her shoulders. "Maybe that's a message from you, Robin, huh?" she asked.

In the distance a horn honked and then another, and sirens roared, and she smiled. "Nope, just another day of business as usual," she said. "Hope you are well, wherever it is you are. Sorry it all happened so soon."

Chapter 21

Tuesday, Late Morning ...

DOREEN CROSSED THE grass, watching as Mugs raced across, heading toward Nan, his ears flapping, as he greeted her with wild enthusiasm. Nan bent down and cuddled the dog, as Goliath, never to be outdone, strolled in like he was some movie star. Nan chuckled out loud and said, "Isn't he magnificent?"

"He certainly is," she said. "He makes Mugs look like an impatient puppy."

"There is something about the way the two of them interact," Nan said, with a big smile. She reached out and gave Doreen a hug. "Don't you look fine this morning."

Doreen looked at her in surprise. "Thank you," she said. "It has been a very strange morning."

"Well, you can sit down and tell me all about it," she said. At that moment, Thaddeus poked his head out from under Doreen's hair, where he'd taken to sitting on the crook of her neck.

"Thaddeus is here. Thaddeus is here."

"And a good morning to you too, Mr. Thaddeus." Nan held out her arm, and Thaddeus immediately crossed over and crawled right up to her shoulder, tucked in against her. Doreen was just going to comment on that, when Thaddeus immediately said, "Thaddeus loves Nan."

Nan placed a hand across her heart and cuddled him close. "Isn't it so lovely to hear that coming from him?"

"It is, indeed," Doreen said. "The trouble is, I'm pretty sure he is eyeing the croissants on the table, and that may be the reason he's doing it."

Nan burst out laughing. "You know what? I wouldn't be at all surprised. And can you blame him?" she said. "They are divine."

"If you say they're divine," Doreen said, "it makes me wonder how many you've already had?"

"Only one. Only one," she said. She motioned to the chair beside Doreen, "Sit, sit, sit. It's so lovely to see you."

"It's nice to see you too. Having Mathew in town just reminded me how much I missed during all the years I was married to him."

"You did miss a lot," Nan said, nodding her head slowly. "But you also experienced a lot that other people never do as well."

"I guess," Doreen said, "but they were all wealth-based things that existed on such a superficial level. I may not have much in the way of money now and don't go to fancy places and events, but I'm so much more alive, and I mean that from an inside level, beaming outward."

"That's a lovely way to put it," Nan said, staring at her in surprise.

"Well, lately I've had some eye-opening experiences, when you consider that river dunking and being shot in the shoulder," she said. "I've really done some thinking."

"Oh, dear," Nan said, "please tell me that you won't

move away."

Doreen looked at her in horror. "Of course not! Why would I do that?" She added, "That would be terrible. You are part of the reason I'm here, and I just found you. I don't want to lose you now."

"Oh, good," Nan said, settling more comfortably into her chair. "Like I said, it's just so wonderful to have you here. I really wouldn't want you to move away. Another reason for you and Mack to hook up. At least I know Mack isn't going anywhere."

"That's hardly a reason for Mack and me to 'hook up,' Nan," she said. "Honestly, what will I do with you?"

"Oh, don't be such a prude," Nan said, unrepentant. She pointed at the plate with croissants and said, "The two biggest ones are on your side."

Doreen couldn't argue with that. She reached for the first one, and it was still warm. "Oh my," she said, as she broke it open gently, then reached for the small tub of what looked like whipped butter. "Is that butter or cream?"

"You know, when you come to this point," Nan said, "there's very little difference between clotted cream and butter, really it's just consistency."

Doreen grinned. "I never thought of it that way."

She dipped her knife into the pot of creamy goodness and gently spread it on the croissant. It melted on contact. She gently buttered the other half and then picked it up and took a bite. She sat back, closed her eyes, and just enjoyed the experience, as her palate rose up and sang. "My goodness," she said. "These are absolutely delicious, Nan. Where did you get them?"

With a chuckle, she said, "One of the inmates here was downtown at that 360 bakery place," she said. "And they're divine. They have the biggest apple fritters ever, and these absolutely wonderful croissants are made fresh every morning."

"So it's a bakery where they make their own pastries?"

Nan nodded. "My friend brought back several dozen, enough for everybody," she muttered. "So I snagged up a bunch and called you down."

"And the cream?"

"He got it from there too. A big pot of it for everyone. I just took a little bit," she said. "You just really must have some with these croissants. They also had a lot of chocolate-covered croissants, if you could imagine," she said, with a sniff. "Who would do such a thing?" she said. "A croissant is meant to be savory. Don't add sweet to savory."

Doreen thought it would be a wonderful idea to have chocolate all over it, but she understood Nan's reticence. "I think it makes it more like a doughnut or a dessert," she muttered. And she took another bite.

Nan nodded. "And nobody should be starting their day with that."

"Well, I've started mine with leftover pizza and a few other weird things in the last little while," she said, smiling. "Things that I never thought I would ever be starting my day with."

"That's because you used to always get your perfect soft-boiled eggs and a piece of toast or yogurt and berries," she said. "One egg and one-half piece of toast is not enough to keep a bird alive. You're looking much better now."

"Well, I was eating just enough," she said, "to maintain my figure. After the divorce, I dropped quite a bit of weight, and now I think I'm starting to put some of it back on." She looked down at her flat belly and shrugged. "The nice thing is, I don't even think about it right now," she muttered. "And I don't want to."

"How did dinner go last night?"

She looked at her in surprise and then smiled. "Who told you?"

Nan just gave a noncommittal shrug, but her eyes twinkled. "You know there are no secrets in a town this size."

"No, there doesn't appear to be," she muttered. There was a long moment of silence, as Doreen enjoyed her croissant. Bringing herself back to the conversation, she smiled. "It was fine," she said. "I mean, dinner itself was absolutely lovely. The company, well, not so much. I found it a very strange experience, almost surreal to think that I was sitting there, having a meal with him again."

"But I hope you didn't enjoy it too much?" Nan asked, looking at her carefully.

She shook her head. "Nope. Once I told him that I had a USB key of his, he was very anxious to get me out of the restaurant and home, so we could grab it."

Nan's jaw dropped. "You have a USB key of his?"

"Well, I found it in my old purse," she said, refusing to mention the other keys that Mack had taken back with him. "But it turned out to only have my stuff on it. He didn't believe me though. So I think he was afraid, and honestly, after a lot of contemplation and conversation with Mack, I think Mathew is here because he's afraid that Robin gave me something before she was killed."

Nan leaned forward. "Really?" she said. "Tell me more."

"But, when I gave the USB to Mathew, he ran off really fast," she said, with a shrug, "and just left me standing there in the doorway."

"Did he try to kiss you?" Nan asked sharply.

"Of course not," Doreen said in surprise. "We don't have that kind of relationship anymore."

"Never could figure out what you saw in that frog anyway," Nan said. "Definitely not kissing material, if you ask me. He would never turn into a prince."

Doreen started to smile, but the image caught her funny bone, and she started chuckling. Soon she was laughing furiously at the comment. By the time she finally calmed down enough and had wiped away the tears, she felt pretty fine indeed. "You do have a lovely turn of phrase," she said to her grandmother.

"Sometimes," Nan said comically, "sometimes."

"So, let's turn this back to you," Doreen said, when she could, eyeing the last little bite of croissant on her plate. She quickly picked it up and popped it into her mouth. "What gossip is it that's going around here?"

"Well, everybody knows your ex is in town." At that, Doreen stopped and stared in shock. Nan nodded. "He has been seen all over, and people have talked. They also know that Mack took him in and talked to him at the station," she snickered. "They were all abuzz, trying to figure out what charges Mack would trump up to keep him in jail."

"I don't think Mack was trying to trump up any charges," Doreen said in surprise.

"Then you don't really understand Mack."

"Well, he will obviously be fair and would never unfairly harass someone."

"Are you kidding? Mack would harass that no-good loser in a heartbeat," Nan declared. "So would I. That's why he doesn't dare show his face around here."

"Well, he already did once," she said, with a roll of her eyes.

"That doesn't count. But, since Mack let him go, every-body is trying to figure out how long before he leaves town. Actually everybody is trying to figure out—"

"Oh, Nan!" Doreen said, leaning forward, staring at her grandmother. "Please tell me that you didn't bet on it?"

"Why wouldn't I bet on something I knew would abso-lutely happen," Nan said. "That's like, you know, money in the bank."

She stared at her grandmother, trying to figure it out. "Oh, good Lord, you're the one who set it up, aren't you?"

Nan twittered. "Of course I did. The man's a menace," she said. "The sooner he is gone, the better. Actually it would be best if he is charged with Robin's murder. That would suit the two of them and serve them both right."

"Well, Robin is dead," she said, feeling a little bit more gratitude toward the woman, after seeing what was on that last key.

"But still, they both did you wrong," Nan said.

"Oh, he's not making any apologies. Don't worry," she said. "He is still talking about bringing me back with him, although why he thinks I would even want to do that, I don't know. And he certainly isn't offering me any money."

"Of course not. Money is all about power for him," Nan said. "And you don't want any exposure to any of that."

Doreen shook her head. "No, I don't. But back to you and this little wager you've got going. If Mack finds out that you're betting again, he won't be happy with you."

"Mack knows," she said, with a wave of her hand. "Be-sides, Richie talks to his grandson all the time. I'm sure somebody there knows."

"You can't get away with this all the time, Nan. You must stop. You have to consider the fact that it's putting their positions in jeopardy too."

"Pish-posh," Nan said, with another wave of her hand. "These guys have known about it for years."

"So, you didn't start it when you arrived here?"

"When I moved into Rosemoor? No, of course not," she said, wide-eyed. "We've been betting on everything in this place for years. I've always had friends here. I just have more now."

"I'm surprised they let you in, if you were the instigator behind all this betting," she muttered, as she snagged up the second croissant.

Nan sat back, with a satisfied look on her face, as she watched Doreen break it open and slather whatever that creamy goodness was on it. Nan said, "You still need to eat up. You're not that rounded yet."

"I'm not trying to be rounded, thank you," she said, looking at Nan in horror. "I think just maintaining my current weight would be lovely."

"Well, you can't maintain it, if you're not eating."

"I had food last night, and it was quite good," Doreen replied.

She nodded. "Lucky you didn't end up with indigestion," she said, "given the company."

"Well, it certainly gave me a lot to think about afterward."

"Did you sleep?"

"Like a baby," she said cheerfully. "Only he woke me up this morning."

"Please don't tell me that Mathew spent the night?" Nan said, looking irritated.

Doreen looked at her in horror. "No, of course not," she said. "I told you that it's not that type of relationship."

"Maybe not," she said, "but I wouldn't put it past that guy to try to wiggle his way back into your bed."

"Well, he didn't," she said firmly, as she bit down onto the croissant and chewed.

Nan nodded wisely. "Good, because that's Mack's bed."

Doreen started to gasp and choke at the same time. "It is not Mack's bed." She leaned forward, hissing at her grandmother under her breath.

"Sure, it is," Nan said. "You just haven't gotten yourself up to snuff yet."

Groaning, she sat back and said, "I'm not ready."

"Good," Nan said. "Glad to hear it. That means you know your own mind."

"Of course I do," she said. "I'm not a fool, but I feel like I can't trust my own judgment yet. Look what I chose."

"Honey, you're not the same person you were back then. You're not that naive young girl. And Mack is a good man."

"He is. Yes, I know that—"

"Don't you *but* me," Nan said.

"I didn't say but," Doreen protested.

"Good thing. Good thing," she said. Nan then sat back, picked up her tea, with a look of satisfaction, and sipped it.

Not exactly sure what that look was all about, Doreen finished her croissant in a hurry and said, "Besides, I think Mathew is leaving town this morning."

Immediately Nan leaned forward. "Which flight?"

"I don't know. He just said he had to leave this morning."

"He wanted to know if there was anything else, I suppose."

"Of course," she said. "He also still seemed to think that Robin had given me something. He didn't understand that

Robin threw a fit when she was at my house, and absolutely no way did she give me anything."

"No, I can imagine," Nan said calmly. "Well, the sooner he is gone, the better."

"I couldn't argue with that." And then Doreen noticed that Nan was writing down notes. "Are you using our conversations for your betting?"

"Of course I am," she said. "All is fair in love and war, and, when it comes to bets, it's war," she said, with a cheeky smile.

"It's also illegal, Nan."

"Don't be a stick in the mud," she said. "You keep getting your nose into Mack's business, and I'm pretty sure he figures that's illegal."

"Not as illegal as yours."

At that, Nan looked up, her eyes widened, and said, "You mean, there are degrees of illegal?"

"You know what I mean," Doreen protested.

"Nope, not sure I do," she said, "and I doubt that you could explain it either."

Flummoxed, Doreen sat back, with the last bit of croissant in her hand. She dropped her hand onto her lap, with a sigh, and Mugs took it right out of her fingers. "Mugs, what are you doing?" she wailed. "That last bite was for me."

His tail thumped like crazy, as he sat there, looking at her, hopeful for more. Thaddeus hopped off Nan's shoulder, then walked across the table to the last two croissants and immediately started pecking away on one.

Doreen reached down, snatched up the croissants, and said, "Oh, no, you don't."

But one of the croissants flew off the plate and landed on the ground. Immediately Thaddeus flew after it, but Mugs got there first, and, with the two of them fighting over the one croissant, she stared in dismay at the chaos.

Nan was too busy laughing to be upset. She said, "Go ahead. Take that last one home with you. But this time make sure you don't share it with the others."

"I didn't intend to share that one," she said hotly. "And that just means they aren't getting treats when they get home, since they just stole mine." Then she stood and called the animals over. "Now it's time to go home, you two." With the croissant gone now, both of them were happy enough to oblige.

Chapter 22

WITH THE LAST croissant in her hand, Doreen marched the critters back home, still miffed that they took the last bite of her croissant and beat her to the one that had hit Nan's patio. Doreen knew that she couldn't really blame them. As much as she had enjoyed the pastries, they obviously had too. Still, it would be nice to have had it for herself when she got home. At least she still had one. Mugs pranced at her side, obviously feeling pretty cheeky and happy with himself.

"Yeah, you should be," she muttered. "You got something that was intended for me." And then she shrugged and let it go. After all, she'd been the one who had dropped it, and, even if it had been hers, she would have shared anyway.

"Now," she said, "what will we do?"

She wished she knew exactly where Robin had died, though it wouldn't help her much. Still, even just seeing the scene would help set it in her mind. She pulled out her phone and sent Mack a text.

Instead of texting back, he called. "Why?"

"I figured you found her at the Welcome sign, in the marigolds, where the murderer left her body, but I just wondered where she really died," she said. "I know it doesn't mean anything. It would just help me to understand, if I could see the crime scene, where she really died."

He hemmed and hawed and then finally said, "Her blood was found in the back of where the little coffee shop is."

She thought about it. "Oh, okay, I know that one," she muttered. "Was her vehicle there?"

"Yes, the blood starts right there at the vehicle," he said. "As if she were either getting in or getting out, something along that line. Waiting for the forensics still."

"Do they always take this long?" she complained.

"No, they often take much longer," he said, chuckling, "as you well know."

"I know," she said, "but whatever. Maybe I'll take a drive down there."

"Maybe you should," he said. "If you think of anything or see anything, let me know."

"Will do," she muttered, then ended the call. She looked at the animals and said, "It's too far to walk."

Immediately Mugs woofed, and she figured that meant he'd like to go for a car ride. "I will start sounding like a batty old lady if I keep interpreting what it is that you're barking. You probably just want to go home and have the rest of my croissant," she muttered.

When they made it home, she put the croissant on the counter and walked through to the front yard where she got into her vehicle, letting all the animals climb in with her. Once everybody was packed up and loaded, she drove down to the coffee shop where Robin had been last seen. At least there or at the restaurant. Then Doreen thought about the witnesses to Robin's will. With that thought, Doreen quickly changed direction, heading to the Chinese food restaurant, where Doreen had gotten Robin's briefcase from. The same waitress was there, and she recognized Doreen.

"Oh, hi," she said. "Is everything okay?"

"It is," she said, "absolutely. I just had another question for you,"

Immediately the waitress frowned.

"It's okay," Doreen said. "I handed the briefcase and everything over to the cops."

Relief washed over the woman's face. "Ever since I gave it to you," she said, "I've been feeling terrible, realizing it should have just gone to the authorities."

"In this case, it went to the cops anyway," she said. "I work closely with Mack, the detective."

The waitress nodded enthusiastically. "I have seen the coverage of you two, so I was hoping it was okay."

Doreen wanted to ask more about that but stayed quiet for a moment. "Did you have anything else to do with Robin? Did by chance you sign something?"

"Well, yeah, me and Mendy, the other waitress, we were witnesses to Robin's signature."

"Do you know what it was for?"

"She said that she had just rewritten her will and needed to have two witnesses sign it. She was such a nice lady, and it was obvious she was so young and wouldn't die. We didn't know any different, and how horrible is that?" she said, with sudden insight. "She must have had some inkling that she would die," she cried out.

"Well, I think that's probably quite true. But she was also a lawyer and was well-known for keeping her wills straight. I suspect she changed it on a regular basis." Doreen didn't know that for sure, but it made sense, given the woman that she knew. "I think this was probably just another iteration of it. Too bad we don't know who she met afterward."

"Right," the waitress said. "She seemed quite miffed that he didn't show up."

"Well, that often happens, depending on how far away they were coming from. It could have been quite a drive."

"The traffic can be really rough at times too," the waitress said, nodding. "She did say he had a long drive, so I think you're quite right there."

"Well, that makes sense too. So she said it was a man?"

"Oh, it was a man," she said, "and she seemed quite excited about seeing him. I really hope they connected first. I'd like to think that she at least died happy."

The waitress didn't seem to clue into the fact that whoever Robin had met was quite likely the murderer, so Doreen just nodded and said, "Isn't that the truth? None of us want to think about our death, but it would be nice to think we would at least be happy prior to it."

"Exactly," the waitress said, with a bright, cheerful smile.

"Like a big fairy tale."

"Well, it should be, but I'm not sure it is. I think you just have to try hard enough," the young woman said earnestly. "Life is what you make it." And, with that, she tossed off a beaming smile, as if she'd given a kernel of absolute wisdom that Doreen needed to snatch up and to utilize. "Anyway, if you want to order something, just let me know."

"Thanks," she said. "I was just hoping you might have remembered something."

"Outside of the fact that he was male, and, oh, she did mention something about that truck of his. About she didn't know why he didn't get a new one."

"Oh, so he was driving a truck then?" Doreen said.

"Yeah, she said something about it being lifted, like it was a truck for a young man. It sounded like something he'd had for a long time, but then she didn't say any more. And, of course, I mean, it's not like I understood very much about who or what she was talking about, since I didn't know the man."

"Right," she said. "That's good though, thank you."

And, with that, Doreen walked out of the restaurant. As soon as she got into her vehicle, the animals crowded against her. "I know. I didn't let you go in there with me. I should have though, shouldn't I? Maybe it would have loosened her tongue a little more." But honestly she didn't think the waitress knew anything else. As Doreen sat here, wondering what to do next, she decided she needed to tell Mack. It wasn't much information, but it was a little bit, and it could be important.

When he answered the phone, she said, "I just talked to that same waitress, by the way, and she and another waitress signed the will."

"Really?" he asked in surprise.

"Yeah." And she explained the little bit she'd learned. "Robin was waiting for some guy driving a truck he'd had forever, and it was lifted. Like a young man's truck, with the suggestion that perhaps he was beyond the appropriate age to be driving it."

"Interesting, but she couldn't give you anything else?"

"No, although I'm tempted to go back inside and ask her again."

"Maybe not now," he said. "Just leave it, and we'll see if something jogs her memory."

"And what? Then you'll ask her later?"

"Well, that would be the proper way to do things," he said in a dry tone.

"Maybe," she said. "I still haven't made it to where she was killed."

"Well, it's not like you're expecting to see anything there, are you? It's just a spot, a location. Her vehicle isn't there anymore. No evidence is."

"I know," she said. "I just, well, it was somebody I knew, and I feel odd about the whole thing."

"Well, go ahead then," he said. "Just stay out of trouble."

"Wasn't planning on getting into any," she said cheerfully. "Besides, I have the animals with me."

"Well, it's not like they'll save you every time," he muttered.

"But you have to admit they do a great job when they are busy saving me," she said, chuckling.

"Fine, they've been a huge help, but you can't count on them all the time. And look at what happened to Thaddeus last time."

"I know," she said, with a groan. "Give him a few inches, and that bird will hang himself."

Chapter 23

Tuesday, Noonish ...

WITH THAT, DOREEN turned on the car and headed back to the coffee shop. There she got out and wandered around the spot, where Robin may have been killed, then her body moved to the Kelowna sign. Her killer probably wanted her found fast. There was a sadness in Doreen's soul, as she thought about such a young life snuffed out like that. "It really does make you realize there is absolutely no way to know when it's our time."

Somebody behind her said, "Who are you talking to?"

She turned to look at the stranger. "Me," she said, staring at him. Something was almost familiar about him. She frowned, studying the man in a black three-piece suit. "Do I know you?"

He gave her a quirky smile. "I wondered if you remembered me. I was sitting inside, having coffee, and was quite surprised to see you pull up."

She shook her head. "Where do I know you from?"

He laughed. "From a time that I'm sure you're obviously happy to be gone from."

She stopped and stared. "Rex?"

He nodded. "Absolutely," he said. "I'm surprised you even remember me."

"Well, it's hard not to," she said. "You lived in the house with me, more or less."

"And yet you didn't see me right off."

She studied him for a long moment and then said, "You shaved your beard."

He laughed. "I did, indeed."

"Well," she said, "it certainly changed your look. You've also let your hair grow long." She couldn't quite understand why he'd shave, then let his hair grow. Seemed more likely for him to trim both or to let both grow. She frowned again.

"Just a different look," he said easily.

"Are you still working for my ex?"

"Yes," he said, "at least for the moment."

"Well, you didn't ever look like you wanted to leave."

"Did you notice?"

She winced at that. "I'll admit that I was fairly oblivious to a lot that went on around me," she said, "but I would like to think that I know various people who worked there at the time."

"I'm sure you do," he said easily, "but part of the whole image is also that you wouldn't be affected by it. We were always told to stay away from you and to keep you in utter quiet. After all, you're of a delicate temperament."

She stared at him. "I'm of a what?"

He chuckled. "I never quite understood that reasoning myself. But I figured it was just Mathew's way of making sure the staff didn't talk to you."

"Well, secrecy was always his big thing," she muttered, staring off in the distance. Had Mathew really said that about her being delicate? "It's pretty insulting to find out *delicate* was in his vocabulary when talking about me."

"Well, I wouldn't worry about it," Rex said. "I don't know if you've figured out yet just what he's like, but he would say whatever needed to be said in order to further his agenda."

"Well, I've certainly been learning that," she said quietly. "I'm surprised you still work with him, if you know that too."

"He pays well," he said, with a shrug.

She nodded slowly. "I'm sure he did. It was all about loyalty for him." He looked at her quizzically, and she shrugged. "I'm not blind to who he is, but I admit to having been fairly blind to a lot that went on back then. I think I was on autopilot, instead of actually living."

"Well, you definitely look more alive now," he said, with interest. "A lot less perfect."

She winced. "I don't know if that's a compliment or an insult," she said, with a wry chuckle, "but remember. Being perfect was the requirement of the day back then."

"It was for you, wasn't it?" he said, sounding amused. "More like a china doll."

"Dumb and stupid," she said cheerfully. "I had to stay quiet because I would always say the wrong thing, according to him."

"I don't think it was so much the wrong thing as that he didn't want you to figure out what was going on."

"Well, I never put any time or effort into it," she said. "My mistake."

He shrugged. "It happens."

"What are you doing in Kelowna?"

"Well, I brought your husband in," he said, "but he is off to Vancouver now."

"Seriously?" she asked. "I'm surprised he left so fast."

"He had business."

"He always says he has business. You didn't drive us to dinner last night."

"No, he told me that he was going out for dinner, but I didn't realize he was with you," he said, his gaze even more curious.

"Yeah," she said, "I was trying to figure it out myself."

"If you say so," he said. "I don't know why you would though." Then he stopped, shrugged, and said, "But it's your business."

"I went out mostly because I was curious as to what he wanted," she said, with half a smile. "He never does anything without a reason, and I didn't quite understand what the reason was for even looking me up."

He nodded contemplatively.

"It would have been due to Robin, probably."

"I imagine so."

"I think he thought I had something that she gave me."

He looked at her in surprise. "Did you?"

"Nope, not at all," she stated. It wasn't a lie because Robin hadn't given it to her; she had dropped it out in the yard. "I had a USB key from when I lived with him, in one of my old purses," she said. "So he made me go back to the house and get that for him."

He laughed at that. "Of course he did."

She shrugged. "I told him that it didn't have anything of his on it, but he didn't believe me."

"He had to make sure," he said comfortably.

She looked at the parking lot. "This is where she died, huh?"

"Apparently," he said, but an odd note was in his voice.

She turned to face him. "Is that why you're here?"

He looked at her and shook his head. "No, not at all."

"That's why I'm here," she said. "She was my friend, before she became his mistress, you know?"

"Well, she was never your friend if she became his mistress. He was your husband."

"Good point," she said, "but I didn't know what a louse my husband was at the time."

"No, I think that's one of his abilities. To be what you want him to be at the time."

She thought about that. "You know what? That's not a bad analysis. There was just something always very different about how he appeared to me versus everybody else."

"And that was part of his talent," he said.

"Well, you obviously respect him, since you've been working for him long enough."

"I don't know about *respect* at this point," he said, "but it's almost like I know him too well to quit."

She gasped at that. "Exactly. Depending on what kind of man he really is, you could be right." She looked back at the coffee shop, then at the spot where Robin had been stabbed, the bloodstains still evident. "You'd think that somebody would have seen this murder when it was happening."

"You'd think so. But apparently not. And it is at the back of the corner, facing into the bush, so …"

"I guess I hadn't really thought of it that way," she said, "so maybe it was deliberate after all."

"Usually a murder is deliberate," he said, with a laugh.

And again, there was that odd note. She studied him quietly. "You never did have a family, did you?"

"Nope, my line of work wasn't conducive to it."

"No, you'd have to get out and to get away from my ex

for that. He wouldn't likely tolerate you having a partner. The competition probably wouldn't go well."

"Competition?" he asked.

"Well," she said, "he wouldn't like you being busy with somebody else. He'd want you at his beck and call, not somebody else's."

He looked at her for a long moment and then nodded slowly. "You know what? It really could be just that simple too."

"What could be?" she asked, confused.

He shook his head. "Nothing," he said. "Don't worry about it." He turned to head back into the coffee shop.

"It was nice seeing you," she said.

He looked back at her, smiled, and said, "Ditto."

Then he walked inside. She didn't know what to do at that point, and it was yet another odd occurrence in her crazy life right now. She didn't even know how to react. What she did know was that she felt even more unsettled now. And she knew of no reason for it.

Chapter 24

DOREEN GOT BACK into her vehicle and greeted the critters again, only Mugs was growling out the window. She turned, and there was Rex again, just standing and watching her. She gave him a half smile and a three-finger wave and started up the engine.

"You don't like him, huh, Mugs?" She couldn't remember if he ever felt that way before or not. He certainly should have known Rex. "You do know him," she muttered. "So I'm not sure why you're acting like you are." But the fact of the matter was, Mugs was definitely not a happy camper.

She rolled down her window, as she drove past Rex. "It doesn't sound like Mugs remembers you."

He smiled. "Hey, that's not an issue," he said. "Have a good day." Lifting his hand, he walked over toward a vehicle on the far side.

As she drove past and headed toward the exit of the parking lot, she saw a green car, as in the green Jaguar. That would also make sense because Rex would likely return it himself, which would also suit her husband. Mathew never picked up rental cars or returned them. He wouldn't do the paperwork required either, so it was always handled by somebody else in order to make his life easier. Plus, he always ordered deep green Jaguars if possible. Was that why Robin had the same vehicle type? To get back at him? Or had she somehow commandeered his connections and automatically received the same type of vehicle that was always delivered?

She pondered that as she slowly drove home. Could it have been Rex who had searched her house? That hadn't even clicked when she was talking to him, but realistically it probably was him. Who else would be here with her ex? Who else would have come to search? At least she told Rex about the USB key and had given it to her ex, but maybe that was a nonissue. She didn't know, but she frowned as she headed toward home.

Still feeling a little unsettled, she stopped at one of the parks and got out with the animals for a walk. They were more than happy to oblige, as she walked toward the beach and sat down on a bench, near a big sign warning that no animals were allowed unless on a leash, so she knew she must watch out, or she'd get in trouble because she had neither Goliath nor Mugs on a leash. She had leashes with her, but Goliath was not impressed with his. He'd handled it for the first few weeks, and, ever since, he was quite upset whenever she tried to put it back on.

She whistled for Mugs and brought him back from the beach where he'd been barking at the waves, caused by powerboats out in the lake. "Come here, Mugs."

As he came back toward her, she quickly clipped on the leash and just sat here at the bench. She had Thaddeus on her shoulder, and her crew seemed to be content to enjoy the fresh breeze. "It's been a very weird day today," she muttered. She brought out her phone, checked her emails and messages, but found nothing. Even as she was checking, a text message arrived from Mack.

Well?

She smiled and sent a message back. **Nothing.**

That wasn't quite the truth. So she sent back a message, telling him that she'd seen her husband's long-term employee Rex, and that he was likely the one who had searched her house. Immediately her phone rang. Laughing, she answered it. "I didn't mean for you to call me."

"Well, after a comment like that," he said, "how could I not?"

She shrugged, but, of course, he couldn't see that. "I just wanted to let you know," she said. "You always get upset when I only give you part of the information."

"With good reason," he said.

She said, "He was very civil, and actually I didn't even recognize him at first. He used to have a beard and short hair, but now he has long hair and no beard."

"Why the disguise?"

She stopped and frowned. "Did I say it was a disguise?"

"No, but you didn't say it wasn't either."

"I don't know then," she said. "I suppose it's possible it's a disguise, but that seems a little odd, although it did take me quite a few minutes to recognize him."

"You think he is here with your husband?"

"He did say he had driven Mathew here," she said quietly, "in a green Jag, so I presume that he is responsible for taking it back. My ex has this thing about not picking up rental cars or returning them. He doesn't like to be bothered with all the paperwork."

"How nice to live like that," Mack said caustically.

"He definitely has his foibles, like everybody," she said. "I don't imagine it's any different for anyone else."

"Maybe not," he said, modulating his tone.

She still wasn't exactly sure if something was going on there or not with Rex. "He did say that my ex had left already."

"Apparently he did. I understood he was scheduled on a flight this morning. I don't know if he showed up or not."

"Well, that would be something else entirely, wouldn't it?" she said. "An awful lot of murder and mayhem is going on here, so there's no way to know if he told the truth."

"Do you have any reason to think he is incapable of leaving?"

"You mean, not showing up at the airport? I have no idea," she said. "I would hope that wasn't an issue."

"No, I would hope not," he said slowly, "but we don't know for sure. Maybe I'll check with the airport to see if he actually got on."

"That would probably be a good idea. Maybe you should just find out for sure," she muttered, frowning. "I do think Rex was probably the one who searched my house, but I don't have any proof. I was just assuming that he was the one because he was here with Mathew, and, therefore, while my ex-husband was keeping me occupied, Rex was the one who went in and searched my home."

"It's possible, but it would be nice if we had proof."

"And," she said, "it would also be nice if I had some way to let him know that nothing was there. I did tell him that I found a USB key and then I gave it to my ex."

"And what did he say?"

"He didn't say a whole lot. He actually seemed pretty oblivious to it all. I did pick up some undercurrents over the mention of Robin though. He said a couple things, and, every time, his voice changed."

MURDER IN THE MARIGOLDS

"Changed in what way?"

"I was trying to figure that out. It just, it just changed. It's not like it softened or he was laughing or mocking or anything. It's not like he was saying, 'Ha-ha, the witch is dead.' It was almost more like he was sad but trying not to show it."

"Do you think they could have had a relationship?"

"If that was the case, my ex-husband would have had a heyday firing Rex."

"Which could be why he's still trying to hide it," Mack said. "But could that have been who she was trying to meet?"

"I don't know if he would have gotten away. Mathew always kept his people on a very short leash."

"What a lovely existence."

"No, not very, and Rex did comment on the fact that he had no family and that it wasn't something my ex would have tolerated because Rex would have gone home to somebody he cared about every night, and, therefore, his loyalty to my husband would have been diminished."

"I keep forgetting and then you remind me what an absolute jerk your ex is."

"I keep forgetting too, until I remember bits and pieces," she said sadly. "And then it comes rushing back. Rex did make several comments about me not understanding everything that had gone on while I was there and how nobody was allowed to talk to me about things because I was *delicate*," she said in a scathing tone. "I was not happy to hear that."

He started to laugh. "Well, I guess Rex hasn't seen you recently, has he?"

"More than that," she said, "I think it was a ploy so that nobody would ever let me in on any of the problems or issues at the house. Mathew kept me in this little panic room, completely isolated." She shrugged. "But I'm out now, and I'm never going back in."

"Glad to hear that," he said, and, indeed, a cheerful note was in his voice.

She shrugged. "I guess maybe I said that a little too loud and strong, didn't I?"

"And that's okay," he said. "This time, at least, I believe you. Now how about going home and just get out of trouble."

"How do you know I'm not at home?"

"I don't know," he said. "I assumed you were still at the coffee shop lot."

"No, I stopped in at Kinsmen Beach. I'm just sitting here, with the animals."

"Good," he said. "Exactly what the doctor ordered."

"Well, he probably ordered that a while ago," she said, with a laugh. "I'm just trying to rearrange all the puzzle pieces in my life."

"I hear you there," he said. "Do you want to do dinner tonight?"

"Absolutely I do," she said, "particularly since we had to cancel last night."

"Well, I don't know about *had to cancel*, and you definitely did better out of the deal because at least you got dinner," he said. "I, on the other hand, did not get a beautiful meal out."

"Nope, you're quite right," she said, "but I paid the price for that dinner, and I had to endure the company."

"And you can keep that anytime," he said, laughing. "I'll be over when I'm done at work. We have a meal to cook."

"Good enough," she said, "looking forward to dinner."

With that, she hung up. Still smiling, she called the animals to her and said, "Come on, guys. Let's go."

With everybody safely back in the vehicle, she drove to her house. On a whim, she opened the garage and pulled inside.

"I don't know why I never use this very much," she said to the animals, as she opened the car door. She let Mugs out; then Goliath slid out as well. Mugs immediately started barking. She turned around to see a tall man with a hood over his face.

She gasped in shock. "What are you doing here?" she cried out. She frowned, when he spoke in a mumble. "I don't understand you."

He just shook his head and reached out an arm to grab her. She pulled back immediately and started to turn away, racing for the kitchen door. Now, because she had pulled into the garage, she had limited space. Mugs immediately jumped and tried to bite the stranger, who was grabbing her. Then Goliath hopped up on the back of her car and jumped on the stranger's shoulders. He immediately flung Goliath off, who hit the roof of the car and slid down the side. Doreen winced as she heard the cat scrambling down the car.

But it gave her a chance to get around Mugs, who was still barking and trying to jump up on the attacker. She raced around the front of the car, and, instead of heading for the house, she headed for the side door. Just as she got it opened, it slammed hard in front of her, and the stranger's hand clamped around her nose, and she was picked up. She kicked and fought and screamed. In this hold he had on her, Thaddeus couldn't get free because he was tucked in close against her neck.

Very quickly, a hood was pulled over her head and was

tightened down. She heard a yelp as Mugs took a hit. She cried out, but a hand slapped hard against her head, and that was the last thing she knew.

Chapter 25

Tuesday Afternoon …

DOREEN WOKE UP in the darkness in a moving vehicle. She could breathe but just barely. The hood was still on her head, and she took a long moment to figure out what was going on. She had to be in her own car. She shifted enough to know that her legs hit a wheel well, and she heard a whine in the background. She tried to call out, muffled, at best, from within a hood, "Mugs? It's okay, Mugs."

A little excited woof came and then some scratching. She must be in the trunk, and the vehicle was moving at a fast pace. Her attacker had shoved her into her own vehicle and then had driven out with her. How fair was that? She shifted a bit, happy that her hands were free and that she could get the hood pulled off her head. She heard the crooning against her ear. "Thaddeus is here. Thaddeus is here." Her heart swelled as she reached up and gently cuddled the bird.

"I wish you were safe at home instead," she whispered. "I really wish you weren't here in this situation with me."

She wanted to kick the trunk lid, but she also didn't want to let her attacker know that she was awake. Cuddling Thaddeus, she quickly explored the little space. She was in the back of her own car, which just drove her nuts. What she needed was for the vehicle to slow down. Also a way to attract some attention. Knowing that whatever damage she caused to her own vehicle, she would have to pay for made her hesitate. But, as she studied the two taillights, she wondered if it was possible to pop one of them out. It was an older car, so maybe it would give her less resistance, if she kicked out one. Then she might stuff something into it and attract some attention.

On the other hand, there was a good chance that she'd end up just hurting her foot. And that's the last thing she needed. Just then the vehicle took a hard right, and she was tossed from one side to the other. And she knew that they were quickly heading to a crunch point.

She had no idea how long she'd been out, and her head was killing her, more so when she explored the sore spot. Her finger came away sticky with blood. It was pitch-black in the darkness of the trunk, but, as far as she could tell from the smell and the texture, it was blood. That just made her madder because no way she deserved to be hit and hurt again. She'd been through enough of that already.

But she was also leery, knowing that the vehicle had taken a rough turn. So, even now, as she bounced around, she was afraid she'd be taken out to some far lonely corner, where he planned to do away with her. And she didn't even know why. That would never go down well. The fact that she also had Thaddeus—and quite possibly the other animals were inside the car with her kidnapper—terrified her. They hadn't done anything wrong and certainly didn't deserve to be treated like this.

Doreen desperately wanted to find a way to get out of this, but, if they weren't in traffic, then nobody would notice, even if she were to break something and were to try to attract attention. The vehicle kept going, as she struggled with an exit plan, wishing she had left something in her car. She managed to loosen one of the taillights by her head. But she would have to shatter it to get just her hand, if that, outside the car. She wished she knew more about cars. She wished she knew more about a lot of things.

Just then the vehicle slowed again and took another turn. She jostled in the back, and Thaddeus cried out, as she shifted. Mugs started to bark, and a yowl came from the front. All the animals were here.

At that, a voice from the front of the vehicle started yammering at them. "Calm down. Stop making such a ruckus. I can't even hear myself think."

She immediately recognized the voice as that of Rex, her ex's henchman. She was surprised enough that she didn't even know what to think for a moment. She needed to tell Mack. That brought her up short, and she immediately checked for her phone. Her kidnapper hadn't even removed her phone. She pulled it from her pocket, turned it on, and noted she was at half battery power, but she had enough light to text Mack. She immediately sent him a text message, with the volume way down, warning him that she'd been kidnapped from her garage, was in the trunk of her car, and was on a rough road after a couple harsh corners. She had all the animals with her.

WHAT?

I don't know where we are. I just know I'm in the trunk, and he didn't tie me up. He put a hood over my head, which I have since loosened, mostly because of Thaddeus.

She had marshaled an army by contacting Mack. She

didn't understand why the kidnapper hadn't taken her phone, but he must have thought that she was contained enough that she couldn't do any damage.

Which just meant that he didn't understand her or Thaddeus. Even now, Thaddeus was pecking at the laces on the hood. But she was free and clear of it, so there was no point. She gently disengaged him from that activity and whispered, "See if you can find a way out of here, Thaddeus. Find a way out."

And, at that, Thaddeus walked around the trunk, pecking and sticking his head into various corners. She wasn't sure that he even knew what he was doing, but she appreciated his attempt.

She just smiled at his antics, wondering how long it would take Mack to find her. She got another text, saying an APB was sent on her vehicle, and everybody was out looking. But they needed an idea of how long she had been out. She immediately responded that she'd been unconscious for a time and didn't know how long, but she was awake now, and Rex would regret not taking away her phone and not tying her hands.

At that, Mack sent back a message. **Stay calm. We're on this.**

She knew what that meant, but she also knew that, if they weren't on it fast enough, she wouldn't get a good outcome. She shifted in the back and tried to push the seat forward, and it budged a little bit, but she couldn't get her hand up to undo the locks. Something here engaged them. Normally they just snapped down. But she remembered that the left side never latched properly. She slipped over to the far side, wincing and barely avoiding crying out as she hit something hard, and it jostled her back.

Immediately Mugs started barking again. And, once more, Rex snarled at Mugs to shut up. Then Rex started talking. "I'll be glad when I get this stupid job done. Shut up! God, you're dirty animals. I hated you when you lived at the house, and I hate you even more now!" he snapped.

She wondered at a man who could hate a dog. What kind of a person was that?

Chapter 26

As Doreen listened, Rex muttered to himself, but it wasn't making any sense, or at least wasn't something she understood. She tried hard to listen, but it wasn't clear enough. Some words were garbled. She only heard something about, "That woman had him so wrapped up. And now he's in deep trouble."

At that, she sat back in shock. Maybe Doreen was wrong. But she quickly texted Mack about the words Rex said. **I think Rex had a relationship with Robin and may have killed her. Maybe because he feared getting caught by Mathew.**

At that, she got no answer for the moment, while she kept listening to Rex's words and sending Mack the little bits and pieces that she heard. It just wasn't very much.

Finally Rex took another left and slowed the vehicle. She immediately contacted Mack and said they were slowing down. Rex hit the brakes, opened the driver's door, and hopped out, then opened up the side door and said, "Get out of here! Go on. Get out!" She didn't know who was getting out, but it didn't seem like it was Mugs or Goliath because she could hear the two of them chasing around inside the car, as Rex yelled and hollered at them.

But, for whatever reason—maybe because the animals knew exactly where she was—they weren't leaving the car. She couldn't imagine what chaos was happening, but she definitely heard chaos, and she silently cheered them on.

Finally Rex groaned and said, "What is wrong with you? Here's your freedom. Here's your one chance." And then he said, "You can't possibly know she's in the trunk."

She shook her head and rolled her eyes at his ignorance because, of course, the animals knew.

"Keep it up, and you'll die with her," he said. "If that's what you want, that's fine. I'm happy to do it."

A shout came from somebody in the distance, and Rex yelled back, "No problem. Just trying to put the leash on the dog."

There was laughter, and the other vehicle drove off.

"Nosy busybodies," Rex said. "Why she doesn't have a leash on you, I don't know. At least then I could just drag you out and dump you on the side of the road."

Her heart clenched in pain at the thought of her animals being stranded like that. What a brute Rex was. He should be dropped off in a strange place and see how he liked it then. She lay tense in the back, just waiting for a chance to move and to get the upper hand in this scenario.

Finally Rex groaned and said, "Fine, but then, when I dump her, you're going too. Enough of your caterwauling. Be quiet, or I'll turn around and shoot you."

It was almost as if the animals knew because immediately they were quiet again. She wasn't sure just what was going on, but, while all that had been happening, she had managed to loosen up the left-hand corner of the seat. She didn't know if it would do any good if she couldn't also loosen the right side, but she could hope so. Her kidnapper got back in, and she felt the vehicle sink slightly. Then the door slammed, as he muttered to himself. "A bloody nuisance, all of you. I don't know why I'm even doing this." He drove off again.

She wanted to yell, "Yeah, so why *are* you doing this?"

But she wasn't sure what kind of reception she would get, and then Rex would definitely find her phone and take it away from her. No, the best thing she could do was hope to delay the inevitable as best she could, giving Mack a chance to find her. She sent him another message. **Hurry please.**

He responded. **Stay calm and stay quiet. We're hunting for you.**

She immediately groaned and sent another message. **Somebody else called out and asked if Rex was okay, and he just said he was trying to put the dog on a leash. So people are around. I just don't know where.**

She heard Rex yelling something and imagined that Goliath must be attacking him. And then she heard barking, and, somehow through it all, Thaddeus couldn't stay quiet, and he started cawing and calling in the background. She heard Rex screaming, and, after driving erratically for a few minutes, he pulled off the road again for a few minutes. He hopped out of the vehicle and screamed at the occupants of the car. "You're nuts! You're all nuts!" he muttered. "Get the hell out of the car!"

But nobody seemed to be budging.

"I'm not listening to any of you."

The sound of another vehicle pulled up, as she desperately tried to kick the seat down. Somebody walked closer, and she stilled, as she heard crunching footsteps.

"Hey, are you okay?"

"No," Rex roared. "My girlfriend's stupid freaking animals, I can't stand them."

"Well, they look to be pretty upset," the stranger noted.

She didn't recognize his voice.

"Of course they are. Whatever," Rex said. "I just have to get them back to her."

"What are you doing with them, if they don't like you?" the stranger asked suspiciously. And the two men got into a slight altercation, but so much anger was in their voices that she struggled to hear the words. She started screaming from the trunk of the car, "Help! Help! Help!"

The stranger asked, "What was that?"

"Nothing," Rex said. "Just shut up and mind your own business."

She banged on the back of the car, kicking and kicking and kicking.

"Whoa, whoa, I don't know what you've got going on here," the stranger said, "but, if a woman is in the trunk, no way in hell I'm letting you out of here."

"You've got no say in the matter," Rex said, taking on an ugly tone. "Now you get the hell away from here and leave me alone."

"Whoa, no need for guns, mister," the stranger said. "I don't know what the hell you're doing here, man, but it's wrong."

"It doesn't matter if it's wrong or not," he said. "You let me disappear right now, or you'll disappear too."

She started screaming and kicking against the seat now even harder.

"You have to let her out," the guy said. "You know that, right?"

"I do not," Rex said. "She has been pissing me off all

day."

"Well, you can't just leave her like that. You'll end up really hurting her."

"Yeah, well, that's the intention," he snapped. "Or are you too stupid to figure that out? Now take off, and leave me alone, or do I have to pop you one right here?"

"I'm leaving. I'm leaving," the newcomer said immediately.

"Well, hurry up and scram. And, next time, mind your own business."

Then she heard the guy retreating, who said, "You know you should just let her go. Like, dump them all out on the side of the road, and let her go."

"Can't do that," Rex said. "Somebody is looking for her."

"So what? You don't have to do anything about it. Just leave her alone."

"Nope, I can't do that. It's got to be permanent. She's the only one who will know."

"Know what?"

"Well, if I tell you, then you'll know too," he said. "Now get lost."

With that, her Good Samaritan returned to his vehicle and immediately drove away. She was still kicking and screaming. Rex yelled at the back of the car. "He can't hear you anymore, and he knows if he comes after me, I will pop him one, so just shut up." Then Rex got back in the car and drove off.

She sank back, tears in the corner of her eyes. All she could hope for was that the guy called the cops and let them know exactly where they were. She immediately texted Mack about the altercation, though she couldn't give him any more information.

He contacted her a moment later and confirmed that a call did come in. **Hold on**, he texted. **We have the location where it happened.**

She sagged back with relief and snatched up Thaddeus and hugged him tight. He immediately cawed and crowed. Letting him go, she said, "Help me get out of here."

She resumed kicking at the back seat, trying to get it loose, so she could at least get into the car. The seat was loose but wouldn't completely fold down. Mugs was barking and chewing away at the seat, and she was desperate to get out of the trunk, but she couldn't quite manage it. Finally she collapsed, but, off in the distance, she thought she heard sirens.

Instead of slowing down, Rex picked up speed and tore faster and faster down the road. Now she was jostled from side to side, as he wove through traffic, swearing heavily. She could hear other vehicles honking at his behavior.

She wanted to call out to him that he could never outrun the cops in her old car, but, considering what trouble he would be in, maybe it was appropriate. What she didn't understand is whether her ex was part of this too or whether it was all about the lawyer. Doreen had no clue, but something bizarre was happening.

She knew that Mack would blame her for it. All she'd done was go home, just like he told her to. The least he could do is understand that. Still fuming, she waited, but the sirens got louder and louder; so it was only a matter of minutes until this nightmare was over.

As Rex kept on driving faster and faster, suddenly she realized that a car accident was likely to be the worst-case scenario. Rex still wove through traffic, sending her flying from one side of the trunk to the other. The frightened animals kept up a cacophony that now drove her crazy too. With her hands clapped over her ears, it was all she could do to stay sane, as she was thrown from side to side and one end to the other.

Finally Rex took a really sharp corner, and she was slammed hard against the other side of the trunk. She lay here, completely dazed, as, all of a sudden, the vehicle came to a screeching halt, and a door opened. Just like that, the car was left running, and she heard no other sounds from Rex.

Mugs barked and barked and barked. The sirens came closer and closer, louder and louder, and finally she heard them right on top of her. She waited inside, hoping that they were here to rescue her.

And then Mack asked, "Doreen, you in there?"

She pounded against the trunk lid.

He walked to the front of the car and said, "Hang on a minute. We'll get you out in a jiffy."

She waited. Then the engine stopped, followed by the sound of the trunk release. And, just like that, he opened it up. She stared up at him with tears in her eyes; then she opened her arms, and he reached down, picked her up, and held her tight against him. She buried her face against his chest and whispered, "It's not my fault." She heard the laughter rumbling up through that great big chest of his, as he just held her close.

"Are you hurt?" he whispered.

She shook her head. "No." Then she reared back and said, "He was going to dump the animals right out on the highway," she said in outrage.

He looked at her. "And that's what you're worried about?"

"They're not used to that kind of treatment, you know? And I don't ever want to see an animal subjected to that kind of treatment."

"Uh-huh," he said, then he turned, and an ambulance was right there.

She looked at him and said, "Oh no."

He nodded. "Yes, you should be checked over. The way he was driving, you had to get tossed around back there."

"I'm fine," she said. "You need to go get Rex."

"Believe it or not, more people are on this police force than just me, and we've got a whole contingency of men out looking."

"Rex couldn't have gone far on foot, and he's pretty upset too. He was really angry at the animals." She shook her head. "I just don't understand people like that."

He laughed. "I'm pretty sure he doesn't understand you either."

"Rex works for Mathew," she said, "but I don't know that this is even about that. I suspect Rex was involved with Robin."

"So you said, but she wasn't the kind to be involved in that type of manipulation, was she?"

"She used her body as a weapon. And honestly she had a heck of a body. Guys were falling for it constantly."

"Well, there's more to life than manipulation," he said. "In this case, she obviously hadn't learned those kinds of lessons."

"No, I don't think so," she muttered. "And I feel sorry for her because there's so much else in life that she could have done."

"Well, let's not get too sad about it all," he said, "because there's still a lot we don't know yet."

"I know," she said. "I still don't understand exactly what it's all about, but I think we're really close to finding out."

"Well, we'll be really close when we get Rex to talk," Mack muttered. "We just have to get our hands on him."

A shout came from the distance, and she looked, still encircled in Mack's arms, but on her feet now, to see Rex being led toward them.

"That's him," she cried.

Rex glared at her. "I should have known you'd be a complete pain to look after," he muttered, turning away.

"Hey, I didn't have anything to do with this deal," she said to Mack, waving at the car. "That's all his doing." She looked at the car and frowned. "I really thought I was in my car."

"No, it's the rental," Mack said.

She shook her head. "Wow, I had no idea."

"No, it doesn't matter," he said, "although the rental company won't be very happy."

She said, "Pretty sure about that. Mugs was chewing through pretty good."

Mack leaned forward, winced, and said, "Yeah, I definitely see a lot of damage. I hope you've got some insurance for that."

"Not me," she said, "him." Nodding toward Rex.

He glared at her and said, "Your husband will pay for it."

"Ex-husband," she said, "and Mathew doesn't pay for anything. You know that. Any damage incurred on the job, you pay for."

At that, he just winced.

"Seriously?" Mack asked.

"Yeah, he doesn't pay for anything, if he doesn't have to.

Money is king to him," she said. She looked at Rex. "I still don't understand what this is all about, Rex."

"It's about Robin," Mack said, "isn't it?"

Rex shrugged. "I loved her."

"Ah," Doreen said, "and you didn't realize she was using you too?"

"She wasn't using me," he said hotly. "No way she was. She loved me."

Doreen stared as she watched another man fall for the woman's wiles. "Robin could have done so much good in the world with her persuasive techniques," Doreen said, "but all she ever cared about was money."

"She had a hard life," Rex admitted. "A really rough childhood that really scared her, and she admitted as much. I understood. I mean, I had a pretty rough time of it too," he said. "I'm only with your ex because I can't walk away from the money, and he pays me a lot."

"Yeah, but is it worth your soul?" she asked.

"Lady, I gave up my soul a long time ago."

"And what about Robin?" she asked quietly. "She was my friend for a short time. At least I thought she was."

"She loved me," he said sincerely. "We were leaving together."

"So, what happened then?"

"I don't know," he said. "I really don't know."

"Well, you must know something because you've kidnapped me for some reason."

"Well, that was your ex," he said.

She shook her head. "No, I don't think so."

"Yep, it was," he said. "I'm not even sure why. I was supposed to just threaten you and make sure you were terrified, then kidnap you and dump you somewhere."

"What about the stranger on the road?"

"Well, if I was really intent on killing you, I'd have killed him too."

"I'm pretty sure he thought that's what you were up to," she said. "I don't know, Rex. You sounded pretty interested in killing me."

"Well, I shut him up though, didn't I?"

She thought about it a moment and said, "There was something in his tone. Did he look familiar to you?"

"I've never met him before," Rex said, with a shrug. "Never seen him before either."

Mack looked at her. "What are you talking about?"

"I'm not sure," she said, "just something about his voice, but I can't be sure."

Mack stared at her and asked, "What are you thinking?"

"I think he might have known who Rex is but didn't quite understand what was happening."

"Well, he couldn't have known me," Rex said. "I've never been in town before."

"Weren't you in town when Robin was murdered?"

"No, I came in afterward with the boss, and he didn't kill her. I don't know who did," he said. "I was hoping I could set a trap and bring the killer out in the open. But nobody took the bait."

"What kind of a trap?" Mack asked in a hard voice.

"Her," he said. "That the boss just wanted to make sure you didn't have any of the goods he was looking for. But I thought whoever had killed Robin might be interested in something I found."

"And what would you do?"

"I would give you to them," he said. "Figured they could take care of you themselves."

"But?"

"He didn't show up. I was supposed to meet him on the road back there. You were still out cold at that point, and I stopped where we agreed, but he didn't show up."

"Unless he did show up and then followed you," she said quietly.

He looked at her in surprise. "What are you talking about?"

But Mack understood perfectly. "You think that's who it was?"

She nodded slowly. "Who was it that you were supposed to meet, Rex?"

"James, Robin's first husband."

"And you never met him or never saw any pictures of him?"

"No," he said. "Why?"

"I think it's the guy who stopped you on the road," she said. "He was just checking to see who and what you were."

Rex stared at her. "Why didn't he talk to me then? Why didn't he say something?"

"Maybe he was just checking you out and realized you had trouble enough of your own and decided to call the cops on you instead. To see what madness he could farm up out of this. Why did you want him?"

"I think James killed her," he said softly. "Robin told me that she'd worked with her ex-husband for many years, and they'd been doing this con for a long time."

"Why do you think that Robin's own partner in this con would kill her?" Mack asked.

"Because she told James that she wouldn't do this any-more, that she was done. That she'd had a change of heart and that she wanted to marry me and to go away together and to stop all this."

"Wow, maybe she did have a change of heart," she said, turning to look up at Mack. But he wasn't looking at her. His arms were across his chest.

"I still don't get it. Why kidnap Doreen?" Mack asked.

"Because I told James that I had somebody who had talked to Robin. Who she'd seen on her last day, and my boss thought Robin had handed something over to this woman. James didn't believe me, said I had to kidnap you, so he could talk to you himself."

"Maybe he figured it was just too messy," Mack said. "It's one thing if you hand over an unconscious person. It's another thing completely if you get involved in something that's a public spectacle."

At that, Rex nodded. "I was thinking that myself," he said, "but I never thought that it would be that guy. He should have just said something."

"Describe him," Mack said.

"Mid-thirties, maybe forty years old. Tall, like me. Blond hair."

"Well, Robin's ex is in town," Mack said. "We ran the airline records, making sure Mathew had left, and James's name popped up too."

At that, Rex's gaze widened. "So, he is here. Damn. I wonder if that was him on the road after all."

Chapter 27

Tuesday, Late Afternoon ...

"WHAT ARE YOU getting out of it though?" Doreen asked Rex. "What if James is here? What if that guy you were talking to was James?"

Rex shrugged. "I wanted to meet him. Honestly I wanted to take him out because I figured he is the one who killed her."

"So this is all about revenge?" Doreen asked Rex.

"Maybe," he said, and she could see the sadness in his face.

"You really loved her, didn't you?"

"I did," he said quietly. "I can't believe that I found someone like her after all these years alone, and now she's gone before we got a real chance."

"Maybe so," she said, "but, using me as bait to get to James, that doesn't make much sense."

"Well, it does," Mack said. "Maybe her ex knew and wanted to take care of any loose threads. And to make sure that you didn't have anything Robin might have given you."

"Why does everybody think she was giving me stuff?" Doreen asked, raising both hands. "The woman cheated me."

"And she was sorry about that too," Rex said quietly. "Honestly she really did have a change of heart."

Doreen didn't know what to believe and stared at the man who kidnapped her. "Didn't you threaten to shoot that guy?"

Rex shrugged. "Yeah, but I don't even have a gun. I just made it look like I did."

"Wow," Doreen said. "Well, I wouldn't be at all surprised if he isn't somewhere close by, watching the circus and laughing."

"He might be," Mack said, "but we've also got guys out looking for him."

"Good," she said, "there are a couple more murders we want to ask James about."

At that, Rex said, "She killed them, you know? The two of them together."

"What are you talking about?" Mack asked.

"His parents. James and Robin, the two of them, planned it all out and made it look like a burglary. Together they killed his parents because they didn't have any money and because the parents wouldn't share."

"Wow," she said, with a glance at Mack. "I was actually right about that."

Rex looked at her and said, "That's another reason this James guy didn't like you."

"He doesn't know anything about me."

"Robin told James that she felt bad and that she wanted to get some money to you. Because you could hardly survive on your own without it. She said she had looked into how you were living. It was bad, and it was her fault, so she wanted to fix it. James got mad, and that's when she told him that she wanted out, but she wanted her share of the money, so she could give something to you."

"Well," Doreen said, "this is just unbelievable."

Rex shrugged. "Like I said, she had a change of heart."

She looked at Mack. "Maybe she really did then?"

"I think she did," he said, "but we still have to find her ex."

"I have a phone number," Rex said. With a nod from Mack, Rex pulled out his phone and held it up for Mack to see.

"Okay," Mack said, "but you're still not walking away from this. You kidnapped Doreen, knocked her out, and crammed her in the trunk, drove like a maniac. You're lucky she'd not hurt more than she is. You risked public safety, terrified her, and all the animals have been traumatized as well."

"You have no idea," he said. "Those animals aren't traumatized. I'm the one who's traumatized," he cried out. "I just want to go back to work and to forget about this whole nightmare."

"How the heck do you think that will happen?" she cried out. "You hurt me."

"Hardly," he said, "you're the one walking away scot-free. And those animals are a nightmare. You have to pay for that."

"Enough of that," she said, "those animals are loyal and brave. More reliable than most people I know."

"James is the one who killed Robin," Rex said hotly. "I want to make sure he is brought to justice."

"And you didn't mind using me as bait." She shook her head. "What if he had killed me?"

"Well, that would have been your problem," Rex said,

with a sneer. "There's been lots of times I wanted to kill you myself."

"And yet you could have easily helped me," she said. "With the tiniest effort, you could have made my life a whole lot easier with Mathew."

"That is one scary man," he said. "I probably don't have a job anymore after all this mess, but you can bet he will make sure that he gets whatever he wants out of it."

"What is it that he wants?"

"He wants money and power, and he wants to make sure that Robin didn't take anything she wasn't entitled to have."

"I think she may have done a lot to bring him down," Doreen said quietly.

"Are you for or against that?" Rex asked, as he stared at her and started to laugh. "Robin said she would damage him if she could, but she also wanted to walk away from her ex, only James wasn't having it."

"Well, what will you do about it?" Mack asked. "Will you do anything to make Robin's sacrifice worthwhile, or will you just let the status quo continue?"

"Well, you'll make sure I'm charged," he said, "and I'll do what I can to make sure James goes down."

"Take him away," Mack told the officers, escorting Rex.

Just then Mack's phone rang, and still watching them put Rex in the nearest police cruiser, Mack stepped away to answer and a few moments later ended the call. "Well," he said, walking back toward Doreen, "they picked up James's vehicle and are tracking his trail now. He'll be heading to the station soon." He looked at Doreen and said, "You go to the hospital and get checked out. I will follow these guys to the station and have a serious talk with both James and Rex."

"You do that," she said, "but the animals are coming in

the ambulance with me," she said defiantly, "or I'm not going." He looked at her quietly, looked at the ambulance drivers, and asked, "Can we make an exception this time?"

At that, the two men looked at each other and shrugged. "Fine," one said. "Let's go."

And, with that, she headed toward the ambulance to find Thaddeus already sitting there in the back, looking at her and calling out, "Thaddeus is here. Thaddeus is here."

"I'm glad you're here, buddy," she said. "And what about Mugs and Goliath?"

They were already in the ambulance too, sitting deeper inside, behind the gurneys. Goliath looked more than a little freaked out, and even Mugs looked like he was stressed. She got into the back, then waved at Mack and said, "Okay, but I'm just getting checked over, and then I'm going home again."

"Okay," he said. "You know where I'll be." He looked at his ringing phone and said, "I need to get this."

"Don't worry about it, just go," she said, waving her hands.

He groaned and said, "Just go get checked out, and make sure you're safe. No hiding symptoms from the doctors either."

She nodded and hunkered down on the seat, as the paramedic went around to the front and got into the driver's seat. And, with that, they pulled away.

She looked down at Mugs and said, "I'm so happy we're all together," she whispered. He barked at her and cuddled her close. She was so tired and stressed, and all she wanted to do was go home. But that was definitely not happening. Instead she had to go to the stupid hospital.

She watched as everybody disappeared in the distance, as

the ambulance headed toward the hospital. She sank back and closed her eyes, grateful that her ordeal was over. As Mugs started to whine at her feet, she reached down and said, "It's okay, buddy. We're good." But he didn't stop whining, so she looked at him in surprise and asked, "What's the matter?"

She peered out the window and didn't recognize the area. She wondered where they were, but then she hadn't known exactly where they'd ended up in the first place, once Rex had stopped driving. She checked for her phone, only to find out she didn't have it. She stared at Mugs in horror. "Where's my phone?" she cried out. She leaned forward to look through the tiny window that separated her from the ambulance driver, and he was all alone. She thought there had been two men, but maybe it was only one. She had no idea. But somebody was strapped to the bed across from her. She winced. "God, he's probably dead," she said.

She leaned over and took a look and saw that it was the other ambulance driver. She stared at him in horror, but he was tied up, and his eyes were closed. She immediately looked for something to cut his ties. By the time she had cut him free and smacked him across the face several times, he groaned ever-so-slightly.

She whispered, shaking him. "Are you okay? Hey, are you okay?"

He opened his eyes and stared at her in shock. "What happened?"

"*Shh.* You tell me. I got into the ambulance to find you all tied up."

He frowned. "I don't know what happened," he said, sitting up and then groaning because his head was killing him.

"Looks like somebody has taken over the ambulance."

"Why would somebody do that?" he asked, staring at her.

She winced. "Probably because of me."

He just stared at her, confused, as she quickly summarized what had just happened.

"Well, we have to get out of here," he said.

"Wouldn't that be nice," she said, "but he took my phone."

He immediately slapped his legs, looking for his, and quickly pulled out his own phone.

"Please phone the cops," she whispered. "I've been through too much already."

He sent out several alerts, and she hoped that maybe this time it would be okay. He looked at the animals and said, "What the devil. No animals are allowed in here."

"Well, that should have been my first clue," she said, "because he said that it was fine."

"Well, it's not fine," he said. "This is a new guy. I met him here, and he told me that he was supposed to come as part of my crew. I let him in, but I didn't have time to even talk to him because we had to take off right away."

"Well, I don't know quite how it all happened," she said, "but I think he took over your vehicle in order to get to me, and his intentions are likely violent."

"Great," he said, groaning. "Normally I'm not alone, but we've been short-staffed right now."

"I'm sorry," she said, "and here I am taking you away from somebody else who really needs your help." She looked over at Mugs. "We have to do something."

"We can go through the connecting door here," the guy said, "and get to the front seat, but he isn't likely to give up without a fight, and we don't know if he is armed. Plus, he could crash the vehicle, and that could kill us."

"I would imagine he probably is armed. We suspect he already killed a woman, but that was with a knife."

At that, the ambulance driver gasped and shrank back into the mattress.

"Right," she said. "It changes your perspective a little, I know. We don't really need to try to be heroes, if he is going around killing people."

"No," he said, "absolutely not. That's the last thing we need."

With the animals watching, and now almost enjoying the ride, the driver took them across the bridge. "Wow," she said, "we're in West Kelowna now."

"I know," he said, "but I don't know where he is taking us. I did get messages out."

"Let's hope they get here fast."

"I don't think they believed me at first," he said, "but, after I sent several more SOS cries for help, they said they're on the way."

"Great," she said, muttering. "It's never easy, is it? He should have just ditched you back there," she muttered. "Now you're a problem too."

He stared at her in shock. "But I didn't have anything to do with this."

"Well, believe it or not," she said in exasperation, "I didn't either."

He looked at her, "Really? You didn't do anything wrong?"

"No," she said, "I was just in the wrong place at the wrong time."

He nodded. "That happens, doesn't it?"

"Way too often," she said, muttering to herself. And, soon enough, they pulled off at the top of the big hill on the other side of the bridge, into what looked like the parking lot of a huge movie theater. The driver turned around and backed up the ambulance against another vehicle. She whispered, "I bet he's planning on changing vehicles."

"Well, he can't do that. Not with the two of us," he said. "We can take him."

She looked at him in surprise. "Well, that's the spirit," she said.

"No," he said, "but I really don't want to get into another vehicle with this guy."

"Me neither," she said, with a bright smile. "So, on the count of three, I suggest we both rush him."

He stiffened, as he straightened up a little bit, and said, "I can do that."

But they didn't even get a chance. Instead James hopped out, turned, and disappeared. She immediately climbed out of the vehicle. She stopped and looked around and said, "There's no sign of him."

"I know," the EMT said, clearly confused.

"I was so sure," she said, looking around in confusion. "I thought for certain he would move us into another vehicle."

At that, a man behind her said, "That would be foolish, since there's two of you. Once you'd gotten the ambulance driver free, I had to change plans again." James glared at her, stepping out and pointing a gun in their direction. "You're becoming a pain in the ass."

"I haven't done anything," she cried out. "If you hadn't killed Robin, none of this would have happened."

"But she told me that she changed the will in your favor and that she'd left you a long explanation," he said. "If you'd like to hand that over, I'll let you live."

"Oh, I don't think so," she said quietly, "because, once that's handed over, you'll kill me for sure."

"Well, look at that," he said, with a smile, "you are smart enough to figure this out."

"It still doesn't make sense that you killed her."

"She was worth half a million dollars a year in income to me," he said. "No way I was letting that go."

"Wow." She didn't even know what to say to that. "Maybe she really did just want to change her life and become somebody else," she said quietly. "According to Rex, she had fallen in love with him."

"She fell in love with everybody. And it would last for a few months, maybe a year or two," he said. "Then she'd find another con or another mark, and she'd fall in love all over again. She would never have stayed with Rex."

"And what if it was different this time?"

"Well, we'll never know now, will we? She did try to get out of the industry, and, for that, I do blame Rex. I should pop him for it too. Because now I'm in the hole, by a lot."

"How could you kill your own parents?" she cried out.

"Easy," James said, with a snarl. "And she helped me. That started us down this pathway."

"So, why become lawyers?"

"Well, it was a great cover for one thing," he said, with a big smile. "Not everybody is a do-gooder though. We knew it would help us stay out of jail and on the right side of the law, while we figured out how to play it on the criminal side," he said. "It was one of the smartest decisions we ever made."

"So you didn't go to law school out of a sense of justice?" she asked. "You went to law school so you could understand how the system worked?"

"Exactly," he said, with a nod. "And it worked just fine."

"My God. And then what happened?"

"We both wanted to move on. To other people, I mean. But you can't really separate from someone once you've committed a crime like that together. You must always keep them close. She just kept playing and playing, bringing me more and more blackmail deals. That was perfect, but then she decided she just didn't want to do it anymore. I couldn't let that happen, could I? And now that I know that you know about the rest of it," he said, "I can't let you go either. I was hoping that I could let you and the driver beside you go, since he really didn't do anything, thinking you didn't really know anything either. Just a case of being in the wrong place at the wrong time."

She looked over at the terrified ambulance driver, then shrugged and said, "Told you."

"I didn't do anything," he said in horror. "I don't even know this woman."

"He really doesn't," she said apologetically to the gunman.

James shrugged. "I don't really care," he said. "I have to clean up the mess that Robin left behind, and, if this is the way it has to go down, so be it."

"But you don't have to do it," Doreen said. "You don't have to sully her memory with this."

He laughed. "God, you're such a romantic. I kept her close because that's what you do when you commit felony crimes with others, since you can't ever trust them not to turn on you," he said, with a smile.

"Ah," she said, "so you didn't care about her."

"Nope, not any more than she cared about me. We had

a shared purpose, but that was it."

"That's so sad," she said. "I really liked her."

"Until she screwed you over."

She winced. "Yes, until she did that."

"That's what she did though. Everybody would really like her, and then she'd find a way to take advantage," he said. "She was really good at it."

"Yeah, she was, but I know Mathew, my ex, was after her too."

"Yeah, what an idiot he is. That man is just a fool," James said, "and I've got tons of blackmail material to use on him now. And just me, so I don't have to share."

"I think you're making a big mistake there."

"Doesn't matter," he said, raising the handgun. "You won't be around to see the consequences."

At that, Mugs started to bark incessantly. James immediately lowered the gun and said, "You shut that thing up, or I will take a great deal of delight in popping all of them while you watch."

"Oh, I don't think so," she said, staring straight at him, because coming up behind him ever-so-quietly was Mack, and he had his handgun out in front of him.

Once she'd seen him, Mack called out, "Police! Hands in the air!"

The gunman stiffened and glared at her. "Now what kind of shenanigans are you up to?"

She shrugged. "I'm getting a little tired of having guns pointed at me," she said, with a smile, walking slightly closer.

Immediately the handgun came up. "Don't you move," he said.

"Well, either way," she said, "you're about to get shot. So what do you want to do?"

"What do you mean?" James asked.

Then Mack called out again, "I mean it. Drop the weapon, and put up your hands."

James glared at her, and she said, "Hey, there's always another day. There's always a guard you can call or another judge you can con. You're the lawyer, remember?"

He groaned and slowly raised his hands.

"Put the weapon down!" Mack said.

She waited tensely to see what James would do, and, sure enough, he slowly bent down, dropped the weapon on the ground, and then straightened up, his hands in the air.

James looked at Doreen and said, "Robin always said that there was something about you that she didn't quite understand."

"Yeah, there's always something about me," she said, "and I get it. Nobody understands me."

"What she really didn't get was how you always seem to come out on top. I don't even know how you managed it."

"Nobody does," she said, "but I'd like to think it has to do with doing the right thing."

He frowned.

"You know? Doing good, being kind to others?"

He shook his head. "And that's just crap."

With that, Mack came up from behind and immediately handcuffed the angry man. Then looking over at her, Mack smiled. "Are you okay?"

Doreen nodded. "Yes, but you'll have to take a moment to reassure Mugs." At that moment, Mugs was circling the two of them, barking in confusion, his tail wagging like crazy. With two other cops grabbing James, apologizing for him getting away from them, and another checking on the shaky ambulance driver, Mack stepped away, so that Mugs could get the greeting he deserved, then spent several moments cuddling him. Goliath came over and rubbed against Mack's legs, and even Thaddeus hopped up on his shoulder and cooed against his neck. Finally Mack straightened and looked at her. "This menagerie is nuts." She smiled and walked a little bit closer. He looked at her, narrowed his gaze, and again asked, "Are you okay?"

She sighed and said, "Yes, but I do have a request."

"What's that?" he asked.

She walked up, opened her arms, and said, "Can I have a hug, please? It's been a very long day."

With a gentle smile, he reached out, pulled her into his arms, and closed them securely around her. "Absolutely."

"Good. I just want to go home and rest." Looking up at him with a glare, she said, "And, no, I'm not going to the hospital. After this time, I may never get back into an ambulance."

Epilogue

Several Days Later ...

DOREEN WAS STILL babying herself, several days later, just sitting at home, doing a jigsaw puzzle that Richie had loaned her from the abundant supply they had at Rosemoor. Doreen had it spread out on the kitchen table, and it provided a mindless enjoyable fun that didn't require abstract thinking. She wanted to get bored for a change and just relax. She had puttered around in the garden, made a sandwich, worked on the puzzle, then puttered in the garden some more. And that was about the extent of her days.

When she heard a car door slam and footsteps, she smiled as Mugs raced to the front door, his tail wagging. When the front door opened, she peered around the corner and said, "Hey, Mack."

He walked in with groceries and said, "You up for some dinner?"

"If I don't have to do a single thing about it, absolutely."

He walked in, then frowned at her. "You're still feeling down?"

"It's not so much about feeling *down*," she said. "I'm just tired."

"Good," he said, "a few more days of relaxation will be good for you."

"If you say so," she said, with a smile. "I was thinking that it would be about time to pick up something else of interest, but so far nothing has really appealed."

"Again, good," he said. "Maybe you'll stay out of trouble for a change."

She laughed. "There isn't anything for me to get into trouble with," she said. "You've got everybody already locked up."

"Yes, that is quite true," he said.

She said, "I was thinking about looking at the Bob Small cases, but nothing jumped out at me for now. I didn't find anything that sparked my interest. I need to look into the Solomon files but not just yet."

He looked at her in surprise. "That's a pretty big serial killer case involving Bob Small," he said. "It won't be a case of a single crime."

"No, but he never was caught, was he? He was only a suspect."

"And we don't know that he is to blame for any of them."

"One of the cases was in Vernon. A young woman, a model, who was found in an orchard. It was originally thought he was to blame, but they caught the killer. So they solved that one, didn't they?"

He nodded. "Yeah, they did. So it's not a case for you."

She stretched, rolled her neck, and said, "Surely something interesting is happening around town, isn't there?"

"I thought you just said you would take a few more days off?"

"I did, and I will," she said, "but, as you know, we just

finished up with the *Murder in the Marigolds* case." He stopped, stared at her, and she chuckled and said, "Well, the name fits."

"So, what's next then?" he asked in exasperation.

"I don't know," she said. "It could be all kinds of things."

At that, Mack's phone buzzed. He looked down and frowned. "I will need a rain check on dinner."

"Why is that?"

"We have a kidnapping," he said, immediately racing to the front door.

"What? What kind of a kidnapping?"

"A gardener," he said, looking at her. "A gardener was kidnapped while working in his garden."

"Wait," she said. "Do you know what kind of flowers he had?"

He frowned, shaking his head, and said, "What difference does it make?"

She shrugged. "Maybe nothing."

He looked down at the text message on his phone. "Nasturtium. He was picking nasturtium flowers for a salad."

"Oh, one of those kinds of gardens," she said, clapping her hands in delight. "Nasturtiums are lovely to eat."

He stared at her. "I'm gone."

And, with that, she felt all her fatigue falling away. She stepped out in the front yard and said, "Call me when you know more."

"Like heck I will," he said. "Go back to your puzzle."

"Nope," she said. "I'd rather work on yours." And, with that, she gave him a huge fat grin and waved him off. She hoped the smile on her face brightened his mood, since he'd been worried about her, and clearly she was much happier

Turning to the animals, she said, "Look at that. We have a new case to work on. It's not a cold case, but it's a case. *Nabbed in the Nasturtiums.*"

This concludes Book 13 of Lovely Lethal Gardens: Murder in the Marigolds.

Read about Nabbed in the Nasturtiums: Lovely Lethal Gardens, Book 14

Lovely Lethal Gardens: Nabbed in the Nasturtiums (Book #14)

A new cozy mystery series from *USA Today* best-selling author Dale Mayer. Follow gardener and amateur sleuth Doreen Montgomery—and her amusing and mostly lovable cat, dog, and parrot—as they catch murderers and solve crimes in lovely Kelowna, British Columbia.

Riches to rags ... Chaos might be slowing ... Only a new murder occurs ... Sending her off the trail again ...

It's been a tough few weeks since Robin and Mathew, Doreen's ex-lawyer and her ex-husband, slid back into her life.

Okay, so maybe Robin isn't here any longer to cause torment, but Mathew is. And he's not planning to leave Doreen alone anytime soon, although thankfully he's gone back home for a while. Trying to recuperate looks doubtful for Doreen, when a local gardener is kidnapped, while picking nasturtiums for dinner.

The case heats up when the missing man's niece appears on Doreen's doorstep, looking for help, including asking Doreen to accompany her to the police station.

Not at all sure what's going on, but willing to help someone in need—particularly after having been a suspect herself—Doreen tags along, looking to do her good deed for the day.

But no good deed goes unpunished, and, when Mathew calls, Doreen gets more than she bargained for, including all the usual suspects: love, jealousy, and … greed. It takes everything from her feathered and furred critter team to keep her safe, as she digs to the bottom of yet another crazy case …

Find Book 14 here!
To find out more visit Dale Mayer's website.
https://smarturl.it/DMSNabbed

Get Your Free Book Now!

Have you met Charmin Marvin?

If you're ready for a new world to explore, and love ill-mannered cats, I have a series that might be your next binge read. It's called Broken Protocols, and it's a series that takes you through time-travel, mysteries, romance... and a talking cat named Charmin Marvin.

Go here and tell me where to send it!
http://smarturl.it/ArsenicBofB

Author's Note

Thank you for reading Murder in the Marigolds: Lovely Lethal Gardens, Book 13! If you enjoyed the book, please take a moment and leave a short review.

Dear reader,

I love to hear from readers, and you can contact me at my website: www.dalemayer.com or at my Facebook author page. To be informed of new releases and special offers, sign up for my newsletter or follow me on BookBub. And if you are interested in joining Dale Mayer's Reader Group, here is the Facebook sign up page.
https://smarturl.it/DaleMayerFBGroup

Cheers,
Dale Mayer

About the Author

Dale Mayer is a *USA Today* best-selling author, best known for her SEALs military romances, her Psychic Visions series, and her Lovely Lethal Garden cozy series. Her contemporary romances are raw and full of passion and emotion (Broken But ... Mending series). Her thrillers will keep you guessing (By Death series), and her romantic comedies will keep you giggling (*It's a Dog's Life*, a stand-alone novella; and the Broken Protocols series, starring Charming Marvin, the cat).

Dale honors the stories that come to her—and some of them are crazy and break all the rules and cross multiple genres!

To go with her fiction, she also writes nonfiction in many different fields, with books available on résumé writing, companion gardening, and the US mortgage system. She has recently published her Career Essentials series. All her books are available in print and ebook format.

Connect with Dale Mayer Online

Dale's Website – www.dalemayer.com
Twitter – @DaleMayer
Facebook – facebook.com/DaleMayer.author
BookBub – bookbub.com/authors/dale-mayer

Also by Dale Mayer

Published Adult Books:

Bullard's Battle
Ryland's Reach, Book 1
Cain's Cross, Book 2
Eton's Escape, Book 3
Garret's Gambit, Book 4
Kano's Keep, Book 5
Fallon's Flaw, Book 6
Quinn's Quest, Book 7
Bullard's Beauty, Book 8
Bullard's Best, Book 9

Terkel's Team
Damon's Deal, Book 1

Kate Morgan
Simon Says... Hide, Book 1

Hathaway House
Aaron, Book 1
Brock, Book 2
Cole, Book 3
Denton, Book 4
Elliot, Book 5
Finn, Book 6

Gregory, Book 7

Heath, Book 8

Iain, Book 9

Jaden, Book 10

Keith, Book 11

Lance, Book 12

Melissa, Book 13

Nash, Book 14

Owen, Book 15

Hathaway House, Books 1–3

Hathaway House, Books 4–6

Hathaway House, Books 7–9

The K9 Files

Ethan, Book 1

Pierce, Book 2

Zane, Book 3

Blaze, Book 4

Lucas, Book 5

Parker, Book 6

Carter, Book 7

Weston, Book 8

Greyson, Book 9

Rowan, Book 10

Caleb, Book 11

Kurt, Book 12

Tucker, Book 13

Harley, Book 14

The K9 Files, Books 1–2

The K9 Files, Books 3–4

The K9 Files, Books 5–6

The K9 Files, Books 7–8

The K9 Files, Books 9–10
The K9 Files, Books 11–12

Lovely Lethal Gardens
Arsenic in the Azaleas, Book 1
Bones in the Begonias, Book 2
Corpse in the Carnations, Book 3
Daggers in the Dahlias, Book 4
Evidence in the Echinacea, Book 5
Footprints in the Ferns, Book 6
Gun in the Gardenias, Book 7
Handcuffs in the Heather, Book 8
Ice Pick in the Ivy, Book 9
Jewels in the Juniper, Book 10
Killer in the Kiwis, Book 11
Lifeless in the Lilies, Book 12
Murder in the Marigolds, Book 13
Nabbed in the Nasturtiums, Book 14
Lovely Lethal Gardens, Books 1–2
Lovely Lethal Gardens, Books 3–4
Lovely Lethal Gardens, Books 5–6
Lovely Lethal Gardens, Books 7–8
Lovely Lethal Gardens, Books 9–10

Psychic Vision Series
Tuesday's Child
Hide 'n Go Seek
Maddy's Floor
Garden of Sorrow
Knock Knock…
Rare Find
Eyes to the Soul

Now You See Her
Shattered
Into the Abyss
Seeds of Malice
Eye of the Falcon
Itsy-Bitsy Spider
Unmasked
Deep Beneath
From the Ashes
Stroke of Death
Ice Maiden
Snap, Crackle...
Psychic Visions Books 1–3
Psychic Visions Books 4–6
Psychic Visions Books 7–9

By Death Series
Touched by Death
Haunted by Death
Chilled by Death
By Death Books 1–3

Broken Protocols – Romantic Comedy Series
Cat's Meow
Cat's Pajamas
Cat's Cradle
Cat's Claus
Broken Protocols 1-4

Broken and... Mending
Skin
Scars

Scales (of Justice)
Broken but… Mending 1-3

Glory
Genesis
Tori
Celeste
Glory Trilogy

Biker Blues
Morgan: Biker Blues, Volume 1
Cash: Biker Blues, Volume 2

SEALs of Honor
Mason: SEALs of Honor, Book 1
Hawk: SEALs of Honor, Book 2
Dane: SEALs of Honor, Book 3
Swede: SEALs of Honor, Book 4
Shadow: SEALs of Honor, Book 5
Cooper: SEALs of Honor, Book 6
Markus: SEALs of Honor, Book 7
Evan: SEALs of Honor, Book 8
Mason's Wish: SEALs of Honor, Book 9
Chase: SEALs of Honor, Book 10
Brett: SEALs of Honor, Book 11
Devlin: SEALs of Honor, Book 12
Easton: SEALs of Honor, Book 13
Ryder: SEALs of Honor, Book 14
Macklin: SEALs of Honor, Book 15
Corey: SEALs of Honor, Book 16
Warrick: SEALs of Honor, Book 17
Tanner: SEALs of Honor, Book 18

Jackson: SEALs of Honor, Book 19
Kanen: SEALs of Honor, Book 20
Nelson: SEALs of Honor, Book 21
Taylor: SEALs of Honor, Book 22
Colton: SEALs of Honor, Book 23
Troy: SEALs of Honor, Book 24
Axel: SEALs of Honor, Book 25
Baylor: SEALs of Honor, Book 26
Hudson: SEALs of Honor, Book 27
SEALs of Honor, Books 1–3
SEALs of Honor, Books 4–6
SEALs of Honor, Books 7–10
SEALs of Honor, Books 11–13
SEALs of Honor, Books 14–16
SEALs of Honor, Books 17–19
SEALs of Honor, Books 20–22
SEALs of Honor, Books 23–25

Heroes for Hire

Levi's Legend: Heroes for Hire, Book 1
Stone's Surrender: Heroes for Hire, Book 2
Merk's Mistake: Heroes for Hire, Book 3
Rhodes's Reward: Heroes for Hire, Book 4
Flynn's Firecracker: Heroes for Hire, Book 5
Logan's Light: Heroes for Hire, Book 6
Harrison's Heart: Heroes for Hire, Book 7
Saul's Sweetheart: Heroes for Hire, Book 8
Dakota's Delight: Heroes for Hire, Book 9
Tyson's Treasure: Heroes for Hire, Book 10
Jace's Jewel: Heroes for Hire, Book 11
Rory's Rose: Heroes for Hire, Book 12
Brandon's Bliss: Heroes for Hire, Book 13

Liam's Lily: Heroes for Hire, Book 14
North's Nikki: Heroes for Hire, Book 15
Anders's Angel: Heroes for Hire, Book 16
Reyes's Raina: Heroes for Hire, Book 17
Dezi's Diamond: Heroes for Hire, Book 18
Vince's Vixen: Heroes for Hire, Book 19
Ice's Icing: Heroes for Hire, Book 20
Johan's Joy: Heroes for Hire, Book 21
Galen's Gemma: Heroes for Hire, Book 22
Zack's Zest: Heroes for Hire, Book 23
Bonaparte's Belle: Heroes for Hire, Book 24
Noah's Nemesis: Heroes for Hire, Book 25
Heroes for Hire, Books 1–3
Heroes for Hire, Books 4–6
Heroes for Hire, Books 7–9
Heroes for Hire, Books 10–12
Heroes for Hire, Books 13–15

SEALs of Steel
Badger: SEALs of Steel, Book 1
Erick: SEALs of Steel, Book 2
Cade: SEALs of Steel, Book 3
Talon: SEALs of Steel, Book 4
Laszlo: SEALs of Steel, Book 5
Geir: SEALs of Steel, Book 6
Jager: SEALs of Steel, Book 7
The Final Reveal: SEALs of Steel, Book 8
SEALs of Steel, Books 1–4
SEALs of Steel, Books 5–8
SEALs of Steel, Books 1–8

The Mavericks

Kerrick, Book 1
Griffin, Book 2
Jax, Book 3
Beau, Book 4
Asher, Book 5
Ryker, Book 6
Miles, Book 7
Nico, Book 8
Keane, Book 9
Lennox, Book 10
Gavin, Book 11
Shane, Book 12
Diesel, Book 13
Jerricho, Book 14
The Mavericks, Books 1–2
The Mavericks, Books 3–4
The Mavericks, Books 5–6
The Mavericks, Books 7–8
The Mavericks, Books 9–10
The Mavericks, Books 11–12

Collections

Dare to Be You…
Dare to Love…
Dare to be Strong…
RomanceX3

Standalone Novellas

It's a Dog's Life
Riana's Revenge
Second Chances

Published Young Adult Books:

Family Blood Ties Series
Vampire in Denial
Vampire in Distress
Vampire in Design
Vampire in Deceit
Vampire in Defiance
Vampire in Conflict
Vampire in Chaos
Vampire in Crisis
Vampire in Control
Vampire in Charge
Family Blood Ties Set 1–3
Family Blood Ties Set 1–5
Family Blood Ties Set 4–6
Family Blood Ties Set 7–9
Sian's Solution, A Family Blood Ties Series Prequel
    Novelette

Design series
Dangerous Designs
Deadly Designs
Darkest Designs
Design Series Trilogy

Standalone
In Cassie's Corner
Gem Stone (a Gemma Stone Mystery)
Time Thieves

Published Non-Fiction Books:

Career Essentials

Career Essentials: The Résumé
Career Essentials: The Cover Letter
Career Essentials: The Interview
Career Essentials: 3 in 1

Made in the USA
Coppell, TX
12 May 2021

55531365R00164